REVIEWS FOR

Kings of the Boyne
'Moving and wonderfully written.'
Irishtimes.com

'The research into the Battle of the Boyne seeps through subtly, but with unfading accuracy. The pacing is perfect ... and the writing is utterly superb. Though it was over 300 years ago the reader is there. An incredible reading experience. Highly recommended.'
Fallen Star Stories

Behind the Walls
'History as it really happened with its gritty and realistic depiction of the terror-struck city of Derry in 1689 ... a vivid evocation of life in a city under siege. Memorable characters ... heart-breaking in places.'
parentsintouch.co.uk

Spirit of the Titanic
'Gripping, exciting and unimaginably shattering.'
Guardian Children's Books

City of Fate
'Will hook you from the start ... historical fiction at its best.'
The Guardian

'A compelling novel, combining rich characterisation with a powerfully evoked sense of time and place.'
Robert Dunbar, *Irish Times*

Nicola Pierce published her first book for children, *Spirit of the Titanic*, to rave reviews and five printings within its first twelve months. *City of Fate,* her second book, transported the reader deep into the Russian city of Stalingrad during World War II. The novel was shortlisted for the Warwickshire School Library Service Award, 2014. Nicola went on to bring seventeenth-century Ireland vividly to life in *Behind the Walls* (2015), a rich emotional novel set in the besieged city of Derry in 1689, followed by *Kings of the Boyne* (2016), a moving and gritty account capturing the Battle of the Boyne (1690), which was shortlisted for the Library Association of Ireland (LAI) awards. In 2018 Nicola delved in to the true stories of the passengers, crew and the legacy of the fated ship *Titanic*, in her illustrated book of the same name. To read more about Nicola, go to her Facebook page, www.facebook.com/Nicola Pierce-Author and on Twitter @NicolaPierce3.

NICOLA PIERCE

Illustrations by Eoin O'Brien

THE O'BRIEN PRESS
DUBLIN

First published 2020 by The O'Brien Press Ltd,
12 Terenure Road East, Rathgar, Dublin 6, D06 HD27, Ireland.
Tel: +353 1 4923333; Fax: +353 1 4922777
E-mail: books@obrien.ie
Website: www.obrien.ie
The O'Brien Press is a member of Publishing Ireland.

ISBN: 978-1-78849-017-7

10 9 8 7 6 5 4 3 2 1
24 23 22 21 20

Cover image: Jon Berkeley
Internal illustrations: Eoin O'Brien

Printed and bound by CPI Group (UK) Ltd, Croydon, CR0 4YY.
The paper in this book is produced using pulp from managed forests.

Chasing Ghosts receives financial assistance from the Arts Council

Published in:

DUBLIN
UNESCO
City of Literature

Dedication

For the Explorer in All of Us

With much gratitude to the Oncology Ward at Our Lady of Lourdes
Hospital, the Breast Clinic at Beaumont Hospital, the Gary Kelly
Cancer Support Centre, and the Drogheda Hospice

Acknowledgements

I am indebted to Brian Walsh from Dundalk Museum for introducing me to
the subject of the John Franklin expedition in his quest to make the name of
Captain Francis Leopold McClintock more widely known.

I contacted writer and explorer Frank Nugent with a question about Arctic
conditions and could not believe my luck when he offered to meet me, a
complete stranger, in the National Library to describe exactly what it is like in
the Arctic. I highly recommend Frank's important book *Seek the Frozen Lands*,
about the Irish polar explorers.

My good friend Peter Heaney, in Derry, sent me wonderful information on
the Coppin family and, also, went to St Augustine's Church to locate the family
grave. Also, I wish to thank Doctor Jonathan Mattison, the curator of Belfast's
Museum of Orange Heritage, for his help and heartily recommend a visit to
the museum too.

My sister Rachel, of Verba Editing House, offered to read the second and
third drafts of the book and gave me much needed, and much appreciated,
feedback.

As always, I am much indebted to my editor, Susan, who has been with me
throughout my five novels and history book, *Titanic; True Stories of Her
Passengers, Crew and Legacy*. I cannot imagine writing a book without her help
and support. With *Chasing Ghosts*, in particular, I needed Susan to be open-
minded about ghosts and spirits – and she did not let me down.

I feel so lucky to have had not one but three talented artists working on the
book. Eoin O'Brien did the wonderful illustrations, while the cover is down to
the genius of designer Emma Byrne and artist Jon Berkeley who performed a
magic trick by accidentally drawing what I had quietly pictured since I typed
the first sentence of the manuscript. I cannot thank them enough.

The Way They Went ...

Home

'There's magic in that little word …'

Christian Melodies

In search of the Northwest Passage

British explorers had long been obsessed with the
possibility of sailing from the Atlantic Ocean, straight
across the top of North America, to the Pacific Ocean.
By 1845, most of this dream had been realised.
All that was left to do was to find the last piece of this
route – some 300 miles – which was known as
the Northwest Passage.

***

The following is mostly based on two
actual events forever entwined despite
their difference in time and location.

***

Let us start with the story that began in May 1849,
in the city of Derry.

1

May 1849, Derry

Poor Weesy is dead

My sister Louisa's was the first dead body that I ever saw. We called her Weesy because that is what she called herself. When she was very little, she could not say her name properly so when we asked her to say 'Louisa', she could only manage 'Weesy', making us squeal with laughter. William, our brother, tried to teach her, pointing to her mouth as he slowly curled his tongue around the 'L' sound. She watched him, fascinated, as he repeated, 'L…ouisa; L…ouisa' and then, confident he had made his point, he invited her to answer the question, 'Now, what is your name?'

Louisa nodded, accepting his challenge, took a deep breath and replied once more, 'Weesy', giggling as William slapped his face in mock horror. Finally, Papa decided he preferred her version and took to calling her Weesy too, and the name stuck.

Weesy was sick for ages, but neither Papa nor Mama had warned us that she would die. Perhaps they did not know. Grandfather did; at least I think he did. He lives with us and so does Mama's sister, Aunt Harriet, who helps to take care of us. We all help to take care of Grandfather, although Mama told us never to say that in front of him. When Weesy fell ill he started to look gloomy long before our parents and Aunt Harriet did, although my aunt had told me that he was still lonely for my grandmother who had died before I was even born.

William, our baby sister Sarah and I were told that Weesy was tired, and therefore needed a lot more sleep than we did. We were only allowed to sit with her awhile in the afternoons. I usually read her one of my short stories, about our dog, Bobby. Her favourite one was entitled 'Bobby Stands Up to Feline Bullies'. I had written it after watching Bobby become enraged at the sight of a large, stray cat stalking pigeons in our back garden. He soon sent the would-be murderer on its way, thus, I assured Weesy, 'saving countless lives and rendering our garden safe once more'. She would smile and murmur breathlessly, 'Thank you, Ann!' Unfortunately, Mama would not allow Bobby in the house as he had a habit of chewing anything he could get his jaws around, including furniture, sheets and expensive slippers, but Weesy seemed content to listen to my stories about him.

Meanwhile, William liked to show Weesy his model ship

that Papa had helped him to build, telling her, 'You can paint the hull, Weesy, when you are better.'

He did not have to explain what the hull was since we were well versed in the different parts that make up a ship because of Papa's shipbuilding business.

'She is only four,' I argued. 'She might make a mess … by accident,' I added, to halt any protest from either of them, 'but you know that I am good at painting, I can do it for you.'

'No thank you, Ann,' he replied. 'I really want Weesy to do it.'

I did not bother to argue with him since I was sure that he would soon be pleading with me to correct Weesy's mistakes.

But then she died.

William wanted to put the ship in the coffin with her so that she would have something to play with in Heaven. It was a clever idea, I thought, and generous too. However, Mama shook her head, unable to speak, leaving Aunt Harriet to explain that there was no space for it. So, I asked if we could see Weesy as it seemed only fair that we be allowed to judge the size of the coffin for ourselves. Buoyed by my support, William pleaded, 'Oh, yes, please. I want to see my sister.'

She was in the parlour and, so far, we had been kept well away, Aunt Harriet confiding to us that our parents thought it would be too upsetting. As the visitors arrived, with cakes and flowers, we skulked around the closed door of the room but it seemed that all were advised to block our entrance. Still, when old Mrs Delaware took her leave, dabbing at her eyes with her lace handkerchief, she fumbled with the greasy door handle and I just had time to note that the coffin was white.

And tiny.

Just like Weesy.

I attempted to take charge of the family meeting. 'I am nearly thirteen so I am old enough now, I promise!'

Papa sighed, 'Alright, Ann, but what about William? He's only seven. Don't you think it might be too painful for him to see her … as she is now?'

William pouted. 'I'm seven and a half!'

'Plus, he's a boy,' I added, 'and you always tell him that he is the man of the house when you are away at sea.'

Papa thought for a moment while the rest of us waited. 'No, Ann, I tell him that if anything happens to Grandfather while I am away then he is the man of the house.'

My brother and I glanced at one another, neither of us brave enough to point out the obvious, that Grandfather was too old and wobbly to be much help if anything did happen. When Weesy died, Grandfather was the only adult to cry in front of us, with proper tears that splattered his jacket because his trembling hand could not catch them in his handkerchief. Yet, it was Grandfather who now addressed us. 'My dears, do you truly feel that you want to see her? You understand that she might appear a little different.'

William shrugged. 'She will look like she's asleep, like Jenny did when we buried her.'

'The cat!' muttered Aunt Harriet when Grandfather looked confused.

Sensing that they were going to give in, I rushed to include our baby sister, saying, 'And I know that Sarah is only two but she should see Weesy as well, just in case she forgets what she looks like.'

We left the dining room together, Papa holding my hand while Aunt Harriet took William's. Mama carried Sarah, with Grandfather shuffling in last. Everyone was so solemn that I almost changed my mind, suddenly preferring to run out to the garden and jump and shout and make lots of noise or even break something. In the hall, golden sunlight trickled through the arc window over the front door, causing specks of dust in the air to sparkle. Earlier, I had overheard whispers between my parents. Mama wanted to cover all the shiny surfaces in the house, the looking glasses and the windows including the one over the door. 'But why,' asked Papa, 'must we add to the awful sadness of the house? Think of the children.'

Mama sounded fierce as she replied, 'The children? They are alive, aren't they? This is nothing to do with them. I am thinking of Weesy only. I do not want her spirit to get trapped in a mirror.'

I am sure that Papa meant to be kind when he then said, 'Oh, Dora, you cannot believe that, do you? That sort of talk is for poor ignorant people who do not know any better.'

There was a long pause before Mama spoke again. 'I don't know what I believe other than our little girl should not have died.'

As Papa opened the door of the parlour and led me inside, I imagined a spell had been cast that instantly exchanged day for night. The heavy curtains were pulled and the candles were lit, making me forget it was not yet evening; and not a sound did we make, our footsteps hushed by the thick carpet while the eyes of our ancestors, in the paintings on the wall, seemed to gaze sorrowfully upon the little white coffin that sat on its own table, just out of reach. It reminded me of a church altar, thus making the coffin seem like some sort of offering to God, a sacrifice. The crackling of the fire, at least, was familiar. Mama insisted on it staying lit so that the room should not be completely dark at night-time. It was too warm and yet, most peculiar, a shiver slithered its way from the top of my head down to my ankles.

And there she was. Even though I knew I was going to see Weesy, I was shocked to find her there all the same. Letting go of Papa's hand, I reached in to touch her, to see if she was real or maybe to see if she was actually dead. She looked well. I had become used to her greyish skin and the shadows beneath

14

her eyes that looked like fading bruises, along with the noisy cough that forced its way through her, hardly letting her sleep. Really, I thought she looked better now, much better. Her face felt cool, but perhaps it had always felt like that since I could not remember touching it before. A large white ribbon sat on top of her hair that looked like it had been brushed a hundred times and she was wearing her favourite dress, white too with ruffles about the neck. She called it her princess dress and was only ever allowed to wear it on Sundays. Flowers had been pressed all around her, forming a colourful, perfumed garland that perfectly framed her. Her fingers were entwined as if she was saying her prayers. I thought she looked as beautiful as a painting even as I willed her to open her eyes, not for me, but for our parents and Aunt Harriet and Grandfather who had grabbed the poker to prod the orange coals on the fire, turning his back to us.

No doubt William felt he had to say something since he was the reason we were all standing here.

'My ship won't fit in there.'

And that was all he said.

Afterwards, we were given a thick slice of lemon cake but only after we agreed to go to bed without a fuss. Oh, I would have preferred to have remained with the adults and be comforted by their solidness, that is, their living, breathing bodies. As I lay in bed, I felt somehow out of place as if I was in a stranger's house and miles away from anything familiar. I imagined that my family's sadness was draining our home of warmth and light. And I could not stop thinking about my sister lying so perfectly still in the parlour.

The next day was the funeral. Mama crumpled to the ground, her arms outstretched, as Papa carried the coffin out our front door. He saw Mama fall but did not stop or turn back. It was horrible. I supposed that Mama hated the coffin leaving the house as it meant that Weesy was being carried away from our family forever. I pretended not to hear Aunt Harriet whisper, 'Oh, Dora, it is time to let her go.'

Funerals last hours. My arms itched from the long sleeves of my new black dress and, in the graveyard, the sun made me sweat unpleasantly. I could not help thinking what a waste of a beautiful day and then was ashamed of my selfish thoughts. I saw my teacher Mrs Lee amongst the crowd of mourners. She was alone and pretended not to see me when she did.

Once the reverend finished reciting the prayers, I followed William as he plucked daisies for Weesy's grave, half-listening to the jumble of conversations floating around us:

'… was such a pretty little thing …'

'The Lord giveth and the Lord taketh away.'

'At least the weather stayed fine; funerals in the rain can be awfully pathetic.'

'She's in a better place now.'

'Is she, then?' asked William.

'Is she, what?' I asked in reply as I swiped a fly from my ear.

'Is Weesy in a better place now?'

I shrugged. 'I suppose so. She must be in Heaven.'

He nodded his head in agreement. 'And Heaven is better than here, isn't it?'

I refused to answer such a silly question because of course Heaven was better than anywhere else or else it would not be Heaven, would it?

'It is just that ...,' said my brother, who began to cry quietly.

'Oh, William, don't cry, please don't cry,' I pleaded.

Of course, neither of us had a handkerchief, but I tore some large leaves from the ground and bid him to rub his face with them. He did so, streaking watery green across his cheeks, and began again. 'Must we really leave her here? I mean, won't she be terribly scared when it gets dark, being here all alone?'

'No, no, William. The real Weesy is safe. It is just her bones and skin and hair that we buried, like an empty tortoise shell. That is what being dead means. Weesy's body can feel nothing, but her soul is in Heaven now.'

William sniffed. 'I am glad to hear that, though I wish we could have kept her at home with us.'

'Just think of her being happy in Heaven, eating as much chocolate as she wants and surrounded by lots of toys,' I said, to comfort both of us.

2

19 May 1845, Greenhithe, England

Sir John bids his family farewell

Sir John Franklin was just fourteen years old when he joined the British Royal Navy. Back then, his dreams of trampling the shores of distant and unknown lands were the only things that mattered to him. He had yearned to be allowed to press his boot into foreign snow or sand, before any other man, and do so in the name of his beloved country. That was a long time ago now, forty-five years to be precise, but perhaps not that much had changed, not about his dreams anyhow. Surely that fourteen-year-old navy apprentice would be impressed to see his grey-haired self about to embark on one more journey.

Lady Jane peered at her husband's face. 'Are you excited, my dear?'

Sir John merely smiled for an answer. The truth was that

any excitement he felt was tainted by the knowledge that several of his peers thought he should not be doing this: leading a great expedition to the top of the world in search of the last trade route, through the freezing Arctic seas to the Pacific Ocean by way of the infamous Northwest Passage. A successful expedition would bring its British commander instant fame while enabling his country to take the lead on the world's stage, in scientific and polar discovery. This would be his greatest moment yet but try as he might, Sir John could not stifle the murmurs that had reached his ears about him being 'too old', 'too fat' and 'too clueless' for the task ahead. Well, nobody could fault his stubbornness. He had persevered, hadn't he, in spite of the naysayers?

So, here he now stood, in the centre of the small group that included his second wife, Lady Jane Franklin, their niece, Sophie, and Eleanor, his daughter from his first marriage. Standing there, he had never felt more at home, surrounded by all his loves that he was about to leave for goodness knew how long. The family busied themselves watching the goings-on in front of them. Over a hundred men were making their farewells, kissing children, wives and sweethearts, whilst bellowing wild hellos to fellow sailors who were glad to be distracted from the sadness of saying goodbye.

To their left, a marching band were tuning up their instruments in preparation for the big send-off. The short, sharp bursts of various trumpets and horns punctured the air every now and then. Newspapermen jotted down their descriptions, keeping a beady eye out for some fresh detail to satisfy their bosses and enable their readers to imagine the scene.

Surrounding them on three sides was a vast crowd of onlookers and well-wishers, growing bigger by the second. And then, in the background, behind the clamour of human activity were the two ships, Her Majesty's Steamships (HMS) *Erebus* and *Terror*, sitting serenely in the water, aside their rippled reflections. Hardy gangs of seagulls darted about their masts, squalling madly, as if demanding everyone's attention.

'Do you think they will try to follow you?' asked Eleanor.

Her father knew she meant the gulls. 'If they do, they'll be disappointed to discover that we are not going fishing.'

Lady Franklin smiled fiercely. How she longed to have Sir John to herself, but he insisted on Eleanor being here, and so she, in turn, brought Sophie. Lady Jane was only stepmother to Eleanor, her real mother having died years earlier. She did her best to love the girl but was thwarted by her own possessiveness of her husband.

She longed to take Sir John's hand but that would not do.

After all, he was Lord Franklin, captain and commander of this fantastic expedition. Oh, he had done well to take command of what might be the most famous sea journey yet. She was so proud of him. So, these last few moments together had to be savoured and, yes, shared with his daughter. In fact, this had been her gift to him, although she could not remember which one of them had mentioned it first: the proposed expedition to the Arctic, to find the Northwest Passage. Well, it hardly mattered who spoke of it first, just that her immediate response was, 'You should do this!'

He pretended to be shocked at her suggestion. 'What, me, at my age? They would never let me, what with so many younger men who are better qualified.'

She, in turn, pretended to believe that he needed convincing.

'My dear,' she said, 'you have faithfully served your country since you were a boy and, in that time, you have captained many ships and have led expeditions to the very same Arctic. Tell me, who is more qualified than you are?'

He again pretended to consider her question, but all he could think was how right she was. Who else indeed?

Reading his mind, she continued, 'You are a perfect fit for this. You know it, I know it and I'll wager the Navy knows it too. Goodness, if they allowed me, I should like to go and see this Arctic for myself!'

Her husband had described to her the seascapes of ice, with mountains that sparkled like crystal glass and the purest, whitest snow as far as the eye could see. It sounded too thrilling for words.

For a moment, Sir John had fretted that she meant him to pressure the Navy into allowing her to accompany him. Now, he loved her dearly and thoroughly disliked the thought of leaving her behind but – no, no, no – that simply would not do. His naval superiors did not agree with women having opinions and a passion for learning. His Jane had both and never tried to deceive people otherwise. Mind you, she was probably better educated and more travelled than most men he knew.

As it was, he suspected that she was the reason he had lost his post as Lieutenant-Governor in Van Diemen's Land. She had refused to play nice and befriend the other wives, and meekly mind her place in mixed company. Instead, she tackled his colleagues over politics, religion and society's ills. In place of hosting lunches and making social calls, she bought books and maps. And rather than hiding these items in her husband's study, she sat out in the open, poring over them, and then inflicted her newly acquired knowledge on Australian politicians who learned to dread the sound of her voice. Lastly, instead of ignoring the brooding presence of the natives like everyone else, she had temporarily adopted a young Aboriginal girl and introduced her to the neighbours, just to watch their faces twitch in dismay.

Lady Jane was fearless and he had allowed her to infect him too, so that he put his name in the pot to lead a hundred and twenty-eight men to the Arctic. It had taken hundreds of years and the courage of many explorers to reach this point. Sir John allowed himself to consider that history might judge his contribution to be the best of all, charting the last few miles through new territory, finally opening up the elusive sea route to allow northwest access to the trading nations of Asia. He would, in effect, be placing a full stop on any further exploration of the Northwest Passage. Yes, his success would mean his name inscribed in history books, the thought of which made him smile once more.

Seeing his smile, his wife sighed, 'I just wish I knew for certain when to expect you home again. It would be so much easier to say goodbye if I knew how long it was for.'

Regarding her tenderly, he said, 'Well, now, I would be a clever man if I could tell you anything more than I already have. Everything depends on the ice; it is the master of our fate.'

'What do you mean, Papa?' Eleanor peered at her father in wonder.

Sir John gave his daughter a guilty look. Had he not already explained this to her? 'Why, my dear, when the water freezes in the Arctic, it turns into ice which traps a ship until it melts back into water once more.'

'Traps?' echoed Eleanor, looking decidedly worried.

Sir John glanced at his wife who took over. 'Oh, come now, Eleanor, I am quite sure that you know this already. Your father will make his explorations during the summer months but, during the winter, the ships will be stuck fast. No ship is strong enough to break through blocks of ice.'

Eleanor shook her head in protest. 'But, Papa, you told me that the ships have steam engines, from the railway trains. And their fronts are stronger than any other ship.'

Her father hastened to correct her on one point. 'Bows, my dear. That's what we call the front of a ship.'

Lady Franklin stifled an impulse to roll her eyes. The child was impossible. She flashed her niece a look that meant: *see, this is exactly why I wanted to leave her at home.* Typically, Sophie understood as much and nodded her sympathy – *my poor aunt, I completely agree with you.*

Sir John was starting to feel somewhat harassed. The sun was high in the sky and his overly-tight starched collar was making itself felt. He had tried to lose weight over the last few weeks but it proved impossible when he and Jane had been invited to so many farewell dinners. As a result, he had rather a difficult time getting dressed; there were so many buttons on his uniform and some had to be forcibly dragged through the holes. At one point he thought he heard the material groan in protest.

Furthermore, he had a dratted cold that he could not shake. And now Eleanor was pouting while his wife's watery smile barely hid her urge to say, 'I told you so! We should not have brought her.'

A fine farewell this was turning out to be!

'How long will you be gone, Papa?'

He considered offering his daughter a vague 'I don't know', but that did not seem fair. So, he was honest. 'We are taking three years of supplies with us, just to be safe.'

Before Eleanor could respond to this, her stepmother sighed, 'Three years! I cannot lie, it is a long time.'

Eleanor gazed at the blue sky above them, doing her best to imagine slabs of ice big and strong enough to stop a ship from sailing.

Captain Franklin declared to his audience, 'Be assured that I am planning on returning home long before that, with food to spare.'

Pleased to hear him sounding confident, Lady Franklin declared, 'You will find that passage, I know you will.'

He agreed with her. 'If it is God's will, we certainly shall.'

Erebus and *Terror* seemed impatient to be released from

their moorings; their hulks swayed together as if they were listening to music, the waves bearing out the ocean's rhythm.

'They are fine ships,' said Jane, 'so strong and sturdy, just like their captain.'

'Well,' sighed her husband, 'like me, they are of a certain age, have fought in battles and have been to the Arctic before. I just hope they are not too weary for the journey ahead.'

She knew what he was hinting at and assured him, 'There is no substitute for years of experience and I am quite sure that your officers and sailors would agree with me.'

'Good morning to you all!'

They had been joined by Captain Franklin's second-in-command, Captain Francis Crozier. Tall in stature with dark hair, he was quite the opposite in every way of his commander. A shy man, he had forced himself to approach the family group because pure manners decreed it. However, it was the second last thing he wanted to do.

His glance lingered longer than it should have on Sophie who plucked at a loose thread on her sleeve. Twice he had asked her to marry him and twice she had said no. Oh, it took guts to stand there in front of her and pretend that all was well. He doffed his hat to Jane who greeted him warmly, 'Good morning, Captain. Are you anxious to be off?'

'Dear me, Lady Franklin, my apologies if I should look so impatient?'

'Why, Captain Crozier,' said Jane, 'you look as impatient as your commander feels though he will deny it.'

Captain Crozier was quite certain that he did not look the least bit impatient to be gone, not at all. And this was because the very, very last thing that Captain Crozier wished to do was undertake this journey to the Arctic. Sir John might well be pitying himself for having to fight a bad cold but Captain Francis Crozier was having a tougher time as he was fighting serious apprehension about what lay ahead.

The only person who was privy to his sentiments was his great friend and fellow explorer Sir James Clark Ross. Two years earlier, the two had spent four years exploring the Antarctic together and owed their powers of endurance to their mutual respect and admiration for one another. Unfortunately, Captain Crozier felt neither for John Franklin, although, as he told his friend, 'I like him and Lady Franklin well enough and always enjoy their company but ...'

'But?' said James with a smile.

'I am tired, James!' declared Crozier. 'Plain old tired.'

And he was. He had believed that his polar exploration days were behind him. To be fair, four years is a long time out of one's life, 1,460 days or thereabouts. Therefore, it is little wonder that Captain Crozier felt he had paid his due to Heaven and to the Navy and now wanted to enjoy ordinary things, like getting married and becoming a father. He wondered at the situation he found himself in: *how can it be easier to travel to the other side of the world than find myself a wife?*

Recently, as best man, Captain Crozier had watched James marry the lovely Ann Coulman. The marriage only went ahead after James promised his betrothed that he would travel no more. In between making speeches and dancing with James's elderly aunts, Captain Crozier found himself heartily wishing that it was his wedding day instead, with Sophie for his bride.

Sophie had said no, but he was not ready to give up just yet. What if he took himself away for a while? Might there be the merest chance that she would miss him? He knew little about love and romance but he was familiar with the quotation 'Absence makes the heart fonder'. Well, then, what had he got to lose?

Sir John rudely interrupted his thoughts with a roar, 'Ah-tish-shoo!'

Everyone jumped as Sir John fumbled with his

handkerchief. He blew his nose, far noisier than any trumpet player, before asking, 'Well, then, how goes it?'

Captain Crozier nodded. 'I should think we are just about ready, sir.'

Without the Franklins realising it, the sailors had drifted away from their relatives to board their particular ship in single file. Right now, over a hundred men were claiming their hammocks while others, like their officers, cooks and surgeons, were surveying their tiny kingdoms that they expected to lord over for the next year or so, or two at most. Hopefully no longer than that. As Lady Jane said, three years was a long time really.

All that was left was for the two captains to board their ships, Captain Crozier to *Terror* and Captain Franklin to *Erebus*, only neither of them seemed eager to make the first move. Finally, Lady Jane took control, her usual approach. Offering her hand in farewell to Captain Crozier, she said, 'I wish you a safe and bountiful journey and I hope it will not be too long until we meet again.'

'Thank you, Lady Franklin. I hope so too.'

Captain Crozier smiled hopefully at Sophie, who duly followed her aunt's lead, presenting to him her own hand with good wishes. 'Take care, Captain Crozier. We shall keep you and Sir John in our prayers.'

Not to be outdone, Eleanor graciously held out hers too.

'Goodbye, Captain. Will you promise to take care of Papa?'

Captain Crozier smiled at the girl, feeling Sophie's eyes upon him. This was his moment to prove himself as a steady and trustworthy gentleman. Flattering Eleanor, he addressed her thus, 'My dear Miss Franklin, we are most grateful to you and Lady Jane for releasing your father to us, for this grand mission. And I give you my solemn word that I will return him to his family as soon as I can. Will that do?'

A beaming Eleanor nodded her acceptance.

3

May 1849

Weesy is come back

Four days after the funeral, Papa had to go away on one of his business trips. It was the first normal thing to happen in a long time. In truth, he went away a lot. His ship-yard kept him busy, but now his new passion was to salvage or re-float sunken ships and his services were in great demand. It was fascinating, I thought, that he could drag drowned ships from the ocean floor and sit them on top of the water again, bringing them back to life.

If only he could do the same for Weesy.

He would be gone for three months and I heard Aunt Harriet quietly promising him that not for an instant would she leave Mama's side. He thanked her and muttered something about feeling guilty, though I could not hear exactly what he said.

The next morning, he was gone before we got up, which was typical because he disliked goodbyes. I hoped he would remember to bring us back presents.

At the breakfast table, Aunt Harriet told me that I did not have to return to school until after the summer holidays. That suited me fine and then I remembered. 'I saw Mrs Lee at Weesy's funeral.'

'Yes, well,' said Aunt Harriet. 'She lost her daughter too, just last year, I think!'

That explained why my teacher never smiled and was always dressed in black.

***

Papa's absence made the days seem even longer. We missed having our early evenings punctuated by his arrival from work, asking us about our day as he shed his coat and papers, rubbing his hands together in anticipation of a tasty dinner. How long could this go on, this dreariness of one day blending into the next? I yearned to escape the sagging atmosphere of the house or, failing that, for something extraordinary to happen.

And then it did.

***

It was Sarah who saw Weesy first, although she showed no surprise since she hardly understood what was real anyway. Laura, our maid, was polishing the staircase the morning after Papa left when she was interrupted by Sarah clapping her hands and exclaiming, 'Weesy! Weesy!' It was one of the few words she could correctly pronounce. The others were 'me' and 'no'. Used to being trailed by Sarah, as she tended to her morning duties, Laura took her time to discover that Sarah was beaming at the wall as if it had made a joke. Feeling obliged to be clear, Laura waved her cloth at the ceiling as she explained, 'No, my pet. Weesy has gone to Heaven.' When she saw that she was wasting her time, because Sarah was too absorbed in her mysterious game, Laura gave up and returned to her polishing.

A couple of days later, on hearing a thud from the landing and William's howl, Aunt Harriet and I dashed up the staircase to find him sprawled on the floor, a perfect dot of blood winking at us from his grazed forehead. Aunt Harriet flung herself upon him. 'Oh my goodness. What happened to you? Did you fall?'

Instead of answering our aunt's questions, William appeared to be looking for something. Aunt Harriet cupped his face in her hands and spoke slowly. 'William, are you alright? Do you know where you are? Do you know who I am?'

It took a moment before he finally focused on her, and then he certainly amazed me with his answer, 'I saw Weesy.

She was standing just there, by the wall. I ran to hug her but …'

The bell went for dinner. Aunt Harriet pulled her handkerchief from her sleeve, wiped the blood away and told us to go wash our hands. We watched her straighten her skirt and head downstairs.

Waiting until Aunt Harriet had reached the lowest step, William asked me, 'Do you believe me? I really saw her. Honest!'

Unwilling to give in straight away, I allowed a tight nod of my head, which he missed. Instead, he exhaled in relief. 'Oh, she is back again! Where did you go to, Weesy? Aunt Harriet was here.'

Realising that we were staring at the exact same spot, he whispered, 'You see her too, don't you?'

For some reason I suddenly felt annoyed. 'Of course I do. Stop asking me stupid questions!'

I wasn't scared. I mean, it was just my little sister. At least, it looked like her for the most part, only there was a light around her, bluish and straining like the flames of a fire. I had never seen anything like it and yet, at the same time, it was only Weesy. I needed to think. Unfortunately, William still had questions. 'Why isn't she in Heaven? You said she was going to Heaven.'

'Don't blame me, William Coppin!' I snapped. 'This is not my fault!'

William bowed his head and mumbled, 'Are you not happy that she is back?'

All the while, Weesy never said a word. She just smiled at us as if she was glad to be home again. Goodness knows how long we stood there before we were surprised by Laura who had been sent to fetch us. 'C'mon, you pair. You are keeping everyone waiting!'

She grabbed us by the hands and Weesy disappeared just like that. In the dining room Mama asked what had kept us. She was seated in her usual place with Aunt Harriet to her left and Grandfather at the head of the table and they were not alone. Before I could stop him, William blurted out, 'How did you get here so fast?'

Aunt Harriet laughed. 'Because I came down ahead of you, remember?'

Peering at his forehead, Mama asked, 'Is your poor head alright, dear?'

'No,' said William, not hearing her. 'I wasn't talking to you, Aunt Harriet.'

He stopped short and everyone stared at him. Mama shrugged and said, 'Ah, you were talking to me then, were you? Well, I was already down here waiting for you and Ann.'

William looked at me as he shook his head.

I became the centre of attention as each adult, including Laura, who still held our hands, waited for me to explain my brother's strange behaviour. It was Weesy who let me feel that it would be alright to tell. So, I just said it straight out as I did not know how else to. 'Weesy is here.'

Laura gasped and dropped my hand. The others made no immediate reaction except that Aunt Harriet and Mama exchanged glances before Mama asked, 'Where, darling?'

'There!' said William, pointing at Weesy's chair, which wasn't even pulled out from the table.

Aunt Harriet tried to persuade us otherwise. 'Children, we all miss her desperately and it is perfectly acceptable to want to see her so badly that you almost think you do …'

William broke in. 'I saw her upstairs just now. I told you. I ran to hug her and that's how I hit my head against the wall.'

'Well, yes, pet,' Aunt Harriet assured him. 'Because she wasn't actually there.'

'I saw her too,' I added. 'She looks the same, except she is not sick anymore. She is happy now.'

'Is she?'

Mother's eyes filled with tears while Aunt Harriet and Grandfather seemed unsure of what to say next. Then, to everyone's surprise, Laura ventured, 'Begging your pardon, Missus, but I think wee Sarah sees her most mornings … that is, ever since the master left. She chats away and acts likes she hears Weesy talking to her. I … well, I just didn't like to say before.'

Mama gave her a watery smile as Laura suddenly choked

up, covering her hand with her mouth.

It was as if Mama was the judge and we all had to wait for her to decide how to react, but I was sure that whatever she said would be agreed upon by the rest of the adults. Then, quite unexpectedly, I heard myself speak, though I hardly knew what I was going to say. 'Grandfather, Weesy says your pocket watch is under your bed.'

I did not think much of my message, but Grandfather's knife fell onto his plate with a right clatter, making us all jump. He slowly rose and left the room. Overcome with guilt, though for what I did not know, I apologised, 'I'm sorry, Mama. I did not mean to upset anyone.'

'Just sit down, Ann, like a good girl. You too, William.'

We took our seats and listened to our grandfather's footsteps on the landing and then the door of his bedroom opening.

Aunt Harriet sighed and asked Laura to bring out the soup. 'Cook must be fretting over our lack of appetites,' she said brightly, trying to drown out any sounds overhead, while Mama stared at the ceiling as if she could see right through it.

'I am hungry,' I offered, wanting to make things better.

Aunt Harriet smiled. 'I am sure you are; breakfast was a long time ago, and what about you, William? Are you hungry?'

'I am always hungry,' William said, to make us laugh.

Cook and Laura bustled in with the trays of soup. Cook, looking irritable, failed to notice anything unusual as she only had one thing on her mind, and hinted about her complaint, 'I only hope that it is still hot for I was not expecting the delay.'

She continued to grumble under her breath as she and Laura doled out the bowls. Stopping at Grandfather's chair, she cocked her head, 'Will your father be wanting his soup then, Madam?'

'Yes, he will,' said Aunt Harriet quickly. 'I hear him on the stairs. Thank you!'

Cook placed the bowl down and turned on her heel. 'I had better go see that the pie hasn't burnt.'

I saw Laura roll her eyes and Aunt Harriet shaking her head at her, putting her finger to her lips. In other words, Laura was not to tell Cook about Weesy; I understood that much. Grandfather came back in as they returned to the kitchen. He sat down and I saw his watch peeking out of his pocket but thought nothing of it. Mama saw it too and quietly asked, as William and I started to blow noisily on our soup, 'Was your watch lost?'

I hardly heard his answer. 'Since yesterday morning.'

The next day, at dinnertime, Weesy's chair was pulled out from the table and her cutlery was set in its usual place.

***

And that's just how it was until Papa's return. He was there one morning, not long after Weesy's first appearance to William, when we came downstairs, with a paint box for me and another toy ship for William, while Sarah was already sitting on his knee, clutching a new doll.

'Oh, Papa, you have been gone for so long!' I said.

He smiled in surprise. 'No more than usual. Though, you're right, Ann. This time it felt especially long for me too.'

He looked different and I realised there were lots of grey patches in his hair and sideburns that I was sure had not been there before. He must have been lonely for us, on his ship, lonely for all of us. At least here, at home, we had one another.

'Anyway, I am here now and that is all that matters.'

We hugged him in agreement until Sarah cried out in annoyance, making Papa laugh. 'Oh dear, are we squashing you, Sarah?'

She pouted and shoved her doll's head at his mouth to be kissed, which he did immediately.

'You have to give her a name. What is dolly's name?' I asked.

Sarah thought for a moment before announcing, 'Dolly!'

Climbing down from Papa's lap, Sarah brought Dolly over to show her off. I opened up the paint box to find different shades of colours, some of which were new to me: four different blues, four different greens and reds and pinks.

'Well, Ann, do you think you could produce some worthy art for me?'

I hugged him. 'Oh, yes, Papa. I love it!'

'Where's Mama and Harriet?' asked William.

'Shopping, I should think,' replied Papa.

Laura came in with a tray of tea and biscuits. 'Are you sure this is enough for you, Captain Coppin? Cook says she can make you something if you are hungry.'

Papa shook his head, 'No thank you, Laura. This is fine.'

I saw Laura give me a funny look but I was too wrapped up in Papa to pay her any attention.

William took Sarah's place on Papa's lap. He could be such a baby sometimes. 'Where did you go, Papa? Did you see any pirates or sea monsters?'

'Not this time, thank goodness. We sailed to a country that was so hot I watched a fellow cook an egg on a rock.'

'How did he do that?' I asked.

'He cracked the egg open with a spoon, turned it upside down and drained the contents onto a rock that was large and flat and, lo and behold, it began to sizzle.'

'Oh,' said William. 'I wish I could have seen it!'

Papa stretched over to the plate. 'I suppose you will all be wanting one of my favourite biscuits?'

'Yes, please,' sang out William and I together while Sarah just said, 'Yes!'

'I thought so!' said Papa. 'Let's see how many we have here and, for goodness sake, do not tell your mother!'

This was just a special treat because he was home, otherwise the only time we saw biscuits was on a Sunday, and even then, depending on Mother's mood, we might only be allowed to look at them.

'Here, William, take the plate and offer them out to your sisters, but I'll take my one first.'

Papa watched approvingly as we politely lined up in front of William. He bit into his as he began his usual habit of counting us out, saying, 'One for Sarah, one for William, one for Ann and for W ... we ... Oh, my God! WEESY?'

William and I were delighted. 'You can see her, can't you? You can see her like us!'

Papa's expression was one of total confusion.

I ran to him. 'Aunt Harriet and Mama and Grandfather can't see her. Sarah saw her first and then William and then me.'

At that moment, the door opened and Mama came in, followed by Aunt Harriet. Before she could say anything, William roared, 'Papa can see Weesy too!'

Mama stared at Papa, who nodded and reached for her, but she moved out of his way, her lips pressed together in annoyance.

4

June 1849

Ann upsets Mama

One night some time later, I woke up with a start, thinking someone had knocked on my door.

Sure enough, my bedroom door was being opened slowly and deliberately as if somebody wanted me to look around. I pretended to ignore it, to see what would happen. Keeping my eyes shut, I breathed loudly and steadily as if fast asleep.

Then came timid footsteps, the slightest brushing against the wooden floor, but still I would not react. It was hard not to jump when I heard the door creak in earnest, the noise it made when it was pushed back and forth as if it were a swing in the playground. I did it myself, sometimes, finding that the squeaking helped me to think better, though usually I would be obliged to stop soon enough as it never took long before someone protested at the noise.

My stubbornness took charge. I would not sit up. I would not call out. I would not show I was afraid, which I wasn't anyway, not even a little bit.

However, I did open my eyes but only enough to see a wedge of moonlit shadow fall across the wall in front of me. It was too late to change my position. I was lying on my left side, with my back to the door.

Instinctively, I clutched my old doll, Mary, closer to me and nuzzled her hair with my nose, glad for the familiarity of Aunt Harriet's perfume. I had given her to Weesy when she got sick but, now, she was mine again. Fancying that she smelled of sickness and gloom, I had begged my aunt to sprinkle her with perfume.

The scent was from some flower I had never heard of, though Papa said it was Spanish and did his best to describe it, saying it was the brightest pink I could imagine, pinker than my lips and pinker than Mama's pink roses. He had brought the perfume back from one of his trips.

What was that?

I felt like I was being studied, that someone was searching for the tiniest hint that I was awake. I forgot to keep breathing loudly and, instead, took minute, rapid gulps of air that were too slight to fill my lungs. My chest began to hurt.

Who was there?

I shivered, only then realising that I was bitterly cold.

Finally, I forced myself to turn around and to see who was there but there was no one. I sat up, in a fury, and hissed at the empty room, 'Weesy! I know it's you.'

Even as I said her name, I considered the chilling possibility that it might not be Weesy. But who else could it be? *Who else could I be talking to?*

I sat there, trembling from the cold, my breath creating brief swells of fog in front of my face. I could see nobody yet I still felt stifled instead of alone.

And then.

And, then, suddenly Mary was tugged right out of my arms. I screamed and reached forward, waving my arms around, scrabbling to find her amongst the bed clothes.

My door swung open once more, this time bringing Mama to me. Without a word, she sat down and folded me into her, holding me as I began to cry tears of grief for Mary and rage too.

When I was able to, I blurted it out. 'Weesy! It's Weesy, she's trying to scare me.'

Mama fumbled in her pocket for her handkerchief. Treating me as if I were years younger, she wiped away my tears, saying, 'Why would she do that?' her tone suggesting that there could be no proper answer to her question. 'I mean, if as you say, it was Weesy ...'

Feeling criticised, I rudely interrupted, 'It *is* her!'

'Hush, Ann. You will wake up the whole house.'

Afraid that the conversation was dribbling away, I prodded myself to think of something interesting to say. 'Perhaps she is in Hell.'

I was shocked to be roughly pushed aside.

'Mama?' I began.

'Ann Coppin! How could you? I do not believe … I just cannot believe that you would say such a horrible, dreadful thing.'

My cheeks burned in the darkness and I felt tears gathering once more. 'I am sorry, Mama. I did not mean it.'

'You must never say that again, do you hear me? Never again!'

I was panicking now. 'I won't. Truly, I won't. Never, ever again.'

She stood up and I was glad that I could not see her face. I felt miserable for spoiling everything. It had been so pleasant to be in her embrace. She was no longer curious or sympathetic, saying briskly, 'Go back to sleep. It was just a bad dream.'

I lay down immediately.

She started in annoyance. 'What on earth? Why is Mary on the floor? I do wish you were more careful with your toys.'

She placed my doll beside me and I closed my eyes. When

I opened them a moment later, she was gone. Her parting kindness was to leave the door partially open, should I have another nightmare and cry out again.

Mary felt cold to my touch. I dragged up my blanket to cradle her against my chest. Her hair seemed wet but that could not be. No matter, she was safe again. I must have dropped her when I got a fright. Yes, that was what happened.

5

Tuesday, 20th May 1845

HMS *Terror*

Captain Crozier's

Journal

Home at last! That is, I am back here in my cabin after another infernal dinner with Captain Franklin and his officers. God help me but I cannot do this night after night, yet how do I refuse? How do I politely decline to leave the comforts of *Terror* in order to be rowed across the water to *Erebus*? Why must I be the one to suffer the cold air?

Surely he will give me a night off to dine here quietly with my books and papers. Does that make me a bad person? I do like him; in fact, I have always liked him.

However, I would prefer to be with him under different circumstances. I cannot shake the feeling that this expedition is cursed and that my genial host is the wrong man for the job ahead.

This evening, I witnessed his flaws as a captain. His men are much too casual, treating him like a favourite uncle at the dinner table on Christmas Day and, goodness, how he enjoys it. At one point, the steward serving us dinner laughed out loud at the officers' jokes. If it had been my ship, I would have had him severely reprimanded for his insolence. But Sir John, his face practically glowing in the candlelight, merely smiled dotingly upon them all. He only wants to be their friend and, in this, he seems to have succeeded.

Several things pester me and I cannot ignore them. The ships are one too many. Two ships require too much crew and supplies. There is hardly room to walk around the thousands of food tins, never mind the tobacco, soap, blankets and mountains of coal.

On top of that, we are like two floating farms, what with the number of live animals on board: sheep, cattle, hens and pigs. Then there is the enormous bear of a dog taking up precious space on *Erebus*, a gift from Lady Franklin. He will surely end up on a dinner plate should we run short of food, which seems hardly fair to him.

This is why I do not agree with pets on my ship. And if the dog wasn't bad enough, Lady Franklin also gave her husband an actual monkey. I mean, a monkey on a ship to the Arctic. What was she thinking? The little wretch tried to steal my watch while I ate. I hear that he spends his days thieving, worse than any professional pickpocket on the streets of London. He seems quite a favourite with the others. Why, I don't know.

I also worry that, with our steam engines and coal mountains, we are too heavy for the troubling seas ahead. We sit deep in the water. There will be storms to sail through, huge gales whipping up waves bigger than houses.

Honestly, I do not believe that there is a single person aboard *Terror* or *Erebus* who has considered that we may well run into bad luck. How can they be so confident? Even as I write that question, I hear the answer immediately, which is that few of them have ever done anything like this before. It is easy to be jolly about the Arctic when you have never been at its mercy.

Apart from all of that, I cannot shake the sense that we are sailing too late in the year to make real progress. For instance, if the weather is already too severe, we will soon be prevented from adventuring further. I dread to think that we will end up repeating the disastrous expedition of 1824 when those two ships – *Hecla* and *Fury* – were late and found themselves losing an entire year to being stuck in the ice, ending with *Fury* being wrecked and abandoned.

How I wish my friend James Clark Ross was here. I am lonely. There, I have written it down, plain as can be. I am lonely. This little room is my sole refuge from the crew and officers. Once I leave it, I cannot escape them. When I walk around, I am continually hampered by the men. No clear walkway exists. Men everywhere but not one real friend amongst them.

The truth is I do not enjoy my solitary cabin and would prefer to share it with a trusted colleague. What a peculiar situation to be in, rarely alone but lonely just the same. I fear it is adding to my discomfort that I cannot ask a fellow officer whether he agrees that Captain Franklin should be more strident when it comes to discipline. And I cannot ask any other man here if he feels, like me, that we may be too late and, therefore, will possibly spend up to a year attached to an iceberg. And I cannot openly criticise the lack of Arctic experience amongst this crew. I am, therefore, restricted to sharing my worries with this notebook.

What would Sir John make of my journal? Knowing him, he would approve and forgive me my doubts.

Tonight, he urged us all to write and draw and 'bear witness to everything from the flea to the whale. Those of you who can draw, fill your sketchbooks with seabirds, big fish and whatever else we find. Remember, we are the eyes and the ears of those who must stay home. To that end, we have a responsibility to record everything, in our journals and notebooks.'

It was the first thing he said that suited me.

If I had a friend here now, I would pour him a glass of sherry and watch him nod his head in agreement as I said something like, if that pest of a monkey ever goes for my watch again, I will fling him out into the middle of the ocean. Not that I actually would do that, just that it would be enjoyable to say it aloud and make my companion laugh, thereby making me feel a little more positive about everything. Or I could pout about the admiralty pointedly ignoring my expertise and placing Officer Fitzjames in charge of all magnetic observations. Are they smarting because I refused their offer to lead this expedition? They have taken away most of my usual duties, leaving me feeling that I am merely an ornament.

Must I always be the outsider in my own life? I have no wife, no children and no real home on land. In fact, all I have is this little room containing my bed, this table and chair, and my few possessions which easily fit into one trunk. Am I rich or am I poor?

I will now retire to bed after a chapter from my novel. I suppose that is something to be considered. Both ships possess two very fine libraries, over a thousand books. If my old school teacher was here, he would wish to persuade me that books are the only friends I need on this trip.

Well, we shall see.

Saturday evening, 31st May 1845

We have reached Stromness harbour, the largest of the Orkney Islands, and our last stop before we head for Arctic waters. Our immediate plan is to replace four bullocks that have died with four live ones. However, we are too late for business today and it seems the good people of Stromness refuse to trade cattle on Sundays so we have to wait until Monday. I do not mind really. It is a chance to send off our letters, our final farewells. There will be no chance to post anything after Tuesday.

My steward finally solved the riddle of my missing tea and sugar. I ordered it from Fortnum and Mason, who promptly sent me the bill onboard *Terror* before we left England. When I could not find the crates, I was told in no uncertain terms that they had made the delivery. Well, it turns out that they were telling the truth, only instead of sending the tea and sugar to me, they sent it to Officer Fitzjames. But didn't they do well to get the right man to pay the bill!

Tuesday, 3rd June 1845

Let me write here that whoever allowed Officer Fitzjames to select the crew is a damned fool. Only seven out of the twenty-four officers he chose have been to the Arctic before. This is Fitzjames's first time too, which explains his choosing one beginner after another, to make himself feel better about his own lack of experience. Now he has proved that he has no control over the men.

Any officer worth his salt knows not to trust ordinary seamen who will take any opportunity to drink themselves into a stupor. This is why I refused to allow any of my crew to go ashore over the weekend. Not so, Officer Fitzjames. He permitted no fewer than four sailors to go to Stromness, and not only did they get blind drunk but they also smuggled alcohol back onto *Erebus*. So, we wasted two precious hours today because Fitzjames was obliged to make a thorough search of the ship to ensure that no illegal alcohol remained.

This is an embarrassing start to our noble expedition. We finally leave tomorrow, a day late thanks to big winds and Fitzjames's stupidity.

Wednesday, 4th June 1845

At last, we have left the Orkney Islands behind, along with one of our men who the doctors believed to be suffering from consumption. We cannot take chances. With so many men breathing in the same air for months on end, any illness would quickly become a shared one. Certainly, it is no laughing matter, yet it seems that there has been some joke about Jacko, the thieving monkey, having a bad cough. Doctor Goodsir, who was obliged to examine him, assured me that the only thing wrong with the animal was his greed. He gorges himself on whatever he can find. Well, I will not have him on *Terror*. Ever.

Wednesday, 25th June 1845

We have reached Arctic waters. Now, it becomes obvious as to who is experiencing their first visit. Some of my crew, on sighting their first iceberg, needed prompting to return to their duties.

Certainly, my third mate, Officer John Irving, betrayed his innocence. I found him on deck, in awe of a colossal berg. 'Do you see, sir? Oh, I had never imagined that they could be so … so … I mean, it is bigger than any church or town hall.'

I was determined not to look so impressed, only saying, 'I suppose one's first iceberg is always a bit of a shock but you soon get used to them. In fact, the size of this berg is quite ordinary for this part of the world.'

The expression on the lieutenant's face suggested that he did not believe me. He was one of those ambitious young men in search of glory and fortune. Quite a few of his fellow officers shared his belief that all that was needed was a trip to the Arctic to be rounded off with the rapturous applause of their fellow countrymen on our return.

The men were in good spirits, roused by the clear, green water and the sharp, fresh air. Even my heart yielded to the cold magnificence of our surroundings. The fog of the last few days has disappeared, making it truly seem that a veil has been lifted.

Lieutenant Irving was still enraptured by our surroundings. For once, there was no breeze and the only movement on the water was the discreet push of waves caused by our ships. 'It is like a painting,' began Irving once more, 'the sky, the water and the icebergs. Nothing moves or makes a sound.'

The Arctic instantly made a fool of the young lieutenant as, at that very moment, there was a deep, guttural rumble before the iceberg seemed to shatter, almost half of it sliding gracefully into the water, the crash causing spray to leap towards the sky. Shouts of excitement sounded out from *Erebus* as the sea, which had been so placid, woken from its slumber by the massive mound of ice, spewed out waves that rushed towards us, billowing with menace. However, we were too far away to be troubled by them, and *Erebus* and then *Terror* merely swaggered in response.

'What happened? What caused it to fall?'

I fancied that I detected anxiety in the lieutenant's tone and may have sounded a trifle smug in my reply. 'Why, lieutenant, this serves as a reminder that nothing lasts forever.'

Saturday, 19th July 1845

Early this morning, I took my cup out on deck, enjoying the relative lull. It was cold with a pearl-grey mist that was disappearing even as I sipped my sweetened tea. A splash in the distance made me reach into my coat pocket for my telescope. I guessed it to be a whale before I could see a thing. In fact, I think that may have been what woke me so early, that strange haunting sound that a whale makes: neither a howl nor a whine. I can only describe it as a song, a ballad. To my delight, there was more than one, including a mother and its calf. They are such unique creatures. I watched them taking turns to break the surface, smacking the water with their tails and, for those precious moments, I pretended that only they and I existed. They soon disappeared and I returned to my cabin to prepare for the day ahead.

After lunch I was back on deck, in conversation with lieutenants Little and Irving when we heard the cry 'Ship ahoy!' We made our way to starboard. Even as Lieutenant Little needlessly declared, 'A whaling ship, I'll wager. Yes, there is the rowing boat', I found myself looking at the same whales from this morning. There was the mother and calf again and it seemed to me that the group was striving to protect them. They swam either side of them, doing their best to form a shield from the hunters who were fast upon them. But it was too late. The mother had already been harpooned. She could swim another hundred miles as fast as she could and not be free of it. The spear in her side enabled the pursuers to follow them, the long, dark rope between the harpoon and the rowing boat never allowed to slacken while she was still alive.

Lieutenant Irving gripped *Terror*'s side with both hands. 'They almost have it!'

The men in the rowing boat hardly saw us, so intent were they on their prize. Nevertheless, they were being championed by our crew and the men on *Erebus* who roared their encouragement at such entertainment.

Meanwhile, their own ship soon arrived on the scene, the captain waving in salute.

'It is starting to slow down.'

The lieutenant was correct. The mother was tiring, her blood streaming behind, the bright red watered down by the sea. Her calf kept pace with her, though it must have been exhausted. This chase could have started hours ago. I suspected neither of them would leave the other. The rest of the whales began to surge ahead. What choice did they have? To stay with the wounded mother meant a violent death for all of them. Sensing that the end was near, the men in the rowing boat stood up together, spears in hand, and prepared to take aim once more.

As the gap lessened between the boat and its quarry, the hunters threw their spears, only this time they included the calf in their attack. There were cheers all around, congratulating the men on hitting their targets.

It was now that the other whales made their escape, abandoning their stricken comrades in the water that was blush and stank of blood. Then, the calf began to fall away from its mother who could do nothing to save him.

Not wishing to see the final killings, I returned here to the calm of my cabin. Now, I am a practical man and a scientist. Men hunt whales for their blubber and oil that provides lamps for lighthouses and train stations and all manner of buildings, while their bones are needed to flesh out women's skirts and corsets. They are thus required by both genders, by everyone. Still, I am made restless by a vague sense of regret.

6

Visiting the grave with Mama
and Aunt Harriet

We were going to visit Weesy's grave. Papa was away on business, as usual, so it was just us: Mama, Aunt Harriet, William, Sarah and me. Grandfather had already been to the grave first thing this morning. I gathered he went every morning and always alone. Aunt Harriet carried bunches of flowers from the garden, whilst Mama pushed Sarah's pram. I could smell the roses as I trailed behind them. William had Bobby on his lead. I had wanted to walk him, obliging Aunt Harriet to toss a coin: heads – the winner walks Bobby; tails – the loser walks alone and sulks. Typically, William won and did not bother hiding his pleasure from me.

As I walked, I enjoyed listening to the clicks of my heels

against the pavement. They sounded so grown up and I made sure to fasten my heel down heavily, step by step. Of course, my brother chose that moment to interrupt me with a grin, saying, 'You sound like a pony!'

I stuck my tongue out at him again. He was lucky we were in company or else I might have boxed his ears for him. He shrugged. 'I thought you liked ponies!'

'That does not mean I want to be one. Sometimes, you can be so rude!'

He looked confused. 'But I did not say you were a pony, just that you sounded like one.'

I rolled my eyes, already weary of the conversation. Why was I even talking to him? He was just a silly little boy. What I needed was another sister.

Oh!

I blushed as I remembered where we were going and why.

'When is Papa coming home?'

Mama was surprised at my sudden question. 'He should be back tomorrow week. Why do you ask?'

I paused, trying to think of a good reason, but Aunt Harriet replied instead, 'She just misses her father, don't you, pet?'

I nodded which satisfied them both. Papa was in Belgium or France or Spain, I think. They were the three countries he visited most, apart from England. Someday I hoped to travel with him. The farthest I had ever been was across the River Foyle. It is quite a thing to look back from a distance on the city you live in. Papa says it puts everything into perspective. I did not exactly understand what he meant, but he assured me that the more travel I did, the better appreciation I would have for my home. Before he left, I asked, 'Can I come with you on one of your trips?'

He looked at me and smiled. 'That is something we can consider for the future, but right now I do not wish your mother to be lonely for you.'

I nodded sweetly to cover my frustration at Weesy's death preventing my own wishes from coming true.

The streets were busy in the sunshine and there was plenty to look at. Ladies in pretty dresses strolled around in small groups, stopping now and then to gaze at the shop windows. Messenger boys, carrying boxes of goods, darted expertly in and out of the crowded paths, in their efforts to get by, as if they were racing time itself. A constant flow of carriages provided lots of noise thanks to the clatter of wheels and horses. The man with the organ was in his usual spot, his little monkey dancing to the music and then holding out its dainty red hat with a flourish, to collect coins from the small crowd that gathered. Of course, Mama and Aunt Harriet steered clear of him lest Sarah or William demanded to watch the whole act through. Bobby pulled on his lead and growled at the monkey, sniffing the air in a fury. It was difficult to hear my heels now, even though I continued walking as heavily as I could.

We all wore black to show we were still in mourning. I envied the girls I saw who were dressed in assorted blues, pinks and yellows. Sometimes it seemed to me that Weesy was now in charge of our every move and mood. I recognised two girls across the road, walking arm in arm, about a step ahead of their chaperone, Betty, their maid. They were the Bradley twins, Tess and Katie, and they were in my class at school. How elegant they looked. Tess's dress was patterned in different shades of greens, while Katie's was checked in red and navy. They were probably visiting their grandmother who lived in a big house, much bigger than ours, to eat dishes of ice cream and pastries, while I was being marched to a graveyard, dressed in the most boring attire ever, from my neck to my ankles.

'How much longer must I wear black?'

I tried not to sound rude, but it did not seem right to wear black when the sky was blue and everyone else looked happy. When Mama said nothing, Aunt Harriet glanced back at me and said quietly, 'For a while yet. We have to show our respect.' She turned away again, not bothering to wait for my reaction.

'Pardon!' I wanted her to face me once more.

Instead, William butted in, repeating Aunt Harriet's last words, 'Show our respect.'

'Who asked you?' I said through gritted teeth.

Suddenly, Aunt Harriet announced, 'Why, here comes Mrs Delaware and Stanley.'

The two figures were waddling towards us, Mrs Delaware flailing her arms at us as if we were miles away. Stanley did his best to keep up with her on his short, stubby legs.

'Hello there, Coppin family. Hello!'

Mama and Aunt Harriet smiled a polite greeting.

'Oh, my, it is so warm today. Poor Stanley has been complaining nonstop.'

Glancing at the dog, I doubted very much that Poor Stanley could ever have an opinion on anything. He was a pug, that's what they called them, with a short, tubby body, the colour of sour cream, although I could see grey hairs about his mouth. For all I knew, he was as old as his mistress. He licked my shoe and, despite my grumpiness, I bent down and scratched his head, accidentally delighting Mrs Delaware, who glowed when anyone was nice to her dog. Bobby whined in protest and stared coldly at Stanley, who was too busy sniffing the ground to realise that anything was amiss. Next to Stanley, Bobby looked scruffy and overgrown, a fact he seemed to realise himself.

'Now, then, Bobby, let me scratch your head,' bellowed Mrs Delaware. 'There is no need to be jealous. See, we are even now, aren't we?'

Bobby had caught a whiff of something from the old lady and turned on all his charm, gazing straight into her eyes. Humming to herself, she reached into her coat pocket, 'Who's a clever Bobby? Did you smell the treats?'

Bobby stretched himself towards her, staring at her, without blinking. Aunt Harriet laughed. 'Oh, goodness, he is showing us up, acting as if he has not been fed this morning.'

'Now, now,' said Mrs Delaware, 'Bobby is the most well-behaved dog. See how he stands and waits patiently for his reward.'

Producing the treat, she first asked for permission. 'Stanley, we are going to share a treat with Bobby, alright, my dear?'

Stanley sat down at the word 'treat'. It was probably the only word that he recognised aside from his own name. 'As I always say,' sang out Mrs Delaware to the rest of us, 'sharing is caring!'

Both dogs gobbled up their biscuits before turning all their attention back to her again, hoping for more. Mama decided it was time to go, possibly after noticing the large bulge of Mrs Delaware's pocket that suggested that the rest of our day was in danger of being lost to the bestowing of biscuits, one at a time. I would have liked a biscuit but that would never have occurred to the old lady. She only ever thought about dogs. I overheard Mama once explaining to Papa that Mrs Delaware was a lonely widow whose only reason to get up in the mornings was to look after Stanley. Papa grunted, 'Well, then, I should hope for her sake she dies before he does.'

I did not hear Mama's reply, only Papa's apology for his unkind words.

'It was lovely to see you, Mrs Delaware, but we must be going on our way. Children, say goodbye.'

'Bye, bye, cherubs!' bellowed Mrs Delaware as she and Stanley watched us walk away from them. I had the feeling that she was used to people rushing off as soon as she met them so I turned and gave her a little wave, which she immediately returned. She tugged at Stanley's lead to make him bark his own farewell.

'She might have liked to come with us?' I suggested.

Mama and Aunt Harriet exchanged a glance but neither answered me. We kept walking, except for William who had been dragged to a halt thanks to Bobby's eager pacing in front of a lamppost. William tugged at him helplessly. 'C'mon boy, come on, now!'

I waited for him, idling, watching the retreating figures of Mrs Delaware and Stanley in the distance. *How odd*, I thought, *I don't remember seeing that man behind her.* Only Stanley persisted in looking around to bark at the man. A perplexed Mrs Delaware turned to see what was causing the dog to fuss. It struck me that she continued to look when it should have been perfectly obvious that the man was upsetting Stanley because he was walking far too close to his mistress. What was he doing? Could he be planning to snatch her handbag? Instinctively, I turned to call Mama, but she and Aunt Harriet were too far away and I was not allowed to shout on the street.

All I had to hand was my little brother and Bobby. 'William, we have to help Mrs Delaware. I think that man is going to rob her!'

'Huh?' was his uninspired reply. In his haste to turn around, he tripped over Bobby's lead and lay sprawled on the ground while Bobby gave him a sympathetic lick on his ear. 'What man? I don't see who you mean.'

Stanley was still barking away while I lifted my arm to point out the would-be robber. 'There!'

Only he wasn't.

How could that be? Even if he had overtaken Mrs Delaware, I should still be able to see him because it was a long street, with no side streets. Quite simply, there was nowhere else to go. Feeling somewhat embarrassed, I shrugged. 'Well, I am glad he is gone. He gave me a fright when I saw him lean toward her bag.'

I was exaggerating to justify my behaviour. Then, as an afterthought, I said, 'Don't tell Mama.'

'I won't.'

Bobby was waiting patiently to walk again and off we trotted after our aunt and mother. Just as we turned the corner, I took a last look backwards. Mrs Delaware and Stanley were tiny now, but it was just the two of them, although I could still hear Stanley barking his annoyance.

In order to reach the church, we had to climb the walls. Well, climb is not exactly the right word. Once we reached Bishop Street, there were steep steps that took us onto the wide board-walk atop the city walls. Papa said the walls were famous all over the world and that he had met people from different countries who had visited Derry to walk them especially.

Aunt Harriet began to stoop down to help Mama get the pram up the steps until a gentleman approached to present his services.

'Please, ladies, allow me!'

He doffed his hat and gave me his umbrella and newspaper to hold while his companion, a woman wearing a dark blue coat and a tight smile, waited for him at a distance. Mama was most gracious. 'Thank you, sir. We were at quite a loss as to how to proceed.'

'Of course, madam, of course.'

He did not look very strong to me, but his manners had pushed him into action. Taking a moment to study the situation, he suggested, 'It might be best to remove the child until we have achieved our goal.'

Bobby gave a woof of approval to this and sat down as if ready to offer his advice, should it be necessary. Aunt Harriet lifted a delighted Sarah out of the pram. She much preferred to be walking alongside us, while I could not think of anything more pleasant than being pushed around in the sunshine.

Advising Mama to keep hold of the handle, the man took a

deep breath and bent down to take the pram by the two back wheels, inching his way to the first step.

'Oh, do mind your back, Horace!'

William and I did our best not to laugh. We had recently found a small hedgehog in the garden and decided we would adopt him. The first thing we did was give him a name. Guess what name we chose!

Hearing Aunt Harriet's warning murmur of 'children', we refrained from looking at one another.

Horace explained his companion's concern with two words, 'My wife!'

Mama and Aunt Harriet took turns to nod graciously at Mrs Horace, with Mama adding, 'He is most kind.'

His wife accepted the compliment with a complacent smile.

It took longer than expected due to Horace's unwillingness to take a single step without checking his measurements and position. He tried not to huff and puff, which would have been most ungentlemanly. Meanwhile, Mama politely struggled with her end of the pram, not wanting to overburden him. Aunt Harriet looked uncomfortable, but there was no room for her to get involved so she stood there, helpless, holding Sarah by the hand.

The handle of the gentleman's umbrella was a duck's head, that is, it was shaped to look like the head of a duck and it was well polished, shiny and smooth to touch. 'Look, Aunt Harriet,

Grandfather used to have an umbrella like this.'

Perhaps fearing that I was accusing Horace of somehow stealing Grandfather's umbrella, my aunt loudly addressed Sarah, 'Look, little one, at the seagulls in the sky.'

Sarah gazed upwards and began to flap her arms in excitement.

I switched hands, swapping the newspaper and umbrella from left to right and, as I glanced down, a heading caught my eye or one word of it did, Mystery. It was a favourite word of mine, both for how it sounded and for what it might mean, which could be anything at all. I read quickly, about two ships that had sailed to the Arctic to find some passageway or other. Alongside the article were two small pictures of the captains. Before I had time to read any more, Mama was thanking Horace profusely while giving his wife a brief wave and looking to the rest of us to follow her immediately.

'Ann, give the gentleman his newspaper.'

I looked up in dismay, making Horace curious about what I had been reading. 'Ah, the missing ships in the Arctic. Yes, a shocking story, isn't it? Over a hundred men and no word from them in over two years.'

Horace spoke quickly as he retrieved his paper and umbrella, glad to be free of the pram and able to continue his morning stroll with his wife. They left in haste amid a flurry of thank yous, obviously planning to be nowhere in the vicinity for when we needed to return to the street once more.

Climbing the steps, I asked, 'Can we buy a newspaper?'

I wanted to finish reading about the two ships. Both my mother and aunt ignored me. Mama shooed Bobby away from her. 'William, pull him out of the way. I almost wheeled the pram over him.'

Sarah was trying to unhand Aunt Harriet, wanting to walk by herself. Aunt Harriet was pleading with her to behave. 'Now, Sarah, good girl. You must hold my hand. We are almost there!'

Nobody was listening to me so I tried again. 'I saw something interesting. Two ships have gone missing!'

This time, Mama and Aunt Harriet swung around to me; Mama, in particular, looking frightened. 'What ships? Gone missing where?'

Surprised at the vehemence in her tone, I answered, 'In the Arctic.'

Mama sagged a little and put a hand to her chest. Aunt Harriet was shaking her head. 'We thought you meant two of Papa's ships. Really, Ann. How could you scare your mother like that?'

I felt foolish and apologised. 'Sorry, Mama. I forgot about Papa being away.'

'Well,' said Mama, a little too loudly, 'I wish I could!'

'Oh, now,' said Aunt Harriet. 'I am almost sure that Grandfather got the paper this morning. He might let you borrow it, provided that you ask him nicely.'

Grandfather! Of course! I had forgotten all about him too. 'Thank you, Aunt Harriet. I will ask him as soon as we get home.'

'Here we are, at last!' Mama announced.

'And we are just in time. Look, it's a wedding!' gushed Aunt Harriet.

We joined the crowd already gathered at the gates. If I was ever getting married, I would want to do it in this church. Everyone stops to admire the scene. Ceremony over, the bride and groom walked outside as their family and friends swarmed around in delight, throwing rice and laughing at the squeals of the women who mistook the rice for insects or bird droppings.

The bride's white dress was covered in lace and bows, and as wide at the church's porch. Aunt Harriet whispered to me, 'So, Ann, what do you think? Would you like to get married one day?'

I considered her question and also the fact that she had never married. Was there a reason? 'I am not sure.'

She put her arm around my shoulders and drew me close. 'I know what you mean,' she said.

It took a while for the wedding party and the audience to disperse. Mama warned William to pull Bobby away in case he was tempted to offer his own congratulations by jumping up on the bride's white dress or the groom's pristine suit. As the

couple moved through the crowd of onlookers, they acknowl-
edged the well-wishers. Unable to contain herself, Aunt Harriet joined in. 'Long life to you both. Many congratulations!'

The bride gave her a warm smile. Somebody clapped their
approval and a few others joined in. What was it about weddings that made everyone happy and giddy, even people who
knew neither the bride nor groom? I asked Aunt Harriet, but
she only said, 'Oh, everyone loves weddings!'

We waited until we were alone before filing into the church-
yard. While Mama sorted out her flowers, I scuffed at the rice
on the ground, wishing I could have followed the wedding
party instead. The headstone sparkled in the sun, thanks to tiny
shards of glass that were strewn throughout, while we stood
side by side to silently read the letters that had been chiselled
out of it, letter by letter:

Louisa Coppin

departed this life

on 27th May 1849

Aged 3 years and 8 months.

Beloved child of

WILLIAM COPPIN

of this city

7
Friday, 10th October 1845

Captain Crozier's Journal

It has been a while since I have written here.

We have now been farther north than any sailor before
us. Sir John was wise to call a halt to further pursuit
of open water. Enough has been achieved for the time
being. September faded away and we rushed to find a
sheltered spot to avoid the storms that were coming. The
experienced few amongst us know all too well how the
Arctic summer signifies her departure with dangerous
winds that would batter us to kingdom come. So, here
we are, moored at Beechey Island, to see out the winter,
taking advantage of its cove to provide a safe harbour
from what just might well be the worst weather on
earth.

Settling in kept us frantically busy for two weeks as

the necessary tasks were performed. The topmasts were dismantled and the carpenters on each ship built us a roof. Made of wood and canvas, they cover the decks, waiting for Mother Nature to take care of the rest, insulating our man-made roofs with thick layers of ice that will help seal in the heat below. From now on we rely on candles to illuminate our days indoors, while outside it will be pitch black, day and night, no matter the hour.

On the island itself, we built two out-houses and a store house that allowed us to free up much needed space below decks. The men spent twelve days bringing out the tins of food, amongst other things, and depositing them in the store house. Once done, the sight of the stacks of tins set out by themselves was rather thrilling. It had been hard to appreciate them on board. This is the first expedition to be so thoroughly supplied with canned food. Over eight thousand tins filled with such delights as potato, meat, soup, peas, carrots and pudding now have a house of their own on Beechey Island. Oh, but it was wonderful to watch the bellies of our ships increase with the removal of each tin.

I ordered a four-foot-high cairn to be built, tall enough to be seen for miles around, in which I will leave written word about where we are going after we leave the island. That way, if a ship is sent out to find us, they will know what direction we went. Let us hope that we will never need it.

Saturday, 15th November 1845

Today, I took a short walk by myself, leaving the voices of colleagues and crew behind me to concentrate on the crunch of my own feet in the fresh snow. It is an exquisite sound that reminds me of slowly relaxing into a leather armchair. Of course, the cold was unrelenting, gnawing at me like a hunger that could not be satisfied. Oil lamp in hand, I walked as fast as I could, which was not easy, yet I never got any warmer. At least I knew what to expect. Most of the others, those Arctic innocents, are dazed by the weather, acting like children whose feelings have been hurt by an inconsiderate adult who was meant to be caring for them.

This morning I overheard a few of them asking each other why it was so cold! I could not help it and had to ask, 'Pray tell me. What did you expect? Did you not know our destination was a world of ice and snow?'

'Well, yes, Captain Crozier,' one of them protested, 'but we didn't realise that it was going to be this bad.'

I knew I was smirking and wishing that Captain Fitzjames was in hearing distance, although I have to admit that this type of temperature has to be experienced. If you have never been, you simply cannot begin to imagine a chill that pierces your body as painfully as any dagger would and can make it sore just to breathe.

The sight of our ships in their winter coats – their roofs – reminds me of Noah's ark. He built it from wood to carry two of everything so it had to have depth for giraffes along with considerable width for elephants and such like. Old Noah must have had to stop up his nose against the exotic smells of his densely populated ship. The downside of my walks is that they make me aware, on my return, of the staleness and smelliness that is inevitable from too many men, along with a few animals, existing cheek to jowl in cramped conditions. Oftentimes, I confess that the only attraction to boarding *Terror* is the thought of being warm again.

Christmas Day 1845

Today was a good day.

It began with Captain Franklin leading the officers and men in morning prayers, making sure we did not forget the spiritual relevance of the day, although we were thousands of miles away from our churches and loved ones. He seems to relish this role, acting as our father and reverend, and would have made an excellent clergyman. There he stood, with a sombre yet kindly expression on his face as he opened his Bible to the relevant passage. His voice is not so very deep nor loud but he commands our attention by the niceness of his manner. He truly cares about the message he is relaying and, in turn, his men feel cherished and honoured by him, even though I suspect he could not be heard much beyond the first rows of listeners.

I got caught up with emotion in spite of myself when he followed me out afterwards to shake my hand and ask, 'Was that alright? Did the men enjoy it?'

All my jagged thoughts about him melted away and I was genuine in my assurance. 'Of course, Sir John. You spoke so very well as always.'

His eyes shone at my words. 'Well, I cannot forget that they are bound to be missing their homes and their families on this special day, as we all are.'

I said nothing, not wanting to point out that they may be away at least two more Christmases and had better get used to it. Imagine my surprise when he seemed to guess my thoughts, saying, 'You must think me a soft sort of leader ...'

Well, what could I say to this? I could not argue with him, which would be the same as lying. He continued,

'And, perhaps, you are right, Captain Crozier, but today it is Christmas and I see no reason for us not to be in good spirits.'

I smiled. 'Yes, Sir John. Merry Christmas to you!'

He patted me on my arm, reminding of my grandfather, as he replied, 'You, too, my boy!'

The two ships had been spruced up and decorated. Some of the men had devoted several evenings to making paper lanterns and long, twisting streams of colourful materials that hung from the ceilings and embellished every wall throughout. They had also made two large Christmas trees out of bits of wood and cloth.

While the men had their dinner, the officers adjourned to our commander's quarters for our party. As usual, we brought our own cutlery with us and handed them to the stewards on our arrival, who then provided us with wine glasses that were topped up again and again with Sir John's good wine and cognac. There was cake and pudding and beef. I was as well fed as if I had been sitting at my dear mother's table. After our meal we sang Christmas carols with Lieutenant Gore on his flute. I smoked too many cigars and drank too much wine and rather enjoyed myself.

Then, on my way back here, I spent a few minutes gazing at the night sky, fancying that the stars that punctured the darkness might be the very ones twinkling upon London and Banbridge. I pretended it was so. On seeing three shooting stars, one after another, a sight that will never bore me, I made a wish or two, the substance of which I refuse to describe even here. And now I am ready to sleep.

Wednesday, New Year's Eve 1845

I have just had a visit from John Peddie, our surgeon. A reliable man, he is the oldest member of the expedition's four-man medical team and not given to hysterics or exaggeration. Just before we left England, his wife gave birth to a baby daughter. Had we been better acquainted, I might have asked him if he regretted his decision to absent himself from their lives for so long. Thomas, my steward, answered his knock and let him in. I looked up from my book and guessed that the news was not good.

'Sorry to bother you, Captain Crozier, but I preferred to tell you myself that the stoker Torrington has taken a turn for the worse and may not last the night.'

'Are you sure?'

The surgeon nodded. 'There is little else we can do for him, except make sure he is comfortable. Doctor McDonald is with him now and will call me when the end is near.'

John Torrington was our leading stoker who spent his days shovelling coal into the steam engine. I hardly knew him, just that he was young, maybe twenty years of age or so, and was permanently covered in coal dust.

Mr Peddie assured me that we were not in danger from some new and contagious disease, adding, 'He must have been sick for a while.'

I raised my eyebrows at this.

'Oh,' offered the surgeon, 'most likely he did not know how sick he was until he started coughing up blood or, if not then, when his strength finally gave out. They found him on the floor, I believe, his shovel still in his grip though he was barely conscious.'

'Is it the usual?' I asked.

'The usual? You mean consumption, the scourge of the lower classes?'

Was he being sarcastic?

'Yes, I should think so. He has all the symptoms anyway. His breathing is wretchedly loud, though I think he is beyond caring now. A blessing for him really.'

'Well, Mr Peddie, let me know when …' I stumbled over how to finish the sentence.

'Will do, sir, although I will be asking the carpenters to begin on the coffin immediately. No sense in waiting until the last minute.'

I can hear the carpenters at work as I write here. A gloomy sound indeed because I know what they are building. I can only pray that this is the first and last coffin that we will require from them.

Thursday, 1st January 1846

The stoker John Torrington is dead. A dismal start to our new year.

We will bury him today. I went to inspect the coffin, and the carpenters have done themselves proud, taking mere hours to produce a mahogany coffin with brass handles. A fitting end for any man. They tacked on a plaque to the coffin's lid, in the shape of a heart, engraving it with Torrington's name, age and today's date.

I understand he was from Manchester. Just nineteen years of age, he had no time to marry or start a family. He lived with his mother who will have another year, at least, to imagine him alive and well since we have no way of contacting her.

Friday, 2nd January 1846

Yesterday's funeral was rather glum. Of course, all funerals are but there is something about the Arctic that is well suited to a funeral. Perhaps, it was the drabness

of the sky and the snow and the wind that whistled
about the marines whose job it was to put the coffin in
the ground. Before they could do so, however, they had
to spend a couple of hours hacking at the ice in tandem,
with their hammers and chisels, doggedly working away
until they excavated a trench deep enough for the coffin.
As I listened to the clanging of their tools against the ice,
I wondered if Torrington minded being stuck here alone
forever. I think we all did.

Sunday, 4th January 1846

Today was *Erebus*'s turn. A twenty-five-year-old able
seaman, named John Hartnell, died rather unexpectedly.
He had been ill for a while but his death so surprised
Surgeon Stanley that he informed Sir John that he
wanted to perform an autopsy.

It is rather shocking, two young men taken within four
days of one another, both on a ship at the world's edge.

While we waited to hear the outcome of the autopsy,
I paid a visit to Sir John. The marines were out battling
the frozen ground once more with their shovels, so
that Hartnell could be laid to rest beside Torrington.
I did not envy them their task. It was a horrible day
and I rushed to take shelter in *Erebus*, where I found

our commander in his quarters, searching his Bible for another relevant passage for the funeral which would be held indoors as howling winds sorely hampered any attempt to pray or spend any decent time reflecting on this second loss of life.

'I am in fear of repeating myself,' he said, not meeting my eye. We could hear the thuds and chimes that signified the carpenters working on the coffin. Sir John looked troubled. No commander wants to lose even a single man. It can knock everyone's confidence and is an unwelcome reminder of the perils involved on an expedition like this. Sounding somewhat apologetic, he said, 'I have never had to perform two funerals in such a short amount of time.'

'Sir John, the surgeons reckon these men might have died anywhere, that they may well have brought the disease with them.'

I wanted to reassure him, and myself too.

He shrugged. 'Two deaths in six months seems like an awful lot.'

'Yes, sir,' I agreed, 'and there is bound to be a proper explanation. It only seems grossly misfortunate because their deaths occurred in four days. The rest of us are healthy. We have a varied diet and heaped dinner plates day after day. Sir, I have heard it tell that a sickness in the lungs can be resting in a person. It can hide somewhere in the body for months on end before making itself known.'

I might have continued on with my medical lecture for several moments or more had not my attention been taken by a flash of colour in the corner of the cabin. Following my gaze, Sir John allowed himself a smile. 'Well, Captain Crozier, how do you like Jacko's new dress?'

In truth, I was speechless. For one thing, I am not practised in making comments about fashion and, for another, the sight of the scrawny, chattering animal wearing a red dress with dark blue bloomers was too much for me. We both watched it munch away on a biscuit, making sure to catch the crumbs in its tiny paw. All I could think to say was, 'Does he mind wearing a dress?'

Sir John smiled again. 'Haven't you heard, Captain? Jacko is not a male. Mr Goodsir was good enough to put me right.'

'I see.'

'Yes,' continued Sir John. 'I believe that someone is at work on a hat and coat and some other fellow is knitting a scarf and mittens. She has had a bad cough and undoubtedly finds it uncomfortably cold like the rest of us. Lady Franklin will be so glad at the kindness being shown to her little gift.'

'It is always beneficial to have the men kept busy.'

It was not much of a response but what else could I say?

I was most grateful when the door opened to admit Surgeon Stanley and his assistant Mr Goodsir. 'Come in, gentlemen, come in,' said Sir John. 'What news have you of poor Hartnell?'

Mr Goodsir sat down at his table. He could be found here every day as Sir John had offered him the use of it whenever he liked. *Erebus*'s assistant surgeon was also our most passionate naturalist. This was his very first trip to sea. His previous job, before now, was a conservator in a museum in Edinburgh and his Arctic dream was to make important discoveries in its natural history. To this end, he devoted his time to sketching or writing about plants, insects and anything exotic that our fish nets dragged up from the ocean. I admired his diligence and neatness. His notebooks and findings never took up more space than they needed to.

Mr Stanley remained standing, shaking his head when offered some refreshment. 'Well, sir, we examined his internal organs – his heart, windpipe and lungs – and, from what we can see, his death was a combination of consumption and pneumonia.'

'It is what we expected,' added Mr Goodsir.

'So?' said Sir John, wanting a medical opinion that would assure him that all was still well.

'So,' obliged Mr Stanley, 'he would have died anywhere. It has nothing to do with our situation and could not have been avoided. The disease had hold of him before he stepped foot on *Erebus*.'

'Why, Captain Crozier,' said Sir John. 'You were right!'

Hartnell's funeral took place this evening. A single man, like Torrington, Hartnell was lucky enough to have had his younger brother Thomas working alongside him. At least someone in his family knows of his demise. I am sure that makes a difference. The brother is quite devastated, by all accounts, fussing about how to break the news to their mother, though he need not worry about that just yet.

At about five o'clock, the marines carried the coffin outside, where the wind was not screaming quite as loudly as it had been. The rest of us, or as many of us that could fit on *Erebus*'s covered deck, huddled around Sir John and listened to him read about the glory that awaits us all after death.

Sunday, 1st March 1846

Nobody has died this month, thank goodness.

It is almost nine o'clock and I am relaxing here in

my quarters. The candles throw out a cheery light that arches and folds across my bookshelf and desk. Beside me is my cup of coffee and some chocolate that I had squirrelled away for such a night as this. I am swaddled in my heaviest blanket. As far as anyone else is concerned, I have taken to my bed with a headache. Sir John wanted me to dine with him, and Officer Fitzjames had challenged me to a game of chess. It seems that he has devised a competition between our two ships. I might have partaken of the first, the dinner, but not with the prospect of spending all night in Fitzjames's company who, I suspect, is a better player than me. I hear he practises for hours every day and is willing to play with anyone, not just his fellow officers. He takes after our commander, wanting to be liked by all and sundry. I should not be at all surprised to hear that he has invited Jacko to a match.

I wonder what Sophie is doing at this moment. I wish I had a picture of her to dote upon.

Friday, 3rd April 1846

There has been a third death. This time, it is one of the Royal Marines who helped dig the graves in January. Thirty-two-year-old William Braine collapsed whilst out on a long sledge ride this morning. According to his friends, he had been losing weight for a while and did his best to hide his ill health, refusing to admit that there was anything wrong with him, which is a peculiar approach. In fact, it makes no sense to me. Perhaps our doctors could have done something for him, but we will never know now. It is foolish to try to hide anything here. The Arctic is a cruel mistress who wheedles out the frail and takes no nonsense from them.

Wednesday, 8th April 1846

A storm blew up delaying Braine's funeral until today, giving Sir John plenty of time to choose a third passage from his Bible. Because there was no way of leaving the ships in safety, the corpse was kept below deck on *Erebus*. I will freely admit that, for that reason alone, I am glad that he was not one of my men. Sailors are easily spooked and I would not relish *Terror* playing host to a body that refused to wait for the burial before it started to rot. The smell, I believe, lingers still.

Furthermore, it duly attracted attention. When the carpenters went to lay him in the coffin, they found that the rats had been feeding on him. Finally, today, the raging gales morphed into spring breezes and no time was wasted in getting poor Braine off *Erebus*. The improvement in the weather allowed the funeral to be held outside, alongside the graves of Torrington and Hartnell.

The carpenters have constructed three wooden headstones to mark the graves, making it impossible to forget that that they are there. Anyone who leaves the ships has to pass by them and not one of us can do that without making some gesture or salute.

I do not think that I am alone in my impatience to leave Beechey Island. It has not brought us much luck.

Saturday, 11th April 1846

Thomas arrived at my cabin this morning with clean shirts and told me that he had sad news to impart.

'Somebody else has died?' I asked. There could be no other kind of sad news.

'Alas, yes, sir. Sir John is most upset for his little pet, Jacko, is dead.'

I stared at him as he laid the shirts on the back of a chair and began to rearrange my bed clothes. For one moment, I thought to bawl him out for having me think that something far more serious had occurred. However, I suddenly worried what was afoot. 'Is there is a funeral?'

Thomas was strangled by a coughing fit that prevented him from answering my question. In fact, when he did look up, he seemed surprised to find me waiting for him.

Wiping his nose, he finally replied, 'Well ... I ... I don't think so, sir.'

I nodded at him. 'Let me know if you hear anything.'

He gave me a strange look, a sort of half-smile, as if waiting for me to smile in return. I ignored him, deciding that if I heard tell of a funeral, I would make sure to be far too ill to attend.

Sunday, 31st May 1846

The weather is beginning to improve. The sun shines and we grow impatient for the ice to thaw in earnest, allowing us to pack up and sail on.

Every morning, the two ice masters, Messrs Read and Blanky, climb the cliffs with their telescopes, in search of the sea.

Night and day, we listen to the crackling, snapping and groans of the ice as it begins to shift around us. It can be rather unsettling, like a ghostly orchestra playing a hellish lullaby. Some nights, it prevents me from falling asleep and I am glad to have a book to keep me company.

One night, last week, I was reading Homer's *Odyssey*. Meant to be one of the oldest stories in history, I first read it in school, about Odysseus's wandering the seas for ten years, trying to get home after the Trojan War. The wind was whistling about *Terror*, grating on my nerves,

playing a duet with the splintering ice. I reached the part
where Circe advises Odysseus, our hero, and his men to
plug up their ears with bees' wax, to block out the voices
of the Sirens, the murderous women who sing out to
passing sailors, enticing them to approach their shores so
as to shipwreck their vessels against the rocky coastline.
How I envied Odysseus's sailors with their bees and
their wax.

The next morning, I was obliged to calm some of the
men who have never heard the likes of it before. At least
one was convinced we had been surrounded by bears or
wolves. He swore that he could heard growls and heavy
footsteps across the roof of the deck. I explained that it
was only the ice talking. Others worried that the cracks
were *Terror* herself, breaking up around them as they lay
petrified in their hammocks, believing they were to be
crushed at any moment. The more superstitious thought
the creaking and the knocking belonged to the spirits of
our fallen comrades, Braine, Torrington and Hartnell,
wanting to shelter inside the ships.

The daily bulletins of the two ice masters is now the
focus of our every waking moment as we grow eager to be
sailing once more. It is hard to settle down to chores when
there is a distinct possibility that we will be leaving soon.

Friday, 12th June 1846

Today, I took a walk with *Erebus*'s ice master, James Reid.

We are most fortunate to number amongst our crew two of the most experienced ice masters around. Scotsman James Reid and Thomas Blanky from Hull read ice like I read books. They can foresee how the ice is going to move and where. Try as I might, it is much too late for me to imitate their talent. For instance, Mr Reid earned his position as master of the ice only after thirty years of working on whaling ships, having made his first Arctic journey at thirteen years of age. He admitted to me that his family and friends had been surprised at his joining Sir John's expedition. 'Aye, they were flabbergasted, I think, especially my wife.'

'And how did you explain yourself to them?' I asked.

'I told them the truth, that it was my patriotic duty to go and that they would do the exact same if they knew ice like I do. As far as I am concerned, I had no right to stay at home.'

At the risk of appearing overly familiar, I asked, 'And did your wife accept your explanation?'

He shrugged. 'Honestly, sir, no, she did not. But I promised her that this would be my last voyage. And I meant it.'

I nodded, saying, 'I hope you keep your word to her. It is a strange life we lead, and no doubt it is a privilege to be here. Yet, I do not think a man should commit to exploring forever. It demands too much of us.'

Tuesday, 23rd June 1846

It is a little after two o'clock on a sunny afternoon and it has finally happened. We are on the move.

It has been a most hectic day that began with my hearing that the ice masters had dashed back to *Erebus* this morning, ignoring the inevitable questions and comments from the others. There was only one explanation for this. I left *Terror* and made my way to *Erebus*, to see Sir John.

On seeing me in his doorway, Sir John bellowed, 'Captain Crozier, we must make haste and prepare to ship off. Mr Reid says there is no time to spare.'

Barely hiding my excitement, I said, 'Very good, sir, and are you still of a mind to travel south as we decided?'

We had spent many hours over the previous weeks, along with Fitzjames and the other officers, debating what route we would take as soon as we were able to move. The Admiralty advised Sir John that the decision – to sail west or persevere to the south westward – was his to make. However, if there was too much ice west and south-west, then we were to head north where we would surely find open water and, thus, be able to sail freely.

It is widely believed that in travelling far, far north, conditions should greatly improve. This theory sprang from an Arctic voyage made a long time ago in 1608 when explorer Henry Hudson claimed that the farther north he sailed, the warmer the weather got. Ultimately, of course, we are at the mercy of the ice and can only go where it allows us.

Sir John's smile was infectious. 'Yes, we will head south, through the Peel Sound (a narrow waterway between two islands, due south of Beechey Island).'

I also knew that should we be unable to follow any of these routes, Sir John had two options: either spend another winter here, if he believed it to be worthwhile, or return home. Well, I doubt many of us would opt to remain here any longer than we needed to, but I wonder how many of us would prefer to be heading homeward instead.

What followed our meeting was a few hours of orderly chaos. There is a lot of work involved in getting two ships on the move again. The roofs over the decks had to be dismantled and the tall masts set back in their place. Our remaining tins had to be brought back onboard along with any other foodstuff we had stored on land. I watched the men run back and forth, in a rush to perform their chores until all was done, whereupon, following a year of residence, we were transformed into sailors once more.

As we pulled away from the bay that had sheltered us from dreadful storms, I stood on *Terror*'s deck and confessed to Thomas, 'What a bleak place this is. I am glad to see the back of it.'

My steward mumbled something that I assumed agreed with my sentiments.

How long would it be before someone else stood over the three graves and wondered about their occupants? What would they make of our pyramid of empty food tins or our three out-houses that provided no warmth and little shelter from the chilly winds that wormed their way through the merest gaps in the wooden slats?

'Sir, I'm afraid I have a confession to make.'

'What is it?'

If it wasn't so cold, Thomas might well have blushed as he said, 'We left in such a hurry that I forgot all about your cashmere gloves. I mended the torn finger and then washed them and laid them out to dry in the sun. I only meant to air them, really. I wasn't going to leave them long.'

His face was a picture of misery as he added, 'I am so sorry, sir.'

I was thoroughly vexed and refrained from telling him not to worry, that it was only a pair of gloves, that no one had died, or whatever else people say to ease a person's mind. Let him suffer for his negligence. Because, in truth, they were not just a pair of gloves. They were a present from my best friends James and Anne. It is true that I had other gloves but this particular pair meant a lot to me and now they remained behind on Beechey Island, no doubt to be picked up by the next visitor.

'You can dock my wages, sir. Please do. I know they were good gloves.'

I got no pleasure from adding to Thomas's shame and I was certainly not about to take any money from him. He had no idea how expensive those gloves were, though it was decent of him to offer to compensate me for their loss. Still, I wished to make my point and showed him no forgiveness as I snapped, 'Have coffee brought to me.'

He almost curtsied in response before he fled.

Alas, my poor gloves were not the only things to be forgotten in our haste to be gone. We should have left a report detailing exactly where we were going, storing it in the cairn we built, for anyone who comes looking for us. Fleeing Beechey Island like this is a breach of the rules and, anyway, it is just unwise to leave no clue as to where we are going. I could have organised it a few days beforehand but we did not know our departure date and the cairn was too far away from the ships. Perhaps we should have thought of that and built one nearer the camp.

Although, as long as there are no more mishaps and we get home within the next year or two, it will matter little one way or the other. No one is going to look for us unless we are gone longer than three years. An empty cairn is hardly a catastrophe when an expedition is successful.

I kept watch on deck for a while with my telescope, surveying the land as we passed it. I thought of asking for my musket to be brought to me. At this time of the year, I expected to see bears and seals and musk oxen, yet all was quiet. There were no moving dots on the mountains or icebergs. Perhaps they heard us coming or they preferred to be further inland. Besides, we had plenty of food. I had no worry in that respect. We had hardly made a dent in our mountains of tinned food.

The going was rather slow and Messrs Reid and Blanky had to concentrate hard on the waterway. *Terror* followed in *Erebus*'s wake, which really meant that Mr Reid shouldered the enormous responsibility for both ships since he led the way.

Oh, but it felt glorious to sail again. I found myself in quite a sentimental mood as I peered over *Terror*'s side to admire the water that was still crusted in places with a layer of ice but one that was thinning and moved with us instead of holding us in place.

So long, Beechey Island. Take care of our friends who must stay on forevermore.

Next stop King William Land.

At least, that is our plan.

8

Papa changes his mind

Papa was home for the next while, for a few months, he said. He had not been to Weesy's grave since the funeral and Mama was hurt that he would not just go and see the new headstone that she had chosen. 'But I will,' he protested, 'in my own good time.'

Mama said bitterly, 'I suppose you have no need of a headstone since you can see her any time you like.'

The following Saturday, Papa asked William and me if we would like to go for a walk. Of course we said yes and raced off for our hats and coats. Aunt Harriet helped us to get ready and lingered in the hallway, smiling nicely at Papa. She was, I felt, hoping that he might invite her along, but he didn't. Neither did he suggest that we fetch Bobby. I was surprised that William did not make a request. It seemed we both appreciated that this was a special moment and, therefore, we should not complicate it.

Off we went, William and I on either side of Papa. 'Anywhere in particular?' he asked.

'No, Papa … although, I do like walking the walls.'

William nodded his agreement. Papa would let him study the old cannons in more detail than Mama would.

Papa replied, 'Alright! The walls it is then.'

Later on, I wondered if I had suggested the walls on purpose. The clock at City Hall clanged to announce it was two o'clock. Instinctively, Papa brought out his pocket watch to ensure that he was perfectly on time.

As usual, the walls were busy; people used them for their regular exercise, circling them once or twice. Furthermore, plenty of the walkers knew Papa and he was obliged to raise his hat frequently in acknowledgement. However, I could see he had no intention of getting entangled in conversation.

'Is Derry very small?' asked William.

We looked at him, Papa leaving it to me to ask, 'What do you mean?'

William shrugged. 'Just that Papa seems to know everybody or they seem to know him.'

'He is a very important businessman,' I said airily, adding, 'Aren't you, Papa?'

Our father only smiled so I answered my own question. 'He

gives people jobs and brings trade to Derry.'

'Yes, I know that,' sighed William. 'I already know that.'

'I suppose you will be wanting William to work for you, Papa, when he is old enough?'

William looked delighted. 'Really, Papa? I can come work with you?'

'*For* him, not with him.'

I looked to Papa to confirm my appraisal of the matter. We had slowed down to approach the wall, from where we could see the River Foyle mirroring the patchwork of clouds in the sky as the sun worked tirelessly in seeking out gaps to shine through.

'Would you like that, William, do you think?'

'Oh, yes, please. I want to be a captain, like you.'

Papa ran his hand across the bricks. 'You will have to work hard as you need to excel in subjects like mathematics and science, but it will be easier if you have a good reason to, an ambition.'

Here, he glanced at William before asking, 'Do you know what I mean by ambition?'

'Not really!' was William's cheerful response.

'It means having something you really want to do, something that requires work and effort but will be worth it in the end.'

William grinned with the wonder of it all as Papa momentarily lifted the veil over his future, showing him a life of promise and purpose. Filled with envy, I demanded, 'What about me?'

To his credit, William looked as keen as I felt to know what lay ahead for me.

'Well, what would you like to do?'

I hoped to be taken seriously but Papa seemed on the verge of merriment. Perhaps sensing my disappointment, he quickly added, 'Is there anything you have given much thought to?'

'Yes,' I replied while my mind began to pinpoint what. Well, what did I want to do? Finally, I remembered one thing at least. 'I want to travel to other countries!'

'Ah, yes,' said Papa, 'you have mentioned that before.'

'I can go wherever I want, can't I – when I am older?' I asked.

'Oh, I shouldn't doubt it!'

Did he think that I was fantasising about something that I would soon forget? In the meantime, William assured me, 'I will take you wherever you wish to go when I have my own ship.'

It was a kind offer but I rejected it. 'I will be long gone before that, William. You forget that I am a lot older than you are.'

A group of young women appeared in front of us, stretching the width of the walkway. Something about them tugged at me. They seemed so jolly and confident. As they approached,

I noticed odd splashes – of what could only be paint – on some of their skirts. Smears of navy-blue were dashed across the hand of one in the centre, who carried a book and was pointing out something for her friends. 'Her name is Catarina van Hemessen and this is her famous self-portrait. See how she presents herself, not just with her paintbrush but also her palette and easel.'

I stopped to watch them pass by. The one with the book, slender and tall, and not wearing a hat, winked at me. I felt winded.

Papa called me, 'Whatever is the matter, Ann?'

'I want to be like them!' I said.

Papa peered after the noisy group and smiled. 'I am not sure what you mean, my dear. They were rather messy and, well, excitable. That is not exactly you, is it?'

Undeterred, I insisted, 'I think they were artists. There was paint on their clothes and they were talking about art.'

'Ah,' said Papa. 'Perhaps they attend the art school in the Diamond.'

'Well, then, that is what I want to do!'

'So, you no longer want to travel far and wide. You would be happier sitting in the Diamond?'

'Papa, I am serious, just as William seriously means to be a captain like you.'

Papa smiled. 'Oh, my dear, I am not mocking you. Sure,

wasn't my own career founded on nothing more than day-dreaming, when I was your age, about building and sailing my own ships?'

'So, I can go to the art school when I am older and, after that, go wherever I want?'

'If that is what you wish to do.'

I nodded to confirm that this was exactly what I wanted to do.

It was only then that I realised where we were going. Maybe it was easier for him to visit Weesy's grave with us than to accompany Mama, who might need him to behave in a certain way. A flower seller had set up her stall beside the church gates. Papa took no notice of her but once he was inside the gates, he fished out a coin and asked me to buy some flowers.

'We cannot turn up without something for Weesy, now can we?'

William laughed and then looked guilty.

'It is alright, child,' said Papa. 'We cannot be sad all the time and your sister would not mind us having a joke. Besides, she did love receiving presents, didn't she?'

William and I smiled in relief. I trotted back to the flower seller. It was thrilling to be able to select what I wanted. Mama would never have allowed this. Grateful that the girl was busy with another customer, I briefly scrutinised what was on sale. I knew little enough about flowers so I decided to choose my favourite colours, pink and blue. I was buoyed by the fact that, however little I knew about flowers, Papa knew even less so he would not criticise my choice. I pointed out what I wanted to the flower seller and we made the exchange, her flowers for my coin. When I turned to leave, she was rather vehement in her thanks. 'Why thank you, miss. Most kind of you!'

'Not at all,' I replied graciously, having heard my mother say this to shopkeepers.

As I re-joined the others, I presented my chosen bouquet with pride. Papa looked at me inquiringly. 'And where is my change?'

'Change?' I repeated.

'Yes, Ann, change. This little selection cannot have cost much.'

I blushed and grew defensive. 'Well, I didn't know. She never said. She just said I was kind.'

'Oh, I cannot argue with her. You were most definitely *extremely* kind.'

He and William chuckled at that, while I felt obliged to highlight a serious truth. 'It was my first time to buy something!'

'There is a first time for everything,' said Papa, 'and mistakes can be good teachers. Remember that.'

We stood in front of Weesy's headstone. I set down the flowers beside the roses that Mama had left. When I stood up again, Papa placed a strong hand on my shoulder, and on William's too.

'Do you think she knows we are here?' asked William in a low voice.

Papa relaxed his grip. 'I thought you two spoke to her every day?'

Was this why he brought us out of the house, to ask about Weesy's spirit?

I spoke first. 'No. She comes and goes, I suppose.'

In truth, I did my best to forget that she might be around the house. Well, I could not be thinking about her all the time, now could I? Furthermore, she did not need me to dwell upon her since I am quite sure that she remained a constant presence in Mama's and Papa's heads and Grandfather's and Aunt Harriet's too. She did not need anything from me.

'She has been playing with my ships again,' said William.

Papa was intrigued. 'What do you mean?'

William shrugged. 'She moves them around. Sometimes it takes me a while to find them.'

'Couldn't it also be Sarah or Laura tidying up?' asked Papa.

William paused to consider this before shaking his head.

'You still believe us, don't you, Papa?

When Papa did not reply, I reminded him, 'You see her too.'

His expression was peculiar. I felt he was preventing himself from being honest and suspected that Mama was behind his reticence. He spoke quietly. 'I was very sad when Weesy died and then I had to go away so soon after her funeral.'

William and I stood in silence. Around us, the birds sang, and then, out of nowhere, a robin landed on the headstone and regarded us with interest. It seemed to be listening to Papa as keenly as we were.

'What I mean, children, is that when I came home again … well, I had no chance to get used to her not being there. In my head, she was still part of our family, part of our home.'

The robin darted down beside my expensive flowers, having seen a small, stringy worm in the upturned earth, which it gulped down with relish.

Sounding disappointed, William said, 'You mean, you didn't see her?'

Papa sighed. 'I don't know. I just don't know. All I do know is that I wanted to see her. I wanted her to be still living.'

I broke away from him, startling the robin, who flew off, and busied myself adjusting the flowers. I was angry at Papa for bowing to my mother's wishes. Perhaps she even told him to take us out today in order to tell us this. She was jealous that Weesy did not appear to her. William was too young to realise any of this, but I decided, there and then, that I would never let someone tell me what I should think about anything at all. Never, ever!

Papa and William were watching me. How was I supposed

to stand up now and what was I to say? I was angry, so angry that it scared me a little. But just when I thought I might explode, the robin appeared once more, on the ground, inches from my trembling hand, whereupon I thought I heard a childish voice whisper my name.

To everyone's consternation, including my own, I began to cry. Taking hold of my shoulders, Papa brought me to my feet, turned me around and wrapped his arms around me.

9

Friday, 11th September 1846

Captain Crozier's Journal

Six weeks of freedom on the water has ended this
afternoon. I watched it happen. Mr Peddie, *Terror*'s
surgeon, and I stood on deck together, gloomily watching
Erebus doing her best to battle her way through the sea
that was getting thicker with every inch we covered. The
waves tried to shrug off the thousands of dinnerplate-
sized pieces of ice that Mr Reid called 'pancake ice'.
'When you see water dotted with what looks like flat
white pancakes,' he had often remarked, 'it is a sure sign
that it is about to freeze. Because those pancakes are
going to join together, like a patchwork quilt, forming a
blanket of ice over the entire area.'

Mr Peddie sighed as we listened to *Erebus* and *Terror*
bumping up against the ice, asking, 'Do you think we can

reach King William Land?'

This was our plan, to make our winter camp on the land there. It was an impossible question for me to answer and I could only offer, 'I did not expect so much ice yet.'

We gazed upon the familiar sight of a vast, white unyielding world that did not wish us to pass by. Mr Reid blames the high percentage of ice on the high winds that announce the end of summer. It is they that have pummelled the ice in our direction – or in the direction that we wished to go.

Erebus was met by a force greater than her, stubborn and silent, a sea sculpted in stone, in white marble, or that was how it seemed to me. The solid lumps and dips were once fleeting waves. And then, just like that, the battle was lost and *Erebus* was stopped. The surgeon murmured, 'So, that is it, again.'

I did not think he was addressing me and made no comment. Moments later we were just as trapped. I stamped my frozen feet against the deck and was nostalgic for something more than this nothingness. As if reading my mind, the surgeon shrugged. 'It feels like we are nowhere.'

'Well, Mr Peddie,' I said. 'We are home.'

He smiled and nodded. 'We shall be here a while, I suppose?'

I did not spare either of us. 'Until the sun sees fit to return next year.'

Thursday, 17th September 1846

Today was my birthday.

Sir John summoned me to *Erebus* to drink to my health and receive my presents, a bottle of his favourite red wine and a woollen scarf.

When I got back here, Thomas had left two good handkerchiefs that he had embroidered with my initials on my desk. Such a thoughtful young man.

I have drunk most of the wine and feel quite content in myself and the universe.

Wednesday, 23rd September 1846

At dinner this evening, Sir John declared that we should have a play for Christmas. Naturally, Lieutenant Fitzjames proclaimed this to be the most wonderful idea, while I held my peace, wanting to see what was involved. However, I could not deny that it was a sensible proposal.

It is of vital importance that the men be kept busy to prevent any boredom or lack of interest setting in. They need, I think, to care about something as it keeps the mind sharp and provides a reason for leaving one's hammock every morning. Once their daily chores are completed, their spare time needs to be filled satisfactorily too. Providing dramatics requires a community effort, giving a role to whoever wants one.

Lieutenant Fitzjames was fast making this his pet project by asking, 'I have spent the last week or so cataloguing the books in *Erebus*'s library. Shall I check what plays we have?'

'Well,' said Sir John, his eyes glinting in the candlelight, 'I was rather thinking of William Shakespeare. Lady Franklin and I always enjoy his plays and are particularly partial to *Romeo and Juliet*.'

He knew that most of the crew would not have read it before but he fancies himself as a teacher, our commander, and takes pride in the idea of young, ignorant crew returning from his expedition with a new thirst for knowledge and books.

Mr Goodsir piped up, 'I enjoy Shakespeare too, sir, but I wonder if the men might enjoy something more modern.'

'Like what?' asked Fitzjames. 'It must be something that we have onboard.'

'I think I have the perfect story here,' smiled Mr Goodsir, as he pulled a reddish book from his pocket and held it up for us to read the title: *A Christmas Carol* by Charles Dickens.

'Bah humbug!' shouted Sir John, startling me.

'Oh, yes, I love Mr Dickens' books, don't you, Captain Crozier?'

'I have not read it,' I admitted.

Lieutenant Fitzjames informed me that *Terror* must have her own copy. 'Perhaps you might like me to catalogue your books too?'

I assured him in turn that that would not be necessary but felt bound to offer my opinion all the same. 'The very fact it has Christmas in the title suggests its merits as a Christmas play.'

Sir John nodded in delight. 'Indeed it does. Well, then, we are all decided. *A Christmas Carol* it is.'

On my return, I had Thomas search *Terror*'s library for the novel. He has just delivered it to me, apologising for taking so long. 'The books are all muddled up, sir.'

I thanked him and sent him on his way.

Thursday, 24th September 1846

I have just finished *A Christmas Carol*. It is after five o'clock in the morning and my candle has little life left in it.

What a wonderful little story about the true spirit of Christmas. Very sentimental in places but I must confess that it made my eyes water more than once, then left me smiling after I turned the final page. I hope that I have nothing in common with the cantankerous Mr Scrooge before he is converted by the trio of ghosts to redeem his ways by showering kindness on his employee, the unworldly Bob Cratchit and his family.

Now, I must try to snatch a few hours of sleep or I will be good for nothing today.

Sunday, 25th October 1846

I wonder what is happening with the rest of the world. We are so cut off here. Today, we had our usual service presided over by Sir John. I felt like taking a walk but could only circulate *Terror*'s covered deck as it was snowing heavily and, in any case, it is not pleasant to walk in darkness. It will be some months before daylight returns. And, so, it is as dark as night whether it be night or day.

Thomas made my excuses for escaping lunch on *Erebus*. 'Just between us, mind,' I told him, 'I need a break from hearing about the Christmas play. You know how Lieutenant Fitzjames is; he seems to be under the impression, with Sir John's encouragement, that he alone knows all that there is to know about the theatre.'

Knowing better than to voice his own opinion about an officer, Thomas merely nodded his head. 'I will say you are taken ill but that it is not serious.'

'Yes, do, and will you quietly see about giving me my lunch here?'

I do not wish to dine on *Erebus* but there is nothing wrong with my appetite.

Thursday, 19ᵗʰ November 1846

This evening, I found myself complimenting Sir John once more about his idea to put on a play. He beamed at me saying, 'It has caused great excitement, hasn't it? I have been reading it aloud to a large group of my crew and they seem quite taken with it.'

'It is all anyone is talking about,' I assured him. I refrained from mentioning that I had had cause to reprimand some of his cast – in particular the young steward Gibson who I found nose deep in the novel when he should have been attending his duties. He was ratted out by a colleague who was impatient to get his hands on the book.

Sir John was still talking away. 'Lieutenant Goodsir is designing the set, while Lieutenant Gore, a talented artist, is helping out with the costumes.'

I thought that Gore's artistry was restricted to charting maps but did not say that aloud.

'It does the heart good to find the men sitting in the mess cheerfully sewing the costumes and curtains. I wish

Lady Franklin could see them so happy in their work.'

I smiled. 'Well, perhaps we could put on a performance in London, on our return.'

He laughed. 'I never know if you are teasing me, Captain Crozier.'

I hardly know myself.

Christmas Day 1846

The second Christmas on our ships. Sir John did his usual, Bible open in his left hand while his right moved in time to his own rhythm as he went on and on, doing his best, I suppose, to provide all the entertainment required. We sang our hearts out:

A child is born in Bethlehem, in Bethlehem
And joy is in Jerusalem, Allelujah! Allelujah!

Afterwards, I heard one man exclaim to his mate, 'I can hardly remember what my missus looks like!'

'At least you have one!' was the unsympathetic reply.

Excitement is building for New Year's Eve, when the play is to be performed.

Friday, 1st January 1847

The men did themselves proud this evening. Mr Scrooge was brought to life by Sergeant Bryant, one of *Erebus*'s

Royal Marines. He stumbled over his words once or twice, but we forgave him because of the earnestness he displayed in his performance.

The ghosts were admirable in their parts, including young Irishman Private Pilkington who threw himself into his role as the third Christmas spirit, who shows Mr Scrooge a dark future and a bitter end.

Of course, it was natural that the audience find itself succumbing to self-pity as we watched Bob Cratchit with his devoted wife and children, including the crippled Tiny Tim. How rich Mr Cratchit seemed to us, sitting at his dinner table with his family. I am sure that we all were reminded of loved ones back home who were celebrating yet another Christmas without us. All those empty chairs, all across England and Ireland.

As soon as the curtain fell, up jumped Sir John to clap his hands as if he were in Drury Lane or Covent Garden. He even shouted 'Encore', summoning the 'actors' out to be clapped individually. A third cry of 'encore' was one too much for me, however, and I slipped away back here to *Terror*.

Saturday, 20*th* March 1847

I am sitting in my heavy coat, sipping my coffee and waiting to feel my toes throb back to life again. It occurred to me that the men were in need of exercise. So many are falling victims to colds and sore throats and such like. Since summer is still a couple of months away, I wish to toughen them up. To that end, I summoned them in groups of twenty or so and had the organ brought on deck so that they would have something to march to. I set the tone by leading Officers Irving, Little and Hodgson to stride up and down the starboard side while the men keep a smart pace on the port side.

I saw no evidence of enjoyment, either on the port side or starboard, though that was hardly the point. However, I was irritated by the expressions of sheer mournfulness on the faces of my officers.

Thursday, 15th April 1847

I dined with Sir John this evening, who echoed my wish to be sitting down to a different meal. When faced with yet another plate of tinned carrots and peas along with some sort of meat pie, our commander paused before lifting his cutlery, to admit, 'How I yearn for something fresh.'

'Indeed, sir,' I agreed. 'I was only dreaming about a hefty, pink salmon myself and how it would be an excellent companion to our canned vegetables.'

'I wish for strawberries,' said Sir John, 'and oranges and roast chicken or succulent lamb with potatoes newly pulled out of God's good earth.'

Typically, he looked suddenly guilty. 'Now, Captain Crozier, please don't repeat my words outside my cabin. I would hate our hardworking cooks to feel under appreciated.'

Why does he care so much about the men's feelings?

Friday, 16ᵗʰ April 1847
Sir John's birthday!

We celebrated in style. All the officers squeezed into his cabin, glasses aloft for their share of wine and rum. A singsong ensued, but not before Sir John told us how much he cared for each and every one of us. I gave him a box of fine notepaper, for which he expressed himself most grateful.

The room is spinning a little. Time for bed.

Thursday, 13ᵗʰ May 1847
Eight months now we have been stuck here and there is no sign of a thaw just yet. I took a walk this afternoon, marvelling once more that I was walking on water, frozen water that is. Still, the ice is impressive. I cannot think of anything else that has the strength to hold our heavy vessels, powered as they are by steam engines, in place. What else could stop over a hundred and twenty men in their tracks?

Looking around me, it is easy to be convinced that the ice has always been here and that there will never be free-flowing water on which to sail away. Meanwhile, I long for colour; for fields of billowing yellow corn and for neat red-bricked houses that sit on greyish streets lined with black lampposts that emit a creamy glow to light the way home.

I miss evenings and towns and even traffic.

As I walked off *Terror* this afternoon, I did my best to conjure up the streets of Banbridge. Instead of a deck, I pretended to have exited my parents' front door and descended their nine steps to the pavement.

Shades of white dominate here, with only *Terror* and *Erebus* providing relief from nothingness, like words on a blank page.

Did we choose the right route? Is there any point to my worrying about this? It would hardly be fair to Sir John if I launched a private investigation of my fellow officers, who would, I think, be unable to say one way or the other since this is all new to them. Indeed, they act as if this is normal and so it is, I suppose. Yet, I feel that there should have been some sense of a break in the ice. It is approaching summer, but the Arctic seems bent on ignoring this fact. There is no life, no movement, beyond us and our ships.

Tuesday, 18th May 1847

Sir John summoned me to a meeting this morning. I found him alone in his quarters, poring over his maps. Mr Goodsir was not at his usual spot and his table was clear of his notebooks and plants. Sir John shrugged. 'They are busy today in the sick bay.'

Before I could question this, he announced that he wished to send out some men to explore the coastline of King William Land. 'We might as well prepare ourselves for release soon enough and I would like Lieutenant Gore to make use of his talents for charting maps.'

'A wise choice, sir,' I replied.

I meant what I said. Gore is a good man. Ten years ago, he was with me in Antarctica, on board *Terror*. A man of many talents, as well as being a skilled artist, he also plays the flute superbly well.

'And,' I said, 'we should take this opportunity to leave word of where we are, sir.'

He nodded. 'We are of the same mind, Captain Crozier. I have asked Officer Fitzjames to fill out a naval sheet describing our whereabouts for Lieutenant Gore to deposit in the cairn at Victory Point.'

'Sir John, Officer Fitzjames should write several notes that can be dropped by Gore throughout his journey.'

Sir John gave me a strange look and asked, 'Do you

think we are in trouble, Captain Crozier?'

Oh, how I wanted to remonstrate with him about leaving that empty cairn at Beechey Island, but it seemed foolish to mention it now. What was done was done. Instead, I fibbed a little to explain my position, 'No, sir, of course not. I am only thinking that we are gone two years and it has been a year since anyone has heard from us. Is it not reasonable to think that ships might be sent out in search of us?'

He made no reply, only staring over my head before taking time to peer at the four corners of his cabin. 'Have you lost something, Sir John?'

'Where is little Jacko?'

The question confused me. 'Jacko, sir?'

'Yes, yes. Where is she?'

'Well, she died, sir. A while ago. Don't you remember?'

His face flushed as he snapped, 'There is nothing wrong with my memory!'

It is almost ten o'clock and I sit here in my cabin, trying not to worry about everything.

Monday, 24ᵗʰ May 1847

Wrapped up in coats, hats and scarves, we gathered outside to bid farewell to Lieutenant Gore and his seven men. Their two sledges carry enough food to last them six

weeks while they scout out the best route for us to take,
once the ships are free to move again and, of course, they
will also be watching for open water. They have a tough
trip ahead of them but at least they are turned loose
from tiny cabins and roaming free. Indeed, the eight were
boisterous in their farewells, laughingly promising to send
us letters.

Sir John smiled wistfully as we watched them leave. I
found myself studying him carefully. Did he wish to be
going with them? He rarely left *Erebus* anymore. Well, he
is an old man compared to the rest of us and, I surmised,
had put on more weight thanks to a lack of movement
and his fancy evening dinners. His pallor is none too good
and there is a stiffness as he walks that must surely be the
result of doing no exercise at all. He looked out of place.
A man of his age and girth should be back in London,
in his gentleman's club, reading a newspaper, drinking a
cognac and smoking a pipe.

If she could see him now, what would Lady Franklin
wish for her husband? Surely she would prefer him to
come home.

Gore and his men took an age to disappear from sight.
The ice did not provide an easy road and they were
obliged, almost immediately, to climb and then drag the
sledges up and over slabs of odd-shaped bergs.

As for the rest of us, we returned to our chores and duties, which included anything from scrubbing dishes to mending clothes, to polishing brass, to reading, to teaching others to read and write, to writing up journals and checking out mathematical equations in relation to the magnetic North Pole.

I am impatient to move on. With food for one more year, Sir John might well be prevailed upon to think about going home within the next few months. Once the ice clears, all our possibilities will be alive once more, that we will find the last link of the Northwest Passage and return victorious. If Sophie allows me, I will echo Mr Reid's promise to his wife and tell her that I have done with exploring and am ready to make a permanent home.

Two years ago, when we sailed away from England, I was so depressed about my immediate future and felt it was no more than a dreary, badly lit tunnel but now, two years later, I have come out the other side. With every ending comes a new beginning. For the first time in a long time I feel that a new future is within my grasp. And this time, I will mould it to suit me.

10

Are you there, Weesy?

William showed me one of his ships this morning. The three masts had snapped off and were hanging on by the threads that kept the sails upright and stretched them wide. Now, the sails dipped in defeat, while the threads were a complicated mess of tiny knots that criss-crossed one another.

'Don't tell anyone,' said William. 'They will only blame me but it is not my fault that it fell!'

I shrugged. 'Fell from where?'

'Here and, see, the window is closed. I pushed it right in, away from the edge.'

The window ledge was wide like mine, wide enough to sit on, which I sometimes did if the sun was shining and I wanted to read in its warmth.

'Was there anything else beside it, maybe a book that could have toppled over and knocked against the ship?'

William shook his head. 'No. It is my favourite one so I made sure it was safe.'

He looked close to tears and I found myself feeling sorry for him. 'I will help you fix it. We can probably glue the masts back together once we sort out the different threads.'

'Ann Coppin, where are you?'

My mother's voice sounded out through the house while William and I tugged at the threads on his ships, folding them over one way and then the other when they refused to unravel. The ship almost landed on the floor a second time in my haste to be free of it. I shoved it at William and ran across the landing to my bedroom where Mama and Laura were standing together, waiting for me.

'What is the matter, Mama?'

My mother's tone was cold. 'I think you know what the matter is, young lady. Did you think it was good enough to leave this for Laura to deal with?'

Laura looked at me sadly. I felt she was sorry for getting me into trouble, while I was mystified as to what the trouble was – that is, until my mother gestured impatiently at their feet or near their feet. She must be referring to the rug on the floor by my bed. Papa had brought it back from one of his trips. I took a step forward to see what was wrong with it.

Normally a chaste white in colour, the rug was strewn with paint, my oil paints. Slashed with thick brushstrokes of black and red, the rug was now something vulgar or even violent. In shock, I gasped, 'Oh, my God!'

Mama was now twice as livid. 'How dare you talk like that! That is no way for a lady to behave. How could you, Ann? This is an expensive rug. How could you waltz off and leave it like this?'

'Those are my best paints!'

'I beg your pardon?' Mama's voice was shrill.

I wished that she would allow poor Laura to leave. She looked miserable standing there, unable to get properly involved or ask Mama to calm herself.

I declared to both of them, 'I did not do this!'

The smell of paint was like a further invasion of my bedroom. Normally, I thrived on it, but now it was making a mockery of me, stinging my nostrils, actually hurting me. Of course, Mother refused to believe me.

'What do you mean? This is your room, is not it? And you are responsible for everything in it!'

'Yes,' I said, 'but I did not do this. Why would I waste my good paints like this?'

Mama was too angry to hear what I was saying. Bending down, she picked up a corner of the rug before tossing it down crossly. 'It is ruined, absolutely ruined. What is your father going to think?'

Surely Papa would not believe me capable of this?

The strange thing was that all my paints were still neatly packed away on my desk. The jam jar was still upright, though I would need to count my brushes to see if any were missing.

'I want the truth. Lying is worse than anything else.'

Mama was striving to speak in a normal tone. 'Were you moving your paints around and they fell onto the rug? Is that what happened?'

'Ann didn't do it!'

William was standing beside me, his ship in his hands. I could see he had made no progress in my absence.

'Well, you didn't do it, did you?' Mama asked him, a note of incredulity in her voice.

How could she be so sure that he would never do anything like this but had no problem believing that I could? It was humiliating.

'And do not,' Mama warned, 'for one moment attempt to sully your little sister's name by dragging her into this mess!'

I knew better than to ask if she was referring to Sarah or Weesy. It hardly mattered, anyway, as I was her only suspect. I could only sullenly proclaim my innocence. 'I did not do this.'

Hoping to distract Mama, Laura suggested that she would take the rug downstairs. 'Perhaps it will succumb to a good scrubbing, ma'am. That new soap can work wonders.'

Looking far from convinced, Mama stared at the rug and then told me to take it downstairs. 'You can clean up your own mess. Laura has enough to be doing.'

Nothing would shake her belief that I had poured paint on the rug and then played the coward, hoping that no one would notice it. I hated to think that Laura shared my mother's belief. She refused to meet my eye when I lifted up the rug. To prevent Laura from helping me, Mama told her to move on to Sarah's room, that there was nothing more to be done in mine.

There was no point in telling Mama that this was Weesy's handiwork. It would only make things worse. I spent over an hour working away at the blasted rug, until my hands were red and I had pains in my shoulders and arms, not to mention the fact that I had thoroughly soaked the front of my dress. Mrs Boxhall had given me a scrubbing brush, and although some flecks of paint came off, they only stuck to the bristles of the brush before finding their way back onto the rug once more. In defeat, I sought to convince myself that the splotches of paint had improved what had possibly been a boring addition to my room. If I was allowed, I would let it dry out and put it back beside my bed. As I worked, my thoughts turned to the real question. Why? Why would Weesy do this and break William's ship?

'Are you here now?'

I thought I might as well ask.

'Weesy, can you hear me?'

With some awkwardness, I put down the brush and listened carefully. Not that I expected to hear her voice announcing her presence but I was prepared to hear something strange. However, when the door suddenly opened, I clamped my sopping wet hands across my mouth in fright. But it was only William. Seeing I was alone, he asked, 'Who are you talking to?'

I was relieved and, then, a little disappointed too.

'Come in and close the door behind you. For goodness sake!'

He quickly obeyed, whispering, 'Is the rug alright?'

I rolled my eyes testily. 'No, it is not. She has ruined it!'

'You mean Weesy?'

'Well, who else?' I asked, my nervousness making me irritable with him, though he was not the one I was annoyed with.

'Just be quiet for a moment.'

'Why?'

'Hush, will you! Move over by the door so you can hear if anyone is coming.'

Looking confused, William did as I told him to and I began again, this time more confident because my little brother was with me, 'Weesy, are you here? Did you break William's ship and pour paint on my rug?'

William's eyes widened in surprise but he kept his mouth

shut and listened hard. Then he jerked his head upwards. 'Did you hear that?'

'What? Is someone coming?' I whispered.

He put his ear to the door. 'No, I don't think so.'

Trying to keep the impatience out of my tone, I asked, 'Well, what did you hear, then?'

'I am not sure. Ask her something else!'

It was my turn to obey him. 'Weesy, are you here now with me and William?'

There was a sound. We looked at one another in wary triumph. How can I describe what I heard? Perhaps it sounded like the air around us had momentarily wrinkled or creaked, or like a piece of paper had been rumpled up. William gestured for me to speak again. 'Is that you, Weesy? Can't you let us know?'

Suddenly, we were running, the two of us, getting caught in the doorway in our efforts to outrun the other. We charged up the stairs, not stopping until we reached William's bedroom and shut the door behind us. There, we stood, panting and straining to get our breath back. Laura was moving around next door and I wagged my finger at William, meaning him to keep his voice low should he speak.

'What did you hear?' I asked him.

He opened his mouth but checked himself.

'What?' I snapped, impatient with his reticence.

'I don't know.'

His look was apologetic.

Feeling foolish, I asked, 'Did you just run because I did?'

'No … No!'

That second *no* was drawn out as if he was still thinking about the question. I wanted to shake him and snarled, 'Oh, for pity's sake!'

William gave me a chance to collect myself before shyly admitting, 'I thought I heard someone laugh.'

'You mean,' I demanded, 'you think you heard Weesy laugh?'

He shook his head. 'No, I don't think it was her.'

My impatience vanished. I sat down on his bed and made my confession. 'I thought I heard a man laugh.'

William nodded. 'Yes. That is what I heard too.'

It was unsettling. I would much rather he had heard nothing at all.

'Ann,' said William, sounding fearful, 'do you think our house is haunted?'

His worried expression reminded me that I was the oldest. I should not be scaring him like this. He was only seven years old after all. Feeling guilty about including him in whatever had just happened, I was obliged to lie to him and say, 'No, of course not!'

He swallowed hard and I glanced around, looking for

something safe and ordinary to concentrate on. It was with immense gratitude that I saw his ship, lying on her side, still in need of repair.

'We better get your ship untied before Papa sees it!'

For the first time in years, William took my hand and I walked us over to his toy.

11

Sunday, 6ᵗʰ June 1847

Captain Crozier's Journal

This, I think, has been the worse day yet. Certainly, it is the first Sunday that Sir John has not led us in prayers. I minded more than I would have thought but any change in our established routine knocks our confidence. When I enquired, I was told he was resting. I sent word to see if I could visit him but heard no reply. Not wanting to deal with Officer Fitzjames and his friends, I kept to *Terror*. A football match, between the two crews, had been planned for this afternoon but was duly cancelled.

Then this evening there was a timid knocking at my cabin door. Having already sent Thomas off for the night, I answered it to find Sir John standing there, looking as surprised to see me as I was to see him.

'Why, Sir John, I heard you were unwell?'

He stared at me in confusion as if I spoke another language. Then I realised that his overcoat was open, exposing the fact that his tunic buttons were done up incorrectly, leaving the last button with nowhere to go whilst just below his collar, a button hole lay vacant. He was shivering with the cold, though hardly seemed to notice his own trembling. The shoulders of his dark coat were heavily flecked with ice, making it look as if it had been dipped in crystals.

How had he left *Erebus* by himself? It was a bit of a trek, over ice, between the two ships, especially for a man of Sir John's age and physical status. This was his first time on *Terror* in a long, long time.

In shock, I left him standing there, in my doorway, for a few petrified seconds, before I thought to bring him inside. In order to get him seated, I had to place my hands on his shoulders and gently push him down. Once that was done, I fetched him the cup of coffee I had been drinking.

'Here you are, sir, this should heat you up.'

He gave me a vague smile as he accepted the cup, 'Thank you, child. How kind!'

This flustered me and, for a moment, I thought I should say nothing but then reasoned that the poor man needed my help. 'Sir John, I am Crozier, your second-in-command.'

He gazed at me in wonder as if I had said something

truly magnificent. 'Ah, and you are in charge here?'

I felt winded but was determined to behave as if we were having a most normal conversation. 'Yes, Sir John. That is correct. I am in charge here on *Terror*.'

I wanted to keep mentioning his name in the hope it might break the spell he was under.

He glanced about the room before leaning forward in his chair. 'Well, I need to talk to you about something important. Is this a safe place?'

'Quite safe, Sir John. It is just you and me.'

He beckoned me to come close to his chair. I grabbed a little stool I rarely used and put it right beside him. Was this about his old age? I was reminded of elderly relatives who had to be looked after because they had returned to a child-like stage and knew nothing about boundaries or precautions. Is this what I was dealing with right now, right here in the Arctic? Although Sir John was hardly in his dotage just yet. Those relatives of mine had been in their eighties and nineties.

'They are out to get me!' He tapped the side of his nose with his index finger and winked at me in a conspiratorial manner. 'But they do not realise that I am on to them.'

I hesitated to respond which made him a little agitated.

'Oh, but you must not tell them, do you hear? Not a word, now.'

'I won't tell them but who are *they*, Sir John?'

Scrunching up his face in disbelief, he whispered, 'But you know who they are. Do not play coy with me, young man.'

I tried another line of questioning. 'What do they want from you?'

Here, his eyes widened in horror and he gripped my arm. 'Why, they want to kill me.'

I was stumped and just sat there, racking my brains as to what to say next. He nodded as if I had made a sensible remark to his outrageous claim, adding, 'I think they mean to poison me.'

He must have registered my torment because he suddenly smiled and kindly assured me, 'Do not worry about me, lad. I am too clever by half for them. I just pretend to eat what they give me.'

I returned his smile, though mine was no match for his, as I replied, 'Yes, Sir John!'

I needed to get him back to his quarters as quietly as possible. I could not allow the men to see him like this.

'Sir John, can I get you more coffee? Your cup is empty.'

He peered into the cup. 'Well, yes, it is empty.'

'Might I suggest that I accompany you back to your ship and we will have more coffee in your room?'

He looked at me. 'My ship?'

I did my best to appear confident and trustworthy. 'Why, yes, Sir John, a mighty fine ship, HMS *Erebus*. You are its captain.'

'Am I, indeed? Well, well.' He sounded amazed.

I stood up and began to pull on my coat. Fearful of panicking him, I moved slowly, doing up my buttons, then reaching for my scarf, hat and my gloves. He watched me with interest. I gestured to his own coat, hinting that he should imitate me in buttoning it. He put the cup down and rushed to comply. So far, so good.

'What did you say your name was?'

'Crozier, Sir John, Francis Crozier.'

'Ah, yes. Well, my boy, I must be going now. My good wife will be wondering where I am.'

I had no idea what to say to this. Perhaps it was best to agree since it was the perfect reason to get him back to his room and so I said, 'Yes, sir. It is late. She must be worried.'

'Is your wife with you?'

I shook my head. 'No, sir, I mean, I am not married.'

'How peculiar!'

In spite of the bewildering circumstances, I laughed. 'Yes, sir, it is peculiar, I suppose.'

His manner changed once more, this time becoming

brisk. 'Well, good night. I need to be getting home.'

I picked up my oil lamp. 'Sir, I would be obliged if you would allow me to accompany you.'

He walked to the door and waited for me to open it. I was relieved to have his consent. All was quiet as I led the way to the gangway. Everyone was asleep aside from the lookouts. I assumed that whoever was in our crow's nest did not recognise Sir John but only knew that someone from *Erebus* had made their way to *Terror*, which was no cause for alarm.

I did not envy them their night shift in the freezing cold but there was nothing else for it. We needed to be on our guard from treacherous foes like bears and wolves and even warring natives. Not that I had ever heard of a ship being invaded by the Inuit, but a royal naval ship had to be prepared for every eventuality.

Besides, I had earned my right to my unbroken sleep in my bunk and cabin. As a young apprentice, I had spent countless nights, over many years, keeping watch in crow's nests, a fact confirmed by the stripes on my uniform.

As we walked down the gangway, I gave a brief wave to satisfy the lookout above us. Sir John stumbled a little as we met the ice but I did not like to take his arm. It might annoy him and I could not have a scene in front of the crew.

'Just watch your step, sir. It is a little tricky in places.'

He made no reply, only humming softly to himself. My God, it was bitterly cold. Within seconds my nose and chin were stinging and I felt as naked as a newborn baby. My breath collected in temporary balloons in front of my face, while I could no longer feel my toes or ankles. We crunched along in silence, except for the tuneless humming. The curious thing was that Sir John appeared quite capable physically for this walk. He almost seemed younger as he kept up the pace nicely, making no complaint about the weather.

Instinctively, my gaze took in the night sky. It was a cloudless night and I was rewarded with the sight of miles upon miles of stars showing off their brilliance in miniature. Their shimmering made it seem as if the sky was alive, pulsating with a million different heart beats. An unforgettable moment for me was when Sir John whispered in delight, 'Isn't it heavenly?'

For the first time that night, my agreement was genuine. 'Yes, Sir John.'

I was obliged to raise my arm again before we were halfway across, this time acknowledging whoever was in *Erebus*'s crow's nest. If they recognised their captain, I would just say we were having a meeting. If they raised the point that one o'clock in the morning was a strange time for a meeting ... well, I am sure they would not dare to question me. It is absolutely none of their business what time Sir John and I choose to meet and that is what I would tell them!

As it happened, there was no need for explanations. For all I know, the lookout was asleep at his post but, for once, I did not care about a possible breaking of the rules. We trudged up the gangway and I hoped that Sir John would not need me to escort him to his cabin. I longed for my bed and for this troubling episode to come to an end.

Striving to keep my voice steady when my entire body was jerking in spasms from the temperature, I said to him, 'Now, sir, you are home again. Will you be needing any further assistance?'

He looked around him in obvious disappointment. If he refused to move then, I would be forced to have the doctor woken up, thereby risking all sorts of problems regarding keeping the situation from the sensitive crew.

'Sir John.' I tried to hide my anxiety. 'Is everything alright? Do you need me to lead the way to your quarters?'

He shook his head. I spared him a few seconds to get his bearings. In truth, I felt undone, exhausted by the chilly air.

I barely heard his reply. 'I thought that I really was going home.'

With that, he offered me his hand. I shook it and he turned away from me, finally heading in the direction of his cabin.

I did not feel it necessary to follow him. Instead, I returned here, only focusing on putting one foot down, one after the other.

Friday, 11th June 1847

I have failed in my promise to young Eleanor Franklin, to bring her father safely home. Alas, Sir John, our esteemed commander, is dead.

I have just returned from his cabin on *Erebus*, having spent the previous two hours watching him die. They did everything they could to save him, both surgeons and their assistants, but, in the end, God took him from us.

I am not sure why I stayed in his quarters; he had no need of company with four attendants. In truth, I was probably in their way. Yet, I could not leave. I brought my notebook in case of final instructions and to be ready to put his last words to paper for Lady Franklin. However, he was unable to fathom his whereabouts and did not seem to understand that he was not at home in London. At one point, he cried out, 'Where are my boots?'

In his final moments, he called for his wife, shouted her name, before his last breath left his body. We stood by his bed in silence. Even though we had guessed that the end was near, it was still shocking to see him gone. Mr Stanley, his surgeon, closed Sir John's eyes and I saw his hand tremble in doing so. Perhaps he was tired. I hoped I was imagining that Mr Stanley's pallor reminded me of Sir John's in recent days. We are all so tired these days.

Someone had *Erebus*'s bell ring out the sad tidings and seconds later *Terror*'s bell replied in sympathy. As I walked back here, the men lined the decks of the two ships, shuffling their feet. Several were in tears. They were so fond of him, as I was too, in my own way. He was a lovely, kindly man but I am almost angry for him. He should not have been allowed to spend his remaining years on an expedition to the Arctic and now, in death, he will never leave it.

Saturday, 12*th* June 1847

We buried Sir John at two o'clock this afternoon. I asked Officer Fitzjames to read from Sir John's Bible since I had not the voice for it.

We placed him into the frozen sea. It took the marines more than two hours to dig their way through to a sizeable trench.

Knowing the type of man he was, I felt he would want us to keep him near the ships. Then, when the ice melts into sea water once more, it will take him wherever he wishes.

Sunday, 13th June 1847

I am just returned from *Erebus*. How strange it was, to enter Sir John's quarters and not see him there, holding court. The atmosphere on board both ships is solemn. I feel solemn too. I am now chief commander of an expedition that I had politely refused to command when asked to do so by the Navy three years earlier. I took coffee with Officer Fitzjames, James Reid and Mr Goodsir, who showed me his portrait of Sir John. 'Do you think it is a satisfactory likeness, Commander Crozier? It is only that I thought Lady Franklin might appreciate it.'

He had drawn an elderly man who looked for all the world like he was in blissful slumber, free of the worries that pursue the living. I complimented the artist, 'You have captured him very well, Mr Goodsir. I am sure that Lady Franklin will be most grateful to have this.'

He smiled at this and we sipped our coffee in silence until Officer Fitzjames suddenly looked up at me. 'Sir, will you be moving to *Erebus* now that you are in charge?'

The thought had not crossed my mind. I looked around the room that was full of Sir John's possessions, his books, clothes and boots. There was his cutlery and delph on the shelf, and there on the table next to his bunk was his telescope, snuff box and his pride of joy, his Royal Guelphic Order medal that he was rarely seen without. There had been some discussion about pinning it to his collar to bury with him but I disagreed. I explained my feelings to the doctors and surgeons, as we stood over Sir John, having watched him take his last breath: 'For a wife to be robbed of her rightful place at the bedside of her dying husband and then, furthermore, never be able to visit his grave, we are surely obligated to return as much of him as we can. This medal belongs to Lady Franklin now.'

To my surprise, young Doctor McDonald became quite emotional as he declared, 'Well said, Commander Crozier. What you say is perfectly sensible and correct.'

In fact, everyone agreed with me. As commander, this was something I would have to get used to. 'No, Officer Fitzjames, I will not be moving to *Erebus* but please see to it that Sir John's belongings are packed away safely for Lady Franklin.'

'Yes, sir!'

I wished to keep talking so I added, 'Lieutenant Gore and his party will hopefully have some news for us on their return. Mr Reid, I take it you have not seen any break in the ice yet?'

Erebus's ice master looked apologetic. 'No, sir, not as

far as we can see. It is awfully peculiar to be this far into June and the ice as hard as ever.'

Catching something in his tone, I stared at him until he shifted uneasily in his seat. 'The truth is, Captain Crozier, I have never seen anything like it. The ice should be melting.'

'Well,' I sighed, 'let us hope that Lieutenant Gore can tell us more. After all, we cannot stay here forever.'

'No, indeed,' agreed my companions.

Tuesday, 29th June 1847

There is a plague on our ships. I have just been in sickbay, at the request of Doctor McDonald and Mr Peddie, *Terror*'s surgeon. Men are getting sick despite our cans of food and lemon juice. I had understood that the canned juice was all we needed to prevent scurvy, the biggest scourge of sailors at sea. However, I have just seen a poor man exhibiting all the usual symptoms.

Able seaman Samuel Crispe, just twenty-four years of age, recently lost the use of his legs and was carried to his hammock. There, his teeth loosened and fell out, some he must have swallowed in his sleep since they could not be found. Next his mouth and tongue turned as black as my boots, along with his saliva. A gruesome sight, perhaps made even more distressing by the appalling smell. It made my eyes water and I begged Doctor McDonald for an explanation. He admitted to being horrified himself by it, saying, 'It is as if his body is rotting away now instead of waiting for him to die.'

Rolling up Crispe's trousers and sleeves, he showed me how his now-wasted limbs were an unpleasant shade of purple.

'Well, isn't that scurvy, then?' I asked. 'Had he not been taking his ration of lemon juice?'

'According to his mates, he was,' shrugged the young doctor. 'For myself, I suspect that the juice might not be enough for some fellows. In their case, there might not be a suitable substitute for fresh vegetables.'

It is a disheartening diagnosis.

Ah, Lieutenant Irving has just informed me of Crispe's demise. I gave orders for his burial to be carried out immediately. I have to rid *Terror* of the stink of death.

Saturday, 10th July 1847

A long week ended this afternoon with the return of Lieutenant Gore and his men. It was a far less boisterous scene in comparison to their departure.

I held back, allowing my officers to explain Sir John's loss, and then asked for the lieutenant to make his way to Sir John's cabin, where I was waiting to see him with

Ice Master Reid and Officer Fitzjames, who had ordered coffee and biscuits.

I had pinned a lot of hope on Lieutenant Gore's party. The men and I were in need of good news and I was impatient to speak with him.

However, when he arrived, I was disappointed to see him looking pale and thin. I greeted him quickly, 'Did you have a good trip?' The question seemed foolish considering our location. The Arctic rarely permits anyone to experience anything as innocent as a 'good trip'.

Lieutenant Gore is not a stupid man and, therefore, he did not waste time trying to impress me. Also, he was in shock over Sir John. He glanced around us as if expecting our commander to suddenly appear, and I wondered at his feelings at finding only me in command instead.

'Sir,' he began, 'we did not find any break in the ice.' He paused, allowing that to sink in before continuing, 'Furthermore, we travelled along the coastline and did not find any signs of life. There was nothing to hunt, I mean, in all these weeks we never saw a single caribou, hare, seal or bear.'

Mr Reid shook his head, whilst Officer Fitzjames gazed at me for my response. The lieutenant succumbed to a coughing fit while I poured myself another coffee, for something to do.

Then I remembered to ask, 'Did you find the cairn?'

Managing to catch his breath, Lieutenant Gore answered, 'Yes, sir, that we did. We stored the report sheet in it and ensured that the cairn was solid before adding a few more stones, giving it a greater height. And we dropped the rest of the notes sporadically.'

'Well, then,' I said. 'That is good news. It is more than we did at Beechey Island and, for that, I am grateful to you, Lieutenant.'

Officer Fitzjames agreed, 'Why, yes, sir. They will have no trouble finding us now.'

Mr Reid stared off in the distance, refusing to meet my eye. No doubt, he was thinking about the fact that the autumn was coming around again and we would still be here thanks to this summer's failure to melt the ice. Our ships cannot move and, likewise, no ship would be able to reach us.

I told the lieutenant to get some sleep before writing up his report of his trip. 'I look forward to reading it.' I do not know why I said that.

Anyway, it is only early July. Who knows what the next few weeks will bring? September ushers in the autumn and, hopefully, we will be long gone from here.

Friday, 3rd September 1847

We face another autumn, winter and Christmas here. I will refrain from writing so frequently as there is little to report. I never imagined that we would end up stuck for another year. No, that is not exactly true, is it? But I find no comfort in seeing my initial worry, about sailing too late in the year, being realised.

12

Ask me no secrets and
I'll tell you no lies

I was excited because our relatives were visiting us that afternoon, all the way from County Cork. Papa had received a letter, last week, announcing the time of their arrival, sending Mama into a bit of a tizzy over the 'state of the house'. Aunt Connie was Papa's older sister, married to Uncle Virgil, with my three cousins, Charles, Charlotte, and baby Virgil the second. Actually, I was not sure if I needed to say 'the second' and meant to check before they arrived.

Charlotte was fifteen years of age, with dark brown hair and brown eyes like mine so that some people mistook us for sisters, which pleased me tremendously. Oh, but she was much more sophisticated, and I had always wished, for as long as I could remember, to be tall like her and as slender too. And she was so clever. 'My dear,' she would say, 'you must read this poem. It is simply divine.'

She helped me see that I should become a painter. When we were older, we planned to visit Paris together. Just the two of us, if we were allowed to, of course. Charlotte said that every sensible person knew that Paris was the most beautiful city in the world, which was why all the best artists lived there. She had met someone who had been there and they described elegant women in the most stylish gowns and hats and how civilised people sat for hours over cups of coffee and pastries outside the coffee houses. 'Can you imagine, ma petite? There they sit, for hours on end, having the most intellectual conversations while watching a parade of the most fashionable persons walk by. Does it not sound utterly heavenly? *Oh lá lá!*'

Her French was ever so good too.

In truth, I felt a little unsure about it but had to believe that if I was with Charlotte I would be brave enough to take my seat at a café. For now, we would keep our plans from our parents as they would be sure to dismiss them, though I was hopeful that Papa, at least, would understand.

When we were not discussing such things, Charlotte would take me into confidences about her little crushes, as she called them, on her brother's friends.

Charles had a lot of friends, it seemed to me, because every time we met up, Charlotte was talking about a different boy who was making her blush and feel anxious by his very presence. I found these talks thrilling. She was living in a completely different world to mine. William's friends were mostly annoying creatures who still needed their nurses to wipe their noses and tie their shoe laces. I wished I had a brother like Charles. He was sixteen, going on seventeen, almost as tall as Papa and brimming with intelligence and social graces as far as I was concerned. I made the mistake of saying something along those lines to Charlotte once and, for ages after, she taunted me about having a crush on her brother. It was mortifying – mostly because, for all I knew, it was true. Certainly, he was the only older boy that I really knew and it was hardly my fault that I found him handsome. Even Aunt Harriet complimented him on his good looks, which made him laugh. And he had such a pleasant laugh, gentle and light, in direct contrast to his father's, Uncle Virgil, which Aunt Harriet once compared to Roaring Meg, the loudest cannon on the walls of Derry, left over from the Siege of Derry.

Aunt Connie did not look anything like Papa but she was serious like Papa could be. She rarely smiled and, in fact, could look quite fierce when she was merely listening to someone. She dressed in black a lot, I mean, even before Weesy got sick. I felt that Mama was slightly nervous of her. Well, she did have an unnerving habit of staring. For example, I would be listening to Papa or Charlotte and, gradually, a sense of unease would pluck at me until I realised that my aunt was studying my entire figure, inch by inch. I got the feeling that she disliked Aunt Harriet as she rarely spoke to her.

They had not been here in ages, probably not wanting to come too soon after Weesy's funeral which they had been unable to attend. Mama dashed about making sure that the house was perfect. Not surprisingly, Papa was locked away in his study while the preparations were being made, only allowing William to share his hiding place if he promised to be quiet. Aunt Harriet was on flower duty and kept moving around vases of our roses to see where they looked best and where we could make use of their perfume. I overheard her telling Mama not to overdo matters. 'You know what she is like.' I assumed she was referring to Aunt Connie.

I helped Laura polish the good silverware, which was only used when we had guests. I did not mind doing this, although I was quite sure that my cousins were never expected to do any housework since they had twice as many staff as we did. Mama did not believe in filling our house with extra servants when there was no harm in doing some things for ourselves. 'There,' I said to Laura, 'I can see my face in all of them.'

'Very good, Miss Ann,' she replied. 'Now, let us set out the places. The napkins are pressed and I have already polished the glasses. We just need to ask your mama for a seating plan.'

'I'll go ask her!'

'Miss Ann?'

I turned back. Laura appeared to be deciding what to say or how to say it. I waited politely for her to speak, although if it was anything to do with the table and dinner, Mama was the one to ask.

'Well, now ...,' said Laura, 'it is only that ... well, you will need to ask her how many places we need to set, not just where everyone will sit.'

Her embarrassment confused me and I said, 'I'll get Mama. She will sort it all out.'

Mama was in the kitchen, gazing in earnest at the custard that Cook was making. Cook stirred her mixture flippantly, hardly bothering to hide her annoyance at being supervised in this way.

'Were those eggs all right?' Mama was asking, wisely ignoring the ill-mannered grunts from her cook.

'Yes, ma'am' was the tense reply.

'What about the goose, did it smell a little off to you? I thought the eyes looked somewhat cloudy to me.'

'Well, it is dead, ma'am.'

Mrs Boxall, for once, looked pleased to see me, obviously hoping that I would rescue her by fetching Mama away. Still, Mama felt the need to explain herself, sounding slightly hurt that our cook needed the situation explained to her. 'It is just that I want everything to be perfect for Captain Coppin's sister and her family.'

Mrs Boxhall increased the speed of her stirring, the wooden spoon chiming tunelessly against the sides of the large enamel bowl. As she punished the mixture, she addressed it, that is, instead of looking up at Mama or me. 'Yes, ma'am, and I want everything to be perfect too!'

I spoke quickly, 'Mama, Laura and I need you in the dining room.'

Mama gave Mrs Boxhall a final look. I was afraid that she was considering chastising her for her rude tone, which would probably produce an almighty row.

'Mama, we need you.'

'Yes, Ann, I am coming!'

Laura smiled nervously at our arrival. 'I didn't know where you preferred everyone to sit, madam.'

'Well, then, where to start?' Mama was not exactly talking to us. 'Yes, so, Mr Coppin sits here at the top of the table and I will be facing him, at the far end. We will put his sister on his left with her husband on her right. Ann, you will sit on your father's right, with Charlotte beside you. Charles will face Harriet, either side of myself.'

'What about William?' asked Laura.

I had to admit that I had forgotten all about my little brother.

'Oh, he can sit the other side of Harriet. I was thinking of leaving him out but that would not be fair to him.'

'What about Grandfather, will he be joining us?' I asked.

'No. He prefers to eat in his room. He is too tired for company these days.'

Perhaps he was just too tired for Aunt Connie and her family. I was never sure if he particularly disliked them or if he did not feel obliged to make an effort for Papa's side of the family.

'Ma'am?'

Laura was giving Mama the same look she had given me earlier. What on earth was the matter with her?

'I … I was just wondering was there anyone else you needed a place for?'

'Sarah will not be eating with us. I want you to feed her in the playroom. She can join us afterwards. I thought we had already discussed this.'

'I did not mean the baby, ma'am.'

Mama looked as confused as I had and gazed at each chair in turn as she mentally placed a person in it. And, suddenly, I understood what Laura was hinting at.

Weesy.

Oh, how nice it would be to forget all about death and dying for just one little day. Surely, we could leave her out of this dinner. If Sarah was missing out on it, then why should Weesy be included?

'Just set places for those I have mentioned, in that order, please! Now, I must be getting back to the kitchen.'

Mama had decided against including Weesy at the table. Thank goodness for that!

Our visitors arrived on the dot of three o'clock, as promised. I had been impatiently waiting to hear the sound of a carriage and horses pulling to a stop outside. William and I were wearing our best clothes and had been threatened with all manner of things if we smudged them in any way. So it was a long wait as I could do very little to pass the time; certainly I was not going to touch my paints or anything else to do with making art. *At last,* I thought, as I looked out of William's bedroom window and saw Charlotte and everyone getting out, Aunt Connie, with Virgil the second in her arms, giving instructions to the driver for the return journey.

'They are here!' I yelled, as I pounded down the stairs, William behind me, both of us oblivious to Grandfather's peace of mind.

'My dears!' said Aunt Harriet, appearing at the door of the sitting room. 'Calm down. I thought we had been invaded by wild animals!'

Mama and Papa joined her, Mama fastening a welcoming smile on her face, while Papa looked vaguely curious as if in suspense about what was to happen next. I ran to the door and flung it open. 'Hello, Cousin Charlotte!'

Laura rushed to take coats and hats as Mama, with Aunt Harriet's help, shepherded us all into the parlour. We had a half-hour before dinner was to be served. In other words, there would be a half-hour of being required to be dutifully sociable with the entire family.

We all found a seat, Aunt Connie with Virgil the second sitting beside Papa as if staking her claim to him. Mama and Aunt Harriet hovered until we all sat down and then they took theirs. The adults led the conversation, which was mostly made up by general remarks on the weather and the cost of hiring a carriage.

Nobody mentioned Weesy, which was quite a feat considering that her death and funeral was the biggest and most recent thing that had happened to our family. Indeed, the longer we sat there, not mentioning her, the more it struck me that there was a false note in the atmosphere.

Aunt Connie suddenly rubbed her arms together. 'My goodness, there is such a chill in the air.'

Seeing how the rest of us stared blankly, she shrugged. 'Oh, it is just me then. Well, perhaps I should fetch my shawl.'

'I can have Laura light the fire,' offered Mama, looking flustered.

'Oh, no, not on my account. Besides, this little man is keeping me warm. Well, Ann and William, what do you make of your new cousin? He is a bonny baby, is he not?'

William and I nodded and smiled, both of us wondering if we were expected to say something. Virgil the second, whose splotchy skin reminded me of Mrs Boxhall's bread and butter pudding, belched and began to cry for no reason at all. Somehow ignoring the noise, Aunt Connie carried on talking, 'He is remarkably intelligent and quite, quite sensitive, a true Coppin, of course.'

I felt that Aunt Harriet was trying to stifle a smile.

'Ah, there's the dinner bell!' sang out Mama.

She probably did not mean to sound so relieved, though it must be said that we all stood up rather quickly, as if grateful to be saved by it. Virgil the second did not appreciate the bell nor the fact that we had all stood up. At least, I assume it was one of those things that made him sob louder and with more determination.

Papa and Aunt Connie led the way, the rest of us following behind. Poor Mama. She had meant to be first to the table so that she could direct everyone to their seats. Perhaps she should have discussed this with Papa because he did not waste any time in making towards his place at the head of the table, followed swiftly by Aunt Connie and Virgil the second, who immediately took the chair beside his. Mama, I am sure, would have preferred to take proper charge at this point. As it was, she had to be content with pointing out our places to the rest of us, while making fretful glances at the crying baby who had finally stopped thanks to Papa reaching for a slice of bread, tearing off the crust and giving it to him. 'My little precious,' muttered Aunt Connie.

'There you go, Virgil. Charlotte here, by Ann. Charles, would you sit there? Thank you, dear. Yes, William, you sit there, and Harriet here next to me.'

The table looked well, even if I say so myself. We had used the best napkins, folded into perfect triangles and the candles had been lit, all five of them, placed centre stage, in their silver holder. I felt a stab of pride at the cutlery that gleamed in the candlelight.

Both Laura and Mrs Boxall would serve us. In they came with the first course, a watery beef soup, not my favourite at all. This is the worst thing about Mama hosting dinners; I am expressly forbidden from questioning, or offering suggestions for, the menu.

'I hope you like beef soup,' I muttered to Charlotte.

She smiled at my glum expression. 'Oh, I don't mind it. We have it every Saturday at our house.'

I was about to say something else when Mama singled me out. 'Now, everyone, before we begin, Ann will say "Grace".'

I had had no inkling of this but to refuse was impossible. They all looked at me through the individual mists that were created by their boiling hot soups. There was nothing for it but to close my eyes, bow my head, and mumble, 'For what we are about to receive, may the Lord make us truly thankful. Amen.'

'Amen,' said everyone, and we all opened our eyes, ready to tackle the soup.

'Oh,' said Mama. 'The candles have gone out.'

And so they had, five creeping wisps of smoke in place of the five darting flames of orange that had been there moments before.

'See,' said Aunt Connie, 'I did say there was a chill in the air.'

'How peculiar!' said Aunt Harriet, while Charles reached into his pockets, retrieving a box of matches.

'Allow me!' he announced to the room, before stretching across his father to strike one match that expertly lit all five candles once more.

'Thank you, Charles,' said Mama. 'Perhaps there is a draught coming under the door.'

Nobody had anything to add to this, apart from William staring around as if he thought he might catch the draught in action. Silly boy!

'So, William,' began Uncle Virgil.

Typically, both my brother and father looked at him, William junior quickly realising that Virgil was addressing Papa.

'Have you any trips planned? Heading off anywhere interesting?'

Papa glanced at Mama and chuckled, 'No. Not yet. I thought

I should concentrate on the paperwork for a while.'

'Ah, yes,' said Virgil, as he skimmed the surface of his soup with his spoon. 'Yes, indeed. Paperwork. There is never an end to it.'

'Now, really,' said Aunt Connie, 'no business talk at the table. Surely you two can wait until after lunch.'

'Yes, Mother,' said Virgil, winking at me. 'I forgot the rules. Please forgive me!'

They always behaved like this. My aunt would pretend to take umbrage at something Virgil said or did and he would pretend to behave like a naughty child. I think this is why Grandfather stayed in his room, while Mama always looked slightly baffled by their behaviour.

'Ow!' said William, my brother.

'Whatever is the matter with you?' asked Mama.

'Is your soup still too hot?' asked Aunt Harriet.

'Em … yes,' he replied.

'Well, blow on it … quietly,' said Mama, trying not to sound impatient.

'Your hair is getting so long, Ann. It really suits you, you know, makes your face look smaller.'

'Thank you, Aunt Connie.'

My tongue was stinging from the soup. I imagined dipping it into a blob of ice cream. Well, dessert was only two courses away.

'Charlotte is doing very well on the piano.'

'Mama, don't!' said Charlotte, squirming in her chair.

'Oh, wonderful! I would love to hear you,' said Aunt Harriet. 'Would you play for us later?'

'Of course she will,' smiled my aunt. 'She'd be delighted to.'

'For Heaven's sake,' said Charlotte, making sure only I could hear her.

'Ow!' said William again, though not as loudly as the first time.

Mama gave him a stern look, while Aunt Harriet, who was sitting beside him, leant in to ask him what was wrong now.

'Someone kicked me!'

Using a louder voice than normal, Mama turned to ask Charles how he was getting on at school, while Papa asked Aunt Connie about the new house that they had their eye on in Cork, making sure to include Uncle Virgil, who immediately launched into a lecture about the madness of property prices. At least, I think that was what he bellowing about. Charlotte was between me and William. She asked me a question but I was too busy watching Aunt Harriet quietly explain to William that nobody had kicked him. 'You know how you love to swing out your legs under the table. I suspect you managed to kick yourself.'

William considered this and seemed to accept it as fact.

Charlotte was asking me a question. 'Ann? Did you hear

me? Have you read any good books lately?'

I only half heard her as something was bothering me but I had no time to think about it further. Mama rang her little bell to let Laura know that we had finished with the soup, ignoring the fact that William had hardly got halfway through his. No doubt she was regretting having him with us.

We all got caught up in the returning of the soup bowls to Laura's large tray and then there was a short break before the bowls of vegetables and potatoes were carried through to us. Last to arrive was the goose which Papa would carve at the table.

We oohed at it, reminding me of Christmas when the turkey was always greeted by a brief round of applause, before being sliced up for our plates. There were sausages, too, along with thick slices of ham. Uncle Virgil rubbed his palms together. 'What splendid sights and smells. Mrs Boxhall, as usual, you have outdone yourself.'

Mrs Boxhall, who was proudly presenting the goose, blushed and nodded her thanks whilst pointedly ignoring my mother's smile, her peace-offering for all that 'supervision' earlier.

'Stop it!' said William.

I barely heard him in all the fuss about the goose and the handing around of plates. Whilst our guests were distracted, Mama made a face at Aunt Harriet, who asked William if he might prefer to be in the playroom with Sarah. He could leave the table right now, if he liked. He shook his head but looked thoroughly miserable. Aunt Harriet shrugged at Mama, who bit her lip but then busied herself in the sharing out of the sprouts and the boiled potatoes.

Meanwhile, Papa had produced two bottles of wine, one red and one white, from the side cabinet and was refilling the grown-ups' glasses with their colour of preference. He stopped before Charles who looked at his parents, his eyebrows raised, his lips stretched in a mischievous grin.

'He can have a small glass, then,' said Aunt Connie to Papa, adding, 'and just the one too, mind, so, Charles, make it last.'

'Yes, dear,' said Charles, mimicking his father, making us all laugh, except William who was struggling to keep up with all the chatter. A possible reason for his discomfort was stirring in the back of my mind.

Aunt Connie was staring at William. Determined to distract her, I loudly asked Charlotte, 'Are you moving to a new house?'

She managed to nod before her mother answered my question. 'Why, yes, just as soon as I find us a house big enough. Your Uncle Virgil is setting up his own practice and I expect I shall have to host a great many dinners for important clients.'

It impressed me how she made it sound that her hosting duties were just as important as whatever my uncle had to do. He was a lawyer and, according to Papa, had quite a fierce reputation, which surprised me. I liked my uncle but would not have considered him to be useful in an argument. He looked more like a jolly reverend, what with his little jokey asides and dramatic winking.

To my surprise, he suddenly asked Papa, 'And what about those missing ships? Do you have anything to do with this infamous Franklin expedition?'

'Fortunately not,' replied Papa. 'They are still searching for them, I believe.'

Charles joined in. 'No sign of them yet, last I heard. The second-in-command Francis Crozier is from Banbridge. He is captain of *Terror*, whilst Sir John Franklin commands *Erebus*.'

Noticing my mother looking puzzled, he added, 'They are the names of the two missing ships.'

'Such depressing names!' said Aunt Harriet, '*Terror* and *Erebus* – doesn't that mean darkness or something to do with the underworld?'

Mama shuddered. 'Is it any wonder that something untoward has happened to them?'

Aunt Connie nodded. 'Lady Franklin must be beside herself. How awful to lose one's husband to thin air. I expect she must feel dreadfully powerless, which is a woman's usual lot, of course.'

The men listened to this politely, Uncle Virgil saying, 'Oh, I don't know about that. Lady Franklin sounds like the sort of wife a man needs if he goes and gets himself lost in the Arctic.

She is putting the wind up the Admiralty and refuses to be ignored. In fact, I have heard that she sold up her house in order to move next door to their headquarters so that she can keep a closer eye on them, making sure that everything that can be done is being done. From what I can gather, she is none too popular with the old gentlemen.'

'Oh, how romantic!' I blurted out.

There was a pause before everyone started laughing, making me feel both embarrassed and doted upon. Uncle Virgil took up the subject once more. 'It seems the good Lady Franklin is trying every avenue possible.'

'What do you mean?' asked Papa.

'Well, I hear that during the last year she has been visited by mediums claiming to have made contact with her husband.'

Typically, before anyone else could respond to this, William asked, 'What's a mee-dee-um?'

Mama looked at Papa, panic slapped across her face. Aunt Harriet opened her mouth to say something – anything – while Aunt Connie answered, 'You are perhaps too young to understand, my dear.'

Of course, Uncle Virgil continued, regardless. 'Well, young William, a medium is someone who believes that they can make contact with a person who has died.'

Unperturbed, William asked our uncle, 'Do you mean that they talk to ghosts?'

Charles smiled. 'You don't believe in ghosts, now, do you, William?'

Glancing at Mama, William caught the warning in her eyes and mumbled, 'Um ... I don't know!'

'Oh, do leave him alone, Charles,' said Charlotte.

'As I was saying,' said Virgil, 'Lady Franklin has had several meetings with such persons.'

'But how do you know all this?' asked Papa. 'I did not read about any of this in the newspapers.'

'His sister, April – you met her at our wedding – is great friends with Lady Franklin's niece, Sophie Cracroft,' said Connie. She had a habit of answering questions that were meant for others.

'I received a letter from her last week, describing Sophie and Lady Franklin's visit to a certain Ellen Dawson and her 'handler'. This gentleman, I forget his name, puts the girl Ellen into a sort of sleep, whereupon she is able to see things. Apparently, not only did she locate a stolen brooch in a pawn shop, but she was able to name the culprit, a servant, who had taken it.'

'So, now she is to find someone's husband?' asked Aunt Harriet, sounding fascinated.

'Indeed,' said Uncle Virgil, who was clearly enjoying telling his tale. 'Ellen is too shy to deal directly with Lady Franklin and so sits in another room with Sophie, who asks the pertinent questions. So far, she claims to have seen the ships.'

'Really?' I asked.

'Yes, she says they are stuck in the ice but that everyone on board has plenty of food to eat and they are in no immediate danger.'

'Marvellous!' said Aunt Harriet.

Uncle Virgil beamed at her, feeling complimented for his delivery. This was too much for my aunt who changed the subject, nodding to Papa, 'Well, we had our own ghostly experience, years ago, do you remember?' Turning back to us, she continued, 'We were only children, no more than eight or nine years of age and had been sent to stay with our grandmother.'

Mama gently protested, 'Maybe not in front of little ears?'

Aunt Connie dismissed her concern with a wave of her hand. 'We were upstairs, getting ready for bed, when we suddenly heard what sounded like a party downstairs, with clinking glasses, laughter and even a piano. Well, I could not believe it and was determined to join in the fun. So, I quickly got dressed again and tried in vain to make you come too but you refused.'

Here, Papa shrugged and took a long sip of his wine. 'Anyway,' said Aunt Connie, 'I headed downstairs, wondering why our grandmother had not mentioned that she was expecting guests. Just as I reached the door of the big hall, Grandmother appeared behind me, shouting, 'Don't open that door!' But she was too late. I opened it and saw …'

'What?' I asked breathlessly. 'What did you see?'

Aunt Connie opened her mouth to answer but was distracted by Charlotte demanding to know, 'What is that infant laughing at?'

I was trying to hang onto the threads of my aunt's story but they were fast disappearing as we were all obliged to gaze at Virgil the second who was giggling helplessly at the air in front of him, his arms outstretched.

'Who are you talking to, my pet?' cooed my aunt, while Papa hurriedly took another sip of wine and refused to look in my mother's direction. For an answer, Virgil the second gave a shout of laughter, startling his mother. Virgil the first, my uncle, helped himself to some more potato, showing little interest in his son.

'Maybe he sees a ghost,' said William helpfully.

A strange noise escaped my mother, while Aunt Harriet dropped her fork noisily onto her plate. Virgil the second jumped in fright at the crash and scrunched up his features, sucking in his breath until he was ready to release a titanic howl that made his face turn red. Clasping her arms around him, Aunt Connie flashed Aunt Harriet a look of disgust as she positively shouted, 'My poor, poor baby. Did you get a nasty fright?'

Papa had to shout too as he asked my uncle and Charles, 'Anyone like a top up, red or white?'

'*Mon Dieu!*' said Charlotte, while Mama told William to go and join Sarah in the playroom, promising to send him the biggest slice of cake.

After the family visit came to an end, the house slumped back into the usual sombre Sunday mood. Mama went to rest in her room, claiming a headache. She had been up earlier than the rest of us, getting things ready, and wilted before our eyes once we waved off Aunt Connie and the others.

I headed to the playroom. I was too restless to read or draw and so thought to entertain Sarah. Also, Charlotte had confided in me how much she longed for a baby sister to look after, so much so that I felt guilty as, most days, I paid Sarah little attention. Well, that was going to change. I was determined to be a better big sister. After all, she was rather cute, with blonde curls that folded back into place when you tried to straighten them, blue eyes and a ready, gummy smile. Furthermore, she hardly ever cried, unlike Virgil the second who had refused to be consoled after Aunt Harriet had dropped her fork. Finally, Aunt Connie had decided they should leave as she became convinced that there might be something seriously wrong with him and wanted a doctor to examine him.

Aunt Harriet came in and found Sarah and me sitting on the floor in front of the mirror that I had propped up against the chest of drawers. 'So, here you are. Oh, Sarah, your hair is lovely.'

I was brushing it with the large hairbrush. Sarah bobbed her head and smiled broadly in agreement. 'Me too! Me too!' she said.

I explained, 'I told her she could brush my hair next.'

'Ouch! Good luck!' laughed Aunt Harriet. 'She can be violent with a brush in her hand. Can't you, pet?'

Sarah had no idea what Aunt Harriet was talking about but gave an ecstatic 'YES!' to the question. It delighted her when we both laughed at this. We swapped places, Sarah clumsily getting to her feet so that she could move to stand behind me. I handed her the brush. 'Now, Sarah, gentle hands. Good girl!'

She over-reacted to my advice and, as a result, the brush barely struck a strand of my hair. I tried again. 'Sarah, just do it like I showed you. Remember how I brushed your hair?'

She gave another ecstatic 'YES!' before almost knocking me out. The clonk of the brush as it bounced off my skull made my ears ring.

'Ow, my head! Ow! Ow!'

Only slightly put off by my cries, Sarah merely shrugged a half-hearted 'Sowee' before lifting the brush towards my head again.

Aunt Harriet was no help at all, giggling helplessly as she said, 'I told you so!'

I had to distract Sarah and fast. 'Eh, why don't we do something else, Sarah? Do you want to do your new jigsaw?

Wouldn't that be fun? Will I set it out on the ground here?'

Aunt Harriet jumped to get it and quickly joined us on the floor, opening up the box and spilling out the contents, to keep Sarah distracted whilst I discreetly threw the brush to the far side of the room.

'Look at all this, Sarah!' cooed Aunt Harriet.

Sarah plonked herself back down and reached for the nearest piece, completely forgetting about hair brushing. I briefly checked my scalp for blood but only felt a small bump that failed to justify the pain I had felt.

'That was a pleasant visit, wasn't it? Charlotte is looking like a proper young lady.' Aunt Harriet's tone was light but it did not fool me.

The three of us moved pieces around the floor, trying to find their partners and slot them into place. Although, when we connected one piece to the next, Sarah would immediately pull them apart as if searching for the magic behind their connection.

'It is strange,' said Aunt Harriet. 'William has a bruise on his leg exactly where he claimed to have been kicked.'

I accidentally nodded to this and stopped abruptly but it was too late.

'Ah!' said my aunt. 'You are not surprised by this?'

I slotted one piece into another and did nothing as Sarah grabbed them apart once more.

'Ann?'

It was no use. I reached for another jigsaw piece and said, 'He was sitting in Weesy's seat.'

I looked up at my aunt's face when she made no reply. After a moment, I said, 'William and I feel we should not mention her in front of Mama and Papa.'

'I understand,' said Aunt Harriet, 'but I don't think your parents would want you or your brother hiding things from them or to be wary of telling them about anything that is troubling you.'

'Well, they get too sad when they hear Weesy's name and Papa now says he never saw her ghost which probably is because of Mama. So, what are we to think?'

Aunt Harriet made no reply to this. Just then something occurred to me. 'Aunt Harriet, did you drop your fork on purpose?'

My aunt grinned and stood up to take her leave of us, saying simply, 'Ask me no secrets and I will tell you no lies.'

13

Saturday, 1ˢᵗ January 1848

Captain Crozier's Journal

Lieutenant Gore died today. Just like the rest, he had been sick for some time and fought bravely to the end.

Our dead colleagues are scattered around us, encased in the icy folds of this petrified water.

It is a bleak and dreadful start to the New Year.

Sunday, 16ᵗʰ January 1848

My day of rest was interrupted by a pathetic scene. I was here reading when I heard the sound of shouting and cheering. I waited to see if anyone would inform me what was happening but then, when no one did, my curiosity got the better of me. I followed the sounds to the lower deck where, to my horror, I beheld a fist fight between Officer Irving and a stoker whose name I have no wish to learn. Their audience, resembling a handful of ill-mannered louts, were cheering them on.

So distracted was everyone that I stood there for a few moments until I was noticed. Lieutenant Little detached himself from the group. 'Sir, I tried to stop them.'

Officer Irving had a bloody nose and his uniform was scuffed and even torn. An absolute disgrace. I was furious, shouting at him, 'What is the meaning of this?'

Irving hung his head and I certainly had no intention of interviewing his opponent whose face was bloodied too. Lieutenant Little spoke. 'The officer was slighted by this stoker, sir.'

To my surprise, the stoker whined, 'He bumped into me, knocking me into the wall.'

Determined to bring the conversation to an end as quickly as possible, I nodded to Lieutenant Little to explain matters further. He obliged. 'A collision, sir, after this man refused to stand aside to allow Officer Irving to pass.'

The stoker opened his filthy mouth to say something but I put a stop to him. 'I will not have officers of Her Majesty's Navy mistreated by inferiors. Is that understood? When you meet an officer in the passageway, you will stand aside.'

I stared at each man in turn until he nodded and

muttered, 'Yes, Captain.'

Addressing Lieutenant Little, I said, 'Sir, you will give this man ten lashes for insubordination while Lieutenant Irving returns to his quarters to make himself presentable as befitting his position on my ship.'

Not wanting to hear another word from any of them, I returned here.

Two and a half years of living like this naturally results in frayed tempers. However, I rely on my officers to maintain a firm discipline or we are lost.

Friday, 11*th* February 1848

It has been eight months since Sir John's death left me in charge of this expedition.

Over seven hundred days and nights of seeing the same faces, eating the same meals, coping with the same weather conditions whilst surrounded by a landscape that refuses to change.

Some days, it feels like our actual lives have been frozen solid. For instance, at home how many miles does a man normally walk in two years? How many different people does he meet whilst out strolling on a Sunday afternoon? How many different things does a man usually accomplish or see in one week?

I might well have continued writing gloomy thoughts

but a wet snout has just nudged my hip, reminding me that I now share my rooms with a colleague, albeit a four-legged one. I did not encourage him in any way but when his minder died a while back, *Erebus*'s dog Neptune set out to convince me that I would make a perfect substitute. I had not paid him much attention before then, but he embarked upon a campaign that involved sleeping outside my door for days on end until I saw sense enough to allow him in here one evening. He never leaves my side and I confess that I have grown quite attached to him. I no longer feel so isolated.

Tuesday, 21ˢᵗ March 1848

Erebus's carpenter, John Weekes, has died during the night. I went over to ask his doctors for an explanation and found Surgeon Stanley with Mr Goodsir and Officer Fitzjames deep in conversation in Sir John's quarters.

'Well, gentlemen, what news?'

The surgeon shrugged. 'He did not die of scurvy, sir. We are all agreed. There was none of the usual, no blackened mouth, saliva or lunatic ravings.'

I considered this for a moment before asking, 'Is that a good thing?'

Mr Goodsir spoke. 'I cannot tell you that, Captain Crozier, but I have a theory, if you care to hear it?'

I sat down heavily, Neptune settling himself at my feet.

Mr Goodsir began, 'The carpenter had a wound on his arm that seemed slightly infected. I checked with Watson, the carpenter's mate, who told me that Weekes had hurt himself whilst fixing that leak a few weeks ago. Something about dashing his forearm on a nail.'

'And you think that this killed him?' I asked.

Surgeon Stanley said, 'He never came to see myself or Mr Goodsir so he did not consider himself seriously wounded. And, ordinarily, it would not be. The cut was not that deep.'

'Alas,' continued Mr Goodsir, 'these are not ordinary times.'

He paused, making me nervous. 'Please be good enough to tell me what you are thinking, Mr Goodsir.'

'Sir, remember when Lieutenant Gore returned from his trip looking less than his usual self.'

I nodded.

'It turned out,' said Mr Goodsir, 'that he had taken a bad fall, cutting his leg. At the time I did not think much about it but now it is beginning to make sense.'

'What are you telling me?' I asked. 'That our medicine cabinet is useless?'

Mr Goodsir tugged at his ear and spoke slowly. 'Sir, our

diet lacks fresh food and has done for some time now. And I think that this lack of fresh fruit and meat could result in a man's health dwindling from a little cut like John Weekes or a bruised limb like Lieutenant Gore. The body needs proper food in order to heal fully.'

I tried to be positive. 'Spring will be here in a couple of weeks. Once the days get brighter, I will send out our best hunters in search of meat or whatever else they can find.'

It is the only remedy to our situation, that and the ice melting this summer.

Thursday, 23rd March 1848

Two more deaths today. I have given the task of investigating and recording the deaths to Officer Fitzjames. I see no point in my having the same conversation with the doctors and surgeons.

Needless to say, no animals have been sighted and, therefore, our diet has not yet been improved with fresh meat.

This morning I bolted awake at three o'clock and, for one moment, thought that someone was in my cabin. Only Neptune's snoring reassured me that all was as it should be.

Sunday, 2nd April 1848

Last June, after burying Sir John, we expected to be
shortly on our way. The ice masters kept up a twenty-
four-hour watch, working in two shifts, and I planned to
make one last try to locate the last section of the North
West Passage. My officers and I agreed that we make a
final attempt dedicated to the memory of Sir John before
turning *Erebus* and *Terror* homewards. Yes, all agreed,
that is, except the Arctic, which refused to co-operate and
release us from its clutches.

Our ice masters, Mr Reid and Mr Blanky, are focused
once more on searching for a thaw, but they cannot hide
their concern. In particular, Mr Reid looks far from
confident. His hair and sideburns have taken on the
same colour as his favourite subject. I waited for him
to approach me with his worries, although I suppose he
feels that it is unnecessary to tell me what I can clearly
see for myself.

This afternoon, following a wretched lunch of tinned
soup of some description, and biscuits, I decided to walk
out after Mr Reid. He was a little way off from the ships,
testing the ice and referring to measurements in his
notebook. It was bitterly cold, of course, but there was
no wind and the sun was shining though providing no
warmth. He looked up at the sound of my feet crunching

into the snow and I saw his shoulders droop as he realised that he would have to face me. We were both muffled up with scarves and hats and wearing goggles, to protect our eyes from the sun's glare off the white ground. 'Mr Reid,' I said, 'I think it is time that we discussed our situation.'

'I am trying my best, Captain Crozier, but ...'

'What, Mr Reid,' I said, trying to keep my tone light, 'are you unable to conjure the ice into melting?'

He made no reply to this and I had to prod him once more. 'We are in the second month of spring and you are much worried.'

He sighed deeply before saying, 'I wish I had better news for you, Captain, but the fact is that every time I detect a softening in the ice, it quickly hardens over again with a new layer. As you say, we are well into spring so my instruments should be able to detect a shift but there is nothing. Absolutely nothing.'

I scuffed my boot against the snow in an effort to awaken my toes, which were numb with the cold. Finally, Mr Reid made his grand confession, 'In all my years, I have never seen anything like it. Sir, I ... well ... I have no reason to believe that there will be a thaw this year.'

Thanking him for his work, I returned here. Mr Reid did not surprise me with his opinion, but to hear it said aloud was shocking all the same. Next month brings our three-year anniversary of leaving home, and being stuck here for yet another year was not part of anyone's plan. I have sent Lieutenant Irving to quietly check with our purser about *Terror*'s supplies and have sent word to Fitzjames to have the same done on *Erebus*.

Wednesday, 5th April 1848

It is half past one in the morning. I cannot sleep and so have re-lit my candles and wrapped my blankets and coat around me in order to write here. At my encouragement, Neptune has settled across my feet, providing some warmth at least.

As I lay in my bunk, chasing sleep in vain, I had the most peculiar experience. I felt ... that is, I thought – or could almost have sworn – that I heard a voice whisper my name.

Am I now going to lose my mind like Sir John and the others? Must I add that to the list of worries that already consume my waking day? At least the carpenters do not work at night. We spend too many days listening to the making of coffins. Indeed, the sound of the hammer has become the heartbeat of this expedition. If they are not building coffins, they are stopping up leaks. The freezing temperatures are taking their toll not just on us but on *Erebus* and *Terror*.

I am going to pour myself a large tumbler of brandy and read my book. Writing here adds to my depression tonight because I have nothing positive to record.

Thursday, 6th April 1848

I finally called a meeting with my remaining officers this evening in Sir John's quarters. We need to decide on a plan of action away from the prying eyes and ears.

These days, we are a much smaller group. Nine officers, including Sir John, have died. What in God's name is killing them? Amongst the crew, fifteen are gone, and that includes the three we left behind at Beechey Island. Twenty-four in total. Like Mr Reid with his rebellious ice, I have never experienced anything like this before. Too many have died for this to be considered natural. In fact, I would go as far as to say that it is unnatural – all these deaths and all this ice.

We sat huddled in our overcoats. There was no comfort to be had, even as our crystal glasses of Sir John's cognac sparkled merrily in the candlelight. It was just too cold. Outside, the wind howled miserably about us, clamouring at the shutters, as if looking for a way in. I opened the proceedings as always, thanking my fellow officers for their hard work to date before stating my reason for calling the meeting. 'Gentlemen, I will come straight to the point. We have reached, I think, a crossroads.'

They surely knew what I was about to say. Only a fool would have been surprised at my declaration.

'Quite frankly, we are facing a dangerous situation. Our supplies are finally starting to dwindle although, even now, the evidence shows us that our diet is not good enough. We have lost some of our best men to scurvy. Neither the lemon juice nor our canned foods are protecting us as they should be. How I wish I could relay this particular important information back to the Admiralty today.'

They all dipped their heads slightly in agreement, a couple of them muttering, 'Hear! Hear!'

'In any case, inadequate food is not our most serious problem. According to Mr Reid and Mr Blanky, there is no sign of the ice melting.'

I nodded to Mr Reid to have him pitch in and he obliged by saying, 'Any softening of the ice is quickly covered up by a fresh layer.'

I paused to allow this to sink in before continuing, 'If the water does not thaw out this summer, we are stuck here for another year, and if that happens, we are going to run out of food.'

They stared at me in gloomy silence. Officer Fitzjames attempted to lighten the atmosphere, scrunching up his face as if he were about to be comical while making his harebrained point. 'With all due respect, Commander Crozier, it cannot be as bad as all that. The ice will soon melt. Of course it will.'

Buoyed up by his words and his devil-may-care attitude, some officers nodded, their eyes full of new-born hope.

I was glad that it was he making the challenge; it was only right, I felt. Keeping my tone neutral, I said, 'You sound so definite, sir. Pray tell, why do you say that the ice will melt?'

He gazed around, waiting for one of his chums to help him out, but he was only met by questioning looks. They wanted him to make his case, to back up his own theory and give us all something to believe in. I knew, however, that they were expecting the impossible. Stuttering a little, he said, 'It just has to.'

I could see his listeners' disappointment, as could he. Unable to give up, he babbled, 'Because that is what always happens ... you know, just like winter follows spring which precedes summer, night becomes day ... and ice melts. It *always* melts!'

His voice sounded as thin and as frail as his argument. I could not help thinking that if the good gentlemen of the Admiralty were here to witness their man's ineptitude, I should feel thoroughly exalted. I imagined myself flinging my arm at Fitzjames in disgust and bellowing at those learned men, with their wealth and their big money, 'See here, what you have given me. He knows nothing about Arctic conditions and, ridiculously, with your blessings, hired few who do.'

In that moment, I cursed the Admiralty, believing that they should shoulder at least some of the blame for the large number of deaths. And only God knows how many more we will lose. Even as I write here, there are a few confined to their hammocks, showing the, by now, all-too-familiar symptoms of scurvy: blackened gums, loose teeth and a damning, all-encompassing exhaustion.

I spoke slowly, as if to a child. 'Officer Fitzjames, you are quite right in saying that the ice always melts as, yes, indeed, that is what usually happens.'

Trying not to sound smug, I explained, 'But, sadly, as we have now since discovered, just because a thing usually happens does not guarantee that it will always happen exactly as before.'

For a moment, I felt that this must be how a preacher feels, as he takes his stand behind the church pulpit, facing his congregation who wait to absorb his words. 'This, gentlemen, is the Arctic, which is governed by a different rule book. For instance, back home, the strike of a match may fail or the button may fall from your coat or the horse and carriage that you ordered may be delayed. No matter, you might say, these things happen. It is not the end of the world. You fetch another match or another button and the erring carriage driver will swear never to let you down again, after which life goes on, just as it should.'

Some of the men were ignoring the fact that their pipes had gone out, knowing that if they attempted to revive them while I was talking, I would come down on them in a rage. I cannot bear it when an officer does not pay me his full attention.

'Here, it is completely different. The ice failed to yield last summer, when it should, which is probably something small and even unremarkable for this part of the world. If we were elsewhere, we would know nothing about it. Yet, here we are, and so must face the consequences of unmelted ice day after day since it prevents our ships from bringing us elsewhere and, thus, has the potential to devastate us.'

'Forgive me, sir, but what exactly are you saying?'

It was one of Fitzjames's recruits, Officer Sargent. He was a young man, on his first visit in Arctic conditions. It troubled me that he was so very pale while his voice sounded raspy, as if he were having to force out every syllable. He was ill and this spared him from my instinct to shout my answer at the top of my voice.

'I am saying that if we sit here until next summer, opening up tin after tin of our remaining food, it will not matter a whit to us if the ice melts or not as we will have starved to death by then.'

Officer Sargent, his eyes downcast, nodded ever so slightly. 'Yes, sir, I see what you mean. So ...?'

'So,' I continued, 'I have decided to abandon the ships. I see no other way out of our predicament. It was always my worry that it could come to this but, in order to survive, we need to start walking.'

A chorus of shocked mutterings was unleashed: how could we leave our ships, our steadfast homes for the last three years? It was not something to which I looked forward myself. If there was any other option, I would have gladly considered it, but there was not, and to delay any further would only be courting sheer disaster.

Officer Sargent felt obliged to have me double-check my proposal. 'Sir, are you quite satisfied that this is necessary? Surely they will send someone after us. I mean, we have been gone the allotted three years and, therefore, a search party must be on its way?'

'You make a sensible point,' I replied, 'but we should remember that we have left too little information about our possible whereabouts. How I wish that we had made the time to write out our plans and deposited them in the cairn at Beechey Island. If we had, then, yes, I could believe that, in a reasonable amount of time, we might definitely be found here. However, as you all know, we left in a tremendous rush so a ship arriving at that island would have no indication of where we sailed next. Pure folly on our part, I'm afraid.'

Now it was Mr Goodsir's turn to ask a question. 'I wonder, Captain Crozier, should we have considered trying to reach out to the natives? I realise we have seen little of them, but should we not have sent out a party in search of them?'

I was surprised by this and hesitated to fathom a response, allowing Officer Fitzjames to make his own reply. 'Whatever for? That would be a waste of time, surely? This expedition is the most advanced of its age. If we, Her Majesty's Navy, cannot battle these circumstances, we can be certain that the lowly Inuit are worse off than we are.'

'Hear, hear!' was the general response to this.

Mr Goodsir shrugged and asked another. 'Is it wise to leave now, sir? The weather is wretched and some of the men are already weak from their illness. Should we not wait for warmer weather?'

It was difficult for me not to agree with him. The storm outside was still in full throttle. Was I really going to lead over a hundred men outside to walk in that? It had been challenging enough to walk the short distance from *Terror* to *Erebus*. I wanted nothing more than to stay put. Just wait and see. But as the leader of this expedition, I was responsible for the lives of a hundred and four men who were relying on me to get them home. I knew this terrain and what it could do to a man. Striving against sounding regretful, I replied, 'We have to leave in the next week or so. If we wait until next month, the temperature may rise just enough to soften the snow on land which means we would be walking in slushy, wet conditions. It is easier to walk across a hard surface to say nothing of the suffering caused by wet stockings and boots.'

'Where will we walk to?'

'Excellent question, Office Fitzjames. That is the second reason I have called you all here. Let us study the maps together and decide which direction serves us best: north or south, east or west.'

Relieved to have something to do, they cleared the table in front of them, pushing glasses, plates and cutlery out of the way. Candlesticks were brought closer as the map was spread out in front of us. Heads bowed down over it, and I felt moved to make one last point.

'The important thing, gentlemen, is to remember that we are naval officers of the British Empire and, as such, we need to follow procedures and work together to get through this. We must be the perfect role models for the crew, with no divisions amongst us officers.'

They all answered me in unison, 'Yes, Captain Crozier.'

I can only pray that it will always be this way. And that I am correct in taking this drastic step.

14

It was only a dream

I cannot seem to find my way home.

There I was, walking to school when, somehow, somewhere, I took a wrong turn and, within moments, no longer recognised my surroundings. There was nothing for it except to walk as fast as I could or I would be late. Mrs Lee insists on punctuality and accepts no excuse as being worthy enough to miss her daily inspection at ten minutes to nine o'clock. But I could not be too far away since my school was only fifteen minutes from our front door.

On the other hand, I have been walking down this street for ages. Where does it end? And why can I not see anything I know, like the walls, the town hall, the River Foyle or Austins' Department Store? Oh, I am going to be so late. I need to ask directions but the street is suddenly deserted. But, wait, I see someone! As far as I can make out, the figure in the distance is not wearing a hat but I am sure that it is a woman. I quicken my pace, although I am already out of breath. 'Wait!' I call out. She does not hear me, does not turn around. The faster I go, the faster she goes. I follow her around corners that I did not know existed.

How could my city be so strange to me? The buildings I pass begin to blur into one another but still the street does not end. Mrs Lee will cane me in front of everyone. I cannot bear the humiliation. I cannot bear being so lost when I should know exactly where I am.

'Ann, Ann!'

Oh, thank goodness. It is Aunt Harriet. She has found me. I cannot see her but I hear her voice.

'Ann Coppin, you are going to be late for school. Get up this minute!'

Relief surges through me. It was only a dream. It was only a dream. Nevertheless, I feel drained, as if I have spent the night searching the dark streets for something familiar.

Mama had kept me home after Weesy's funeral, but this morning brought an end to my lengthy break that had stretched out across the summer months. It was time to return to school, where everything looks exactly the same as if there had been no death and no funeral. As usual, Mrs Lee did not smile as we lined up in front of her. Avoiding eye contact, she checked each of us for neat hair, spotless hands and fingernails, and clean boots. We stood in silence until she finished, telling us to take our places.

I managed to sit perfectly still and not draw a single thing while she spoke about what it is to be humble, our first lesson. This was no mean feat as my fingers itched to take up my charcoal and copy the portrait of Queen Victoria that hangs over the blackboard. Or even draw Mrs Lee herself, with her pale skin and thick, dark eyebrows that nearly meet over her nose. Or the rows of the heads in front of me, hair in a variety of brown, yellow and black, long, in plaits or falling straight, some decorated with bows in blues and pinks.

The morning passed slowly as we moved from humbleness to arithmetic, to grammar and, finally, handwriting before the clock over the door struck twelve o'clock, lunchtime. As usual, I walked home for lunch, falling in beside the Bradley twins. No one had said a word to me all morning, but Tess was now eyeing me up before asking, 'Are you terribly upset?' while Katie added, 'You know, about your sister dying.'

I nodded dumbly.

'How old was she?' asked Tess.

'Nearly four.'

'How sad,' sighed Tess, 'although our cousin Virginia died last year and she was only two.'

'From what?' I asked, not out of any curiosity, just that I felt

I should be interested.

'Imagine,' gushed Tess, her sister nodding along. 'The poor little thing fell out of her bedroom window. Her nanny had only left her alone for five minutes, she said.'

'How awful!' I exclaimed.

'Anyway, she was so badly hurt that there was a hole in the back of her head the size of a plum.'

I was intrigued in spite of myself. 'Could you see into it? What was it like?'

'No, silly!' said Katie. 'Nobody would let us see her though we asked and asked.'

'Oh,' I said, a trifle disappointed.

'What did your sister die of?' asked Tess.

'A fever. The doctor said that she probably had it a while before she died.'

'Lots of people die of that, though,' said Katie.

'Yes,' agreed her sister. 'Not like falling out a window, now that is really different.'

'Yes,' I murmured. 'I suppose it is.'

We walked in silence until I forced myself to ask, 'Has anybody seen your cousin since she died?'

The sisters were confused. 'What do you mean?'

'I mean,' I said. 'Has she been seen or heard in the house?'

'But,' insisted Katie, 'she died. She is actually dead. How could she be in the house?'

Tess, who was sharper than her twin, looked at me. 'Like a ghost?'

I shrugged, possibly regretting my question.

The two girls exchanged a glance before Tess asked, 'Do you believe in ghosts? You must, or you would not ask such a thing.'

Wishing it was possible to take back my words, I pretended to shudder. 'I ... that is, I don't know ... well, no, probably not.'

It was too late to protest. By this stage, we had reached my front door and the girls suddenly regarded me with fresh interest. Tess persisted, 'Have you seen your sister? Is she a ghost?'

I hesitated, which was as good as a confession.

Staring at me in delight, they chanted, 'You have a ghost! You have a ghost!'

'Please, stop it,' I begged. 'My mother will be upset if she hears you.'

Just then, the front door opened, but it was only Aunt Harriet. 'There you are, Ann. Your lunch is getting cold.'

'Goodbye then,' I mumbled, without looking at either twin.

They said goodbye in unison and burst out laughing. 'We shall see you later, Ann Coppin.'

Aunt Harriet smiled after them. 'Well, they are very cheerful. Are they always like that?'

'Sometimes.'

'Mrs Boxhall has dished up your soup. In you go now. How was school? Are you glad to be back?'

'Not really,' I answered truthfully as I took my place at the table alongside William and Sarah. William's shorter walk to his school meant he was always home before me. The soup was vegetable and it was steaming. William was pulling faces, making Sarah roar with laughter. I did not join in their fun. Even as I spooned the hot soup into my mouth, I felt a chill around me as if I had thrown open a door that should have remained closed.

I tried not to think about the twins but was dreadfully aware of the ticking clock in the dining-room counting down the minutes until it was time for me to leave for school again. Aunt Harriet flitted in and out, busy finding new threads for the cushion she was embroidering. Laura and Mrs Boxhall were talking about gallstones in the kitchen.

'Where's Mama?' I asked William.

'Out shopping, I think' was his reply. Then, 'What's wrong?'

'Nothing!' I said rather fiercely.

'You look strange!'

'Oh, do be quiet, William!'

It was not his fault but everyone else seemed so innocent and proper. I was jealous of them not having a care in the world. Aunt Harriet called to me, 'Are you finished, Ann? It is almost a quarter to one.'

Nodding, I left the table, stopping in the hall to put back on my coat and hat. Misinterpreting my feelings, Aunt Harriet began to laugh, exclaiming, 'Oh, come on, pet. It cannot be as bad as that. Sure, you are halfway done now, only another three hours or so to go.'

Thinking of this morning's dream, I rather fancied the idea of taking a wrong turn and missing out on the afternoon's classes. Anyway, I told myself, the twins might not have told anyone. Who would they tell anyway?

Thanks to my dawdling, I was one of the last to arrive. Sitting down, I was immediately approached by Polly Sherrard, who rarely bothered with me, but now asked, 'Is there a ghost in your house?'

The twins had told. Of course they had. I stared at Polly, grappling for a simple answer. To my relief, Mrs Lee strode in. 'Right, girls, we will have a spelling test. Put your books and slates away.'

Polly shrugged and returned to her desk, while Marjorie Sweetman, who sat next to me, gave me the most peculiar look. I welcomed Mrs Lee calling out the word 'merciful' and looking to pounce on the pupils who did not put their hand up to spell it.

'Please, Miss,' called Polly.

'What is it, Polly?' asked Mrs Lee.

'Do ghosts really exist?'

Mrs Lee, already irritated by the interruption, snapped, 'What sort of question is that? I would ask you to concentrate on what we are doing instead.'

A part of me was in awe of Polly as she persisted, 'Oh, but, Miss, it is not my fault. Ann Coppin says she has a ghost in her house.'

My cheeks were aflame as everyone, including our teacher, looked in my direction. I waited for whatever was coming, meeting my teacher's gaze as best I could. After what seemed like an awfully long time, Mrs Lee finally spoke. 'Spell merciful, Ann!'

'M–e–r–c–i–f–u–l.'

'Very good. The next word is "understanding". Who can spell it?'

Feeling dazed, I decided to concentrate on my lessons so that I would be too busy to notice the girls who were watching me. Mrs Lee was my rock. I kept my eyes chained to her, not daring to look left nor right.

At three o'clock, I left the schoolroom, meaning to hurry home, but the twins raced to join me. 'Wait for us!' they chanted.

'Do you want to play with us?' asked Tess.

Katie smiled sweetly. 'You could come back to our house, if you like.'

This was a surprise. 'Oh, well, I will have to ask my mother!' I said.

'Yes, do,' said Tess. 'We will come with you.'

'And, sure,' said Katie, 'if she says no, we could always play at your house instead. We don't mind.'

It had been a long time since I had brought friends home with me. 'I will see what my mother says, but it should be alright for me to come to your house.'

They smiled at me.

'What do you normally do after school?' I asked.

'It depends,' said Tess. 'On Tuesday, we have piano practice. Then, we visit our grandmother on Wednesdays. On Thursdays, Mother insists on us practising boring needlework as it is her favourite thing to do. Fridays are the best because we usually go to a café and have ice cream.'

'Which,' said Katie, 'is our favourite thing to do. Isn't it, Tess?'

I envied them having one another. 'What about Mondays, today?'

'Oh,' said Katie. 'Mondays are for our friends. We only invite girls that we really like.'

They seemed rather excited, and buoyed by their mood, I gushed, 'I love painting. In fact, I want to be an artist.'

The twins smiled politely, with Tess affirming, 'I am useless at drawing. I much prefer eating ice cream.'

'Me too,' said Katie, laughing.

We had reached my house and, once more, the door swung

open before I could knock, only this time it was Mama in the doorway, ignoring my companions and looking impatient for me to come inside.

'Mama,' I said, 'Tess and Katie wondered if I might go to their house for a while.'

I smiled brightly to encourage her to smile too, in front of my friends, but she refused to. 'No,' she said, 'not today.'

Tess tried, 'Oh, but Mrs Coppin, our mother won't mind. You see, we always have friends with us on Mondays.'

'Not today, I'm afraid. Say goodbye, Ann!'

Confused, I looked at the twins, noting their amazement at their offer being so soundly rejected. 'Goodbye, I will see you tomorrow,' I said, trying to make it sound normal. Why couldn't my mother be like other girls' mothers, cheerful and friendly? They moved away reluctantly, possibly hoping that Mama would change her mind and only understanding that she would not when the door closed immediately after me. Aunt Harriet was in the hallway, looking distracted, saying, 'Now, Dora, let us …'

I stumbled forward, my hat falling to the ground, thanks to my mother slapping me in the face. 'You little fool!' my mother hissed. 'You stupid little fool. You told them we had a ghost.'

Aunt Harriet ran towards us, dragging me out of my mother's reach and pushing me up the stairs. I howled from shock. I had never been slapped before and my cheek was stinging. Even so, I tried to defend myself. 'It was an accident. I never said it. They just guessed!'

'Is that so?' sneered my mother. 'They just happened to guess that we have a ghost. Do you expect me to believe that?'

Aunt Harriet took charge. 'Ann, go upstairs and do your homework. Now!'

I did exactly that, not stopping until I reached my room, whereupon I flung myself on my bed and cried and cried. At some point, I ran out of tears and fell asleep. The room was dark when I woke to Aunt Harriet's touch, as she said softly, 'Ann, your parents want to talk to you. They're waiting in the parlour.'

Striking a match, she lit the lamp beside my bed and on seeing my tear-streaked face whispered, 'Oh, you poor wee lamb. Come on, it will be alright.'

I followed her downstairs, dreading seeing my mother again, and Papa too. As if guessing my thoughts, Aunt Harriet said, 'Don't worry, I'll be with you.'

Papa was sitting in his favourite armchair, while Mama perched beside him on a wooden chair, her back as straight as always, her hands in her lap. I shied away from looking at her face, while Papa told me to sit down. I took to the settee, thus allowing Aunt Harriet to sit next to me.

'Now, Ann,' began Papa, 'it is time for us to have a proper talk about what is happening and has been happening for some time. I only wish we had done this earlier. If we had, today's outcome might have been avoided.'

Hardly daring myself to speak, I pressed my lips together and felt rather forlorn as Papa continued, 'Your mother and I would have preferred to have kept all the goings on a secret.'

Here, I interrupted. 'I know, Papa. I'm sorry. But I didn't tell; they just guessed.'

'How?' asked Mama. 'I mean, how on earth could that have happened?'

'Well, they were asking about Weesy, and then they told me about their cousin who died last year. She was only two and she fell out of her bedroom window. So, I just them asked if anyone had seen or heard her in the house.'

The three adults exchanged looks I could not read. Papa nodded at Aunt Harriet who spoke. 'My dear, you know that what has happened with Weesy is quite extraordinary. It is not normal, if that is the right word.'

'In other words,' said Mama hotly, 'the next time someone speaks about a death in their family, please do not ask if the dead person has been seen alive again.'

'Yes, Mama.'

'Oh, look,' she said, to Papa and Aunt Harriet, 'can't we sort this out? Is this to continue? My child died months ago. We buried her. This cannot be right for any of us.'

Aunt Harriet rubbed her nose and sighed. 'I have an idea but you may not approve.'

'What is it?' said Papa.

'Well,' continued Aunt Harriet, 'I can ask a friend who has a friend, a lady, who deals with this sort of thing. We could ask her to come and meet Ann and just see what she thinks, I suppose.'

Papa scrunched up his features. 'Do you mean someone claiming psychic powers or whatever, that they can somehow converse with the dead? Isn't that somewhat ridiculous?'

To everyone's surprise, Mama said, 'Yes, it is. It sounds completely ridiculous but how else would you describe what has been happening here? Who are we to stand in judgement?'

Aunt Harriet nodded. 'I think it is worth a try. If nothing comes of it, well and good, but we owe it to ourselves and even to Weesy to at least try.'

Still waiting to be convinced, Papa asked Aunt Harriet, 'Who is your friend? What do we know about them? Are they the discreet sort? I cannot have my business colleagues and competitors being made privy to this.'

'Do you really think,' said Aunt Harriet, 'that I would bring some mad woman here who could not be trusted? Firstly, Ann knows my friend Mrs Lee.'

'My teacher?'

'Yes, dear. Now you must promise me never to mention any of this to your friends. Not just for our sake but also for Mrs Lee. Do you understand?'

It was my turn to feel indignant. 'Of course. I will not say a word.'

Aunt Harriet smiled. 'Very well. Mrs Lee has indulged in these practices since losing her own daughter. So she understands the nature of our loss. Her friend is a Mrs Powell, who is, I believe, an extremely discreet woman who take her duties very seriously.'

'I hardly dare ask what you mean by her "duties",' sniffed Papa.

The two women stared at him, obliging him to put up his hands. 'Oh, alright. If both of you agree that this is for the best, then I agree so too.'

'It is settled, then,' said Aunt Harriet. 'Let's do this as soon as possible. What about eight o'clock tomorrow night?'

Mama and Papa nodded. Just then the door was opened, revealing my brother in his pyjamas, his hair askew and a dazed expression on his face. Mama exclaimed, 'Good gracious, William, what are you doing out of bed?'

'I had a bad dream,' said William, lingering in the doorway until she reached for him.

'What about, pet?'

He opened his eyes wide to solemnly announce, 'I dreamt of the ships sinking and no one knew where they were.'

'Whose ships, darling? Papa's?'

'No,' replied William, 'the ones in the Arctic.'

Papa laughed. 'I must take the blame for this. We were talking about Sir John's expedition earlier. It was just a dream, William.

There is no way that the ships would sink, not the two of them anyway. Do not worry, they will be found very soon.'

'Oh, dear,' said Mama, 'I fear you are becoming obsessed with those ships. Ann, bring your brother up to bed and perhaps read him a story to take his mind off his dream. A short one, mind you! It is way past your bedtime too.'

We kissed everyone goodnight and I led the way up the stairs. 'What were you talking about?' asked William.

'You wouldn't understand,' I said.

'I bet I would,' grumbled William.

'It was about Weesy, if you must know, but I cannot tell you any more than that.'

We had reached his room. As he climbed back into his bed, William muttered, 'See, I knew it was about Weesy.'

'How?'

'She woke me up, didn't she!'

'But you said you had a bad dream about those ships.'

'I did,' said William. 'But Weesy was in my dream too. She was there in the Arctic with the ships.'

'Well,' I said, 'it was just a dream.'

And dreams don't come true, do they?

15

22nd April 1848

Captain Crozier's Journal

We leave the ships today.

Such a nice, short sentence that is as easy to write as it is to read and leaves out all the hard work and anxiety that goes into our departure.

This is what being a leader involves, making a tough decision and sticking to it. And this is exactly what I am doing but, my goodness, it is lonesome to struggle with doubt in silence. Can I truly walk my men to safety? Have I got what it takes? I never wished to be in charge as I have always felt more secure as a second-in-command.

I am abandoning ships because, at this stage, I truly feel that we have no other choice. It is either that or we remain cooped up on board *Erebus* and *Terror* and risk

starvation. Furthermore, it is wise, I think, to give the
men a mission, something grand to do. We will confound
the Arctic by taking our lives into our own hands. I
shudder to think of the strain involved in spending
another year here. We must go forth, one footstep at a
time, while sticking together at all costs. It is our only
chance.

I can hear the men hard at work as we follow the
proper Royal Navy procedure regarding the abandoning
of ships.

Officer Fitzjames was here earlier, with his checklist,
anxious that all is in order, telling me, 'Everything that
can be is either being tied down or hammered into place.'

I have made no formal announcement, but it seems
that he promoted himself to the position of my second-
in-command. To his credit, he treats me with respect
and shows himself to be in complete agreement with my
proposals. I imagine that he now appreciates the voice of
experience. Meanwhile, it is my duty to instil confidence
and leadership in the remaining officers, just in case they
lose another commander, which is to say, me. I pretend
not to see that the doctors are watching over me with
Thomas's, my steward's, help. Last evening when I told
Thomas that I had no appetite for dinner, I was visited
first by Doctor McDonald and then Mr Goodsir. As soon

as I recognised that my refusal to eat was causing undue concern, and distracting the doctors from their true patients, I changed my mind and had Thomas bring me a bowl of soup.

The truth is that there are scant few who could take my place.

Officer Fitzjames raised his voice to be heard over the pounding of hammers. 'Also,' he said, 'I have some men sealing up the windows and all doorways. Once we have all disembarked, the final door on both ships will be sealed up.'

I nodded. 'Yes, it is the least we can do for the ships, try and keep them safe from the weather, just in case they are needed once more.'

'Is there anything else, sir?'

I thought hard and then remembered. 'Ah, yes, the flags. That will be the last task, to raise the flag, the Royal Navy colours on both ships.'

'It is on my list, sir.'

'Good, good. I will entrust to you the job of burning the code books, just to be on the safe side. Take them out onto the ice and reduce them to ashes. We cannot have any foreigners stumbling upon them and then, thanks to us, having the means to communicate or attempt mischief with any British ships.'

Just then *Terror*'s bell sounded out and I could hear *Erebus*'s too. I checked my pocket watch to see it was ten o'clock. Until we are actually leaving, every passing hour will be marked by the bells, making it impossible to forget that we are up against time itself. It adds a certain solemnity to the occasion, making me think of funerals that I have attended.

Believe me, I do not wish to dwell on such morbid thoughts, but I suppose that is the nature of the bell. When rung repeatedly, it signifies great joy, like weddings or the beginning of a brand new year, whereas the solitary chime lulls the listener into reflecting upon melancholic times.

Officer Fitzjames scribbled something onto his checklist, admitting, 'I had almost forgotten about the bells. I will have them tied up when we are going.'

'It is a strange thing to have to do,' I said, 'to silence the ships. I suppose it is a blessing for them more than anything else. We cannot have them ringing out with every sea breeze, attracting the attention of the natives, if there are any around. They will take anything that is not nailed down. Although, it is peculiar that we have found no sign of human life in all the time we have spent here.'

'Aye, sir! I have given orders to pack up beads, matches,

buttons and anything else that we may barter for food, should we meet up with locals.'

I thought of something else. 'I want us to retrace Lieutenant Gore's footsteps and make an addition to the note he left in the cairn last year. It is important to leave a message as to what has happened to us thus far and where we are now headed.'

Officer Fitzjames was enthusiastic in his reply. 'Absolutely, sir. I am quite sure that the Navy will send out search parties for us. For all we know, they are already on their way. We should make it as easy as possible for them to find us.'

'Well, then,' I said, 'I am glad we are in agreement. How are the men by the way? Any trouble today?'

'Oh no, sir. No trouble at all. In fact, their overall mood is very positive. Anyone I speak to is cheerful because we are finally going home.'

His words, said so confidently and assuredly, made me quiver. I leant over to pat Neptune's head and shake off my fears. It seems that my second-in-command sensed my moment of panic for he said, 'The men believe in you, sir. We all do.'

I picked up this pen to bring the conversation to an end. As anxious as I am to nurture this cooperation with Fitzjames and the others, I cannot, nay, will not share any maudlin thoughts with him. If I was him, I would want my commander to be a hundred per cent solid and capable. I would need to believe in him because, otherwise, what would be the point of following him into the wilderness? My lapses of dismay, or whatever, can be poured onto the pages of this diary and heaped onto the glossy head of Neptune, who knows how to keep secrets. Neptune also knows how to do a few other things too. For instance, he shepherded Fitzjames to the door, who could not help laughing, 'It seems that I am being escorted off the premises.'

I smiled and did not like to say that Neptune was reading my mind. I wished to be alone for a while. To soften his being hurried out, I said, 'Perhaps, when it is time to leave, you and other officers will join me in Sir John's quarters for a glass of cognac. I would like to mark the moment of our leaving in true style.'

When he left, I gave Neptune a biscuit to thank him for his excellent work. 'Clever boy!'

Our plan is to walk south, to the mouth of the Canadian Great Fish River. It is, I have calculated, about two hundred and fifty miles away and we should reach it by June. With God's help, we will find plenty of game there at that time of the year, birds and animals that will provide us with enough food to make the second stage of the journey. We have plenty of guns and ammunition amongst us.

As always, everything depends on the weather. I would hope that along with fresh food we will find the Great Fish River thawed out enough for us to boat our way to the nearest fort. This is Hudson Bay Company territory where we shall surely meet some of their fur traders and their families.

It sounds impossible and maybe it is.

No, I cannot think like that. My plan is as wildly ambitious as it is simple. We just have to walk to the river.

The men will have to drag our three lifeboats along on sledges. It is not going to be easy but, should we be successful, it will be worth all the hardship that awaits us still.

Thomas has arrived to help me pack up my belongings. One good thing about bringing the lifeboats is that we can treat them like colossal suitcases and fill them with our possessions. They allow us to bring bigger and heavier items, like our iron stoves. After all, there are over a hundred of us needing to be fed which makes the stoves a necessity. Other necessities include as much, if not all, of our canned food as we can squeeze in, medicine cabinets and, no surprise, lots and lots of blankets to combat the freezing temperatures at night.

Of course, the officers can bring more possessions. Thomas is packing my good silver cutlery. Well, it cost me a pretty penny and there is no way I am leaving any of it behind. Also, I will be needing books – novels and Bibles – along with this journal, of course, and extra paper to write notes upon. Writing is our sole means of helping any rescuers to find us and, therefore, is of immense importance to all of us. To this end, I will also take my writing desk and a healthy supply of pencils, pens and ink.

Thomas has just interrupted me to discuss my wardrobe. 'Sir, I have several changes of clothes, outer and under, and all your good handkerchiefs. If it is alright with you, sir, I shall pack just one tin of polish for the buttons on your tunic. If used sparingly, it should last long after we return home again.'

I thanked him and reminded him about Sir John's good cutlery. I imagine that Lady Franklin would like to have it returned to her.

Thomas nodded. 'Indeed, sir. I have placed his cutlery in one of the boats with his Royal Hanoverian medal. I wrapped it up in a silk handkerchief just as you asked me to. It should be perfectly safe.'

The earthly chorus of hammering is dwindling. In the future, when I have the luxury of looking back on this trip, I will undoubtedly hear those hammers. Thomas has made two trips from my cabin, carrying my things to the boats, which were, I was assured, perched on their sledges, on the ice that should be a sea.

I sit here, greedily snatching the last remaining moments of being able to relax, just Neptune and I. God knows when we shall next have a room to ourselves. These private quarters of mine have been my home for three years. I know every inch of them, the small spidery crack in the wall, the eye-shaped gap between the floorboards, right beside my bed, into which I have watched a multitude of insects disappear and the coffee stain on the wall from the time that I knocked my cup over, after we buried Sir John and I had had too much wine.

In truth, I love this ship and *Erebus* too. We have been through a lot together and I truly regret leaving them like this. But my first responsibility is to the men. I need to get them home, back to their mothers, wives, girlfriends, sisters and daughters. We have done all we can here. Too many have been lost as it is, including poor Sir John. I hope I have his blessing, although I wonder what he would think if he was still alive. Somehow, I doubt he would agree to this madness and, perhaps, that is why the Lord took him from us so that he would not stand in our way from undertaking this next adventure.

I am writing as fast as I can because I can hear the men calling to one another that all is ready. Ah, there is the knock on my door. Fitzjames is telling me that the officers are waiting for me aboard *Erebus*.

Neptune and I, along with our crew, must leave *Terror*. May God bless her and keep her and *Erebus* safe from harm. How we will miss them.

16

Aunt Harriet's friend takes charge

Just as the clock struck eight o'clock, the doorbell rang. Mama had given Mrs Boxhall and Laura the night off so Aunt Harriet went to open it and returned almost immediately with Mrs Lee and her friend. Were they expecting to see so many of us? Papa, Mama, me and Grandfather, who had surprised us all by wanting to take part in the proceedings. Only I had guessed that he hoped to hear something about his wife, my grandmother. He and Papa had dressed as if for a proper dinner. They stood up rather stiffly as the women appeared, only Mama actually welcoming them, with the words, 'How do you do?'

I was struck dumb at the sight of my teacher in my house. She seemed a lot smaller than usual. Too shy to greet her, I busied myself in watching the adults respond to one another.

Mrs Lee stood aside, allowing my family a better look at her companion, Mrs Powell. Her clothes were perfectly respectable and her features rather plain though her engaging smile made her instantly likeable. Possibly, I had been hoping that she would look somewhat unusual; not exactly like a witch, but I had fancied that she would stand out on entering a room. Yet, there was something about her. As I stared, I was convinced I could see an actual light radiating from her figure, a mistiness about her head and shoulders. She was a woman of colour. I mean that, though her coat and shoes were brown and her skirt a mute green, I somehow felt shades of pink, orange and blue wafting about her. I wished I could fetch my paints and try to capture what I felt on paper.

To my surprise, she approached to shake my hand. Normally, adults who were not relatives ignored me. But here was this lady, a most gentle one at that, addressing me, 'And you must be Ann.'

All eyes were on me as I replied, 'Yes, madam.'

She held my hand steady for a moment longer than I expected and, for some reason, it did not make me uncomfortable. Instead, I felt that a conversation had begun, a private one between the two of us. 'You are not scared, are you, dear?'

'No, madam. At least, I do not think I am.'

'Good girl! Well, just remember that you are surrounded by your loved ones. More than you know. All I need you to do is trust me and everyone else in this lovely room. Do you think you could do that?'

I felt myself melt into her kindness. I had never met anyone like her before and was determined to do whatever she asked of me.

'Would you care for some refreshment?' Mama asked.

'No, thank you, Mrs Coppin. I think it is best that we get on as I have another appointment this evening.'

Grandfather and Papa, unsure of their role, kept quiet, but now Mrs Powell spoke to them, directing them towards the table. 'If you gentlemen could place enough chairs for all of us around this table. How many of us are there?'

'Seven!' I declared, proud to help.

'Also,' said Mrs Powell. 'Could I ask for the lamps to be turned down? I prefer to work in twilight.'

Mrs Lee and Mrs Powell removed their hats and coats and we all sat down together, taking our places around the table on which had sat Weesy's coffin. I only noticed Mrs Powell's large carpet bag when she opened it and brought out a small bell, setting it down in front of her. There was a strong smell of lavender that I assumed was coming from Mrs Powell or her bag. This was exciting, though I saw Papa looking puzzled and glancing at my mother for reassurance. She ignored him.

'Well, now,' said Mrs Powell, smiling at each of us in turn. 'I hope everyone is comfortable. If we could place our hands palms down on the table, in a relaxed fashion, we shall begin with a prayer, as proof of our good intentions.'

'I say,' Papa suddenly blurted out, 'I am sorry but I must ask what it is that you are proposing to do. I thought you just wanted to speak to Ann. What is this all about?'

'I assure you, Captain Coppin,' replied Mrs Powell, 'that I will not be doing very much as I rather feel that Ann will be doing most of the work.'

'But is she old enough for … this?' Papa asked. Grandfather nodded to support him. It struck me that the men were nervous while the women, I felt, were impatient to begin.

Mama and Aunt Harriet exchanged a grim smile, leaving Mrs Powell to explain, 'She must be, otherwise I would not be here. I promise you, sir, if I think it is proving to be too much, I shall bring the session to an end.'

He had no choice but to accept her solution. Just then, she shuddered. 'Hmm, yes, it would be best if we had some paper and pencils to hand. I have a feeling that they might be needed but we shall see.'

Happy to oblige, I offered to get some and rushed out of the room, taking the stairs two at a time, knowing that no one would dare criticise me for being unladylike. None of that mattered tonight.

'What is going on? Who are those ladies?' William shuffled out of the shadows, a ship in his hand, and would have frightened me only I had just seen that his bedroom door was wide open and knew he must be on the prowl.

'Nothing!' I said. 'It is just a tea party. Go back to bed.'

'Are you going to bed now?'

'Well, no, I have been asked to get some paper and pencils.'

'Why?'

'So that I may draw something for them.'

'Like what?'

'I don't know,' I said crossly. 'I am in a hurry. Stop asking me questions.'

'Can't I come down with you? I want to see you draw.'

A likely story! However, I did feel a little sorry for him. It had crossed my mind that he should be at the table since he knew as much as I did about Weesy's doings. My parents would never allow him, of course, but I had an idea: 'If you want, you could hide behind the folding door. I think we are going to be calling Weesy, that's all. But you have to be really quiet. And if you get caught, do not tell them it was my idea.'

'I won't, I won't.'

He waited for me to get what I needed and tiptoed downstairs after me, holding his finger to his lips, proving a point. In the parlour, I took my place once more and Mrs Powell suggested that I keep the paper and pencils in front of me. Pausing to make sure we were ready, she then said, 'Now, I want everyone to close their eyes and say with me:

Our Father who Art in Heaven
Hallowed Be Thy Name
Thy Kingdom Come
Thy Will be Done ...

A few lines from the end of the prayer, I could not resist peeping and cracked open my eyes to see everyone else dutifully praying, eyes shut tight, voices loud and clear. Everyone that is except Mrs Powell who winked at me, making me smile in spite of my embarrassment at being caught out.

Once we said the 'Amen', Mrs Powell rang her bell, to signify, she explained, that we were beginning our session. The rocking chair in the corner began to rock ever so gently. 'My wife's chair,' gasped Grandfather.

'I think,' said Mrs Powell, 'that we should remember what tonight is about. We are here for Ann and her sister. There may be other 'guests' but, perhaps, I could return another night to concentrate on them.'

Seeing the disappointment in my grandfather's face, Mrs Powell told him, 'It is enough for her to know that you recognise that she is near.'

Mama and Aunt Harriet gave Grandfather encouraging smiles. He nodded to himself, saying, 'Thank you.'

The chair ceased to rock and a wonderful calm spread throughout the room. At the same time, the air around us grew chilly. I shivered, feeling the hairs on my head stand out.

My feet were numb, a familiar sensation. Mrs Powell looked at me. 'Well, my dear, have you anything to report? But I do not want you to stress or strain to produce a feeling that you do not have.'

My voice was a whisper. 'I do not think that Weesy is here yet.'

'No matter,' said Mrs Powell. 'I will call her now on everyone's behalf: Weesy, do not be afraid. We are here to help you, your parents, your grandfather, your aunt and sister. They love you very much and only want to know that you are alright.'

Silence.

Papa shifted in his chair. I wondered if he saw Weesy tonight, would he admit it. Suddenly, he asked, 'Did someone kick the table?'

'Did you feel that too?' asked Aunt Harriet. 'I thought I imagined it.'

Mama's face had paled in the half-light. She jumped as the table beneath our fingertips lurched.

'Please remain calm,' said Mrs Powell. 'This is quite the usual, I assure you. We must provide as warm a welcome as we can.'

'Is my daughter doing this?' asked Mama. 'Ann, are you kicking the leg of the table?'

'No, Mama,' I said, quickly adding, 'and neither is Weesy,' before anyone could ask.

The table lifted once more, prompting Mrs Powell to say, 'If your name is not Weesy Coppin, I urge you to pass on your way, with our thanks and respect.'

'But who is it?' persisted Mama.

Mrs Lee, who had not said a word, spoke gently. 'It could be someone just passing through, as Mrs Powell has said. They might not be known to any of us here. It is like they are travelling around and on finding us sitting like this together, they see an opportunity to communicate.'

Mama bit her lip, still looking worried, but the table had stopped moving. We all studied it but it remained in place. I felt that whoever had been shaking it had left, thereby allowing someone else to come through. Weesy had, I felt, been waiting to do so and now moved closer. My hair felt like it was being tugged and a gust of cold air sped past my ear. 'Mrs Powell, Weesy is here. I cannot actually see her but I know she is here.'

'At last,' said Mrs Powell with a gentle smile. 'Weesy, dear, do you have something that you would like to say to us?'

Silence. Of course, everyone looked at me, so I said, 'I do not think that she likes the question.'

'Weesy, can you tell us why you are here?' asked Mrs Powell.

I hardly knew how she would answer and, once more, found myself explaining her silence. 'She does not understand the question.'

Mama sighed, causing Mrs Powell to look at her. Blushing,

Mama said, 'This is what happens. I neither see nor hear a thing, and yet must believe that my dead child is in the room with me.'

'Let me try again,' said Mrs Powell. 'Weesy, is there something you can tell us to prove that it is you?'

Again, we waited in vain for something to happen. The clock ticked on and I found myself checking it. We had been sitting here for over thirty minutes. 'I do not believe,' laughed Mrs Powell, 'that I am asking the right questions. Small children can be a stubborn lot.'

No one else laughed, and I sensed my family's impatience that this had all been for nothing. 'I wonder,' said Aunt Harriet, 'if Ann should ask her something.'

'If that is alright with Captain and Mrs Coppin?' said Mrs Powell.

My parents glanced at one another before nodding their permission.

'Now, consider, Ann, what would be a good question,' Aunt Harriet said, 'something that no one here would be able to answer.'

I stared at her blankly, thoroughly stumped. Without thinking, I picked up a pencil, just to have the feel of it in my hand, rolling it back and forth between my fingers and thumb. I shivered and wondered what William was making of this. Perhaps he had already returned to bed, satisfied that he was not missing out on anything special. And then, just like that, I thought of a question, startling everyone when I leant forward and said, 'Oh! Weesy, where are the two ships in the Arctic, the ones that have gone missing?'

'For heaven's sake,' said Mama. 'As if that has anything to do with us.'

'Hush, Dora,' said Aunt Harriet. 'She might as well try. Nothing else is working.'

'Exactly,' said my mother. 'Perhaps we are wasting Mrs Powell's time.'

Mrs Powell assured my mother that this was not the case. 'This sort of thing can require a huge amount of patience with very little in return.'

'It is not for everyone,' agreed Mrs Lee.

'Pardon me for asking, Mrs Lee, but have you heard from your daughter since she died?' asked Mama.

'No, not as such, but that is not to say that I don't feel her around me sometimes,' said Mrs Lee.

'I just don't know,' said Mama.

Their voices faded pleasantly into the distance, though I did hear Grandfather say, 'Look at Ann.'

Closing my eyes to shut out their expectations and con-versations, I had begun to draw, allowing the pencil to roam where it wanted to, soothed by the sound of its sketching busily. The page felt like iced water against my wrist and hand, reminding me how cold I was.

I had no idea how long I sat there, wondering what it was that I was creating. Would it be better than good? Or a web of meaningless squiggles? All I could fathom was that I seemed to be filling the entire page because my arm, not just my hand, was involved.

Back and forth.

Right and left.

And back again.

All the while the only sound I could hear was the forlorn chime of a distant bell.

The last thing I did was a full stop, that is, I drilled a dot into the page with the pencil standing upright just before I thought I heard the word 'victory!' from somewhere, maybe inside my head. We all have an inner voice after all. I took pride in knowing when to stop, even with my eyes closed. I had ruined many a decent picture by over drawing, accidentally producing an image on paper that was out of shape and completely at odds with the one in my mind. Well, this drawing had to be different since my mind had been free of expectations aside from the whiteness of the page.

I opened my eyes, curious to see what I had accomplished, and was immediately disappointed. I had hoped to see a face of a human or an animal, or a landscape, maybe a typical Derry scene with the walls in the background, or in the foreground.

But, this? This was nothing, just outlines of odd-looking rectangles and oblong shapes, not a straight line to be seen. Everything was crooked, with lots of nips and tucks. It made no sense at all. Sarah might have drawn it. Oh, why couldn't I be as wonderful, as talented, as I dearly wanted to be? It was such a let-down that every picture I had ever done was nowhere as good as the picture I had planned to draw. Sometimes I wondered why I bothered trying. How long did I have to wait before I found any kind of satisfaction in what I did? Even as I was caught in my thoughts, I was scribbling words I hardly recognised: *Terror, Erebus*, Lancaster Sound, Prince Regent Inlet, Point Victory and Victoria Channel.

I felt tired, too tired to draw anything else, and stifled a yawn. My aunt touched my arm and pronounced it to be freezing. She pressed the back of her hand against my face. 'Oh, she is so cold!'

Meanwhile, Papa was peering at the page and sounded most strange when he declared, 'Oh my God, I think … but, surely not … though it does look like one.'

'What?' said Aunt Harriet. 'What does it look like?'

'A map,' said Papa.

'Oh, yes,' I said. 'That is what it is.'

Aunt Harriet was positively giddy as she looked from my drawing to Papa. 'Do you really think that is what it is?'

'Well, I will have to check it against the atlas in my study but there are the ships' names, *Erebus* and *Terror*. I am familiar with some of the other words as place names but not all of them.'

Mama was sceptical. 'But we all know the ships' names. Surely Ann was just remembering them from previous conversations?'

'Ann, dear,' said Mrs Powell, 'is Weesy still here?'

'No, she has gone again.'

'Well, then,' said Mrs Powell. 'Let me ring my bell, closing us for business, as it were. Captain Coppin, would you be so good as to turn up the lights?'

The light returned us to normality. Mama looked disgruntled while Aunt Harriet was torn between comforting her and wanting to march to Papa's study to fetch his atlas. The two ladies began to put back on their coats and hats. 'Are you quite sure,' asked Mama, 'that you cannot take a cup of tea?'

'Quite sure, Mrs Coppin. I hate to rush off like this but I have another family to attend to this evening,' said Mrs Powell. She knew that my mother was struggling to compose herself as a good host. Their eyes met and Mrs Powell said, 'I know that you probably expected something more. It can be unpredictable and I am not in control of the results. We can try it again, if you like. I can come back another time.'

Even I could see that Mama had little interest in doing that. Grandfather, who had taken himself to sit in the rocking chair, now cocked his head and asked, 'What is that?'

'What is what?' asked Aunt Harriet.

He shook his head, wanting her to listen. No one moved and, then, we heard it. Whatever it was it seemed to follow its own pattern or rhythm. Mama looked accusingly at Mrs Powell and whispered, 'Is it whoever was moving our table? Are you leaving something here in our house?'

I had never heard my mother speak so rudely to someone before but Mrs Powell did not seem to hear her. Looking perplexed, she was studying the air as if waiting for an explanation. In the meantime, Papa had crossed to the other side of the room, saying quietly, 'It sounds louder over here.'

At exactly the same time as he slid open the folding door, I recognised the sound but pretended ignorance when Papa laughed and beckoned my mother and Aunt Harriet to come see what he was looking at. I followed them to find, as I had guessed, my little brother fast asleep on the carpet, curled around his favourite ship, snoring like a steam engine.

17

Tuesday, 25th April 1848

Captain Crozier's Journal

Today, we finally reached Victory Point and made camp while Lieutenant Irving fetched Lieutenant Gore's report from the cairn. It was a sobering experience to read Gore's words from almost a year ago, when he wrote in blissful ignorance, '*Sir John Franklin commanding the expedition. All well.*'

Officer Fitzjames stood beside me and shook his head. 'I had not realised that he wrote this two weeks before Sir John's death.'

'Yes,' I sighed as I handed him the paper. 'What a different expedition we were last May.'

'What would you have me add?' asked my second-in-command.

'Start with today's date,' I instructed him, 'and then

take down the following:

H M Ships Terror *and* Erebus *were deserted on 22nd*
April, 5 leagues NNW of this, having been beset since 12th
September 1846. The officers and crews, consisting of 105
souls, under the command of Captain F.R.M. Crozier.
    Sir John Franklin died on the 11th June 1847 and the
total loss by deaths in the expedition has been to this date 9
officers and 15 men.'

Officer Fitzjames was obliged to squash his sentences
onto the outer edges of the report with the result that
his writing, I am sure he will agree, was not entirely easy
to read. After signing his name, he returned the sheet
to me for my signature. I quickly reread what he had
transcribed and then, at the last moment, decided to
supply some more detail, writing, '*And start tomorrow 26th*
for Great Fish River.'

We handed the note back to Lieutenant Irving so that
he could bring it back to the cairn which was, he told us,
less than two miles away. Fitzjames and I stood watching
him for as long as we could, before he faded into the mist.
I silently recited a prayer that our note would be found.

Instead of my cosy cabin aboard *Terror*, I am writing
this huddled in my tent. Writing with a gloved hand

is one of the most difficult things I have ever done. A simple task, writing, that I normally enjoy is now bound up with frustration as I try to keep this pencil upright. Yet, I refuse to give up. I am relieved I thought to bring the pencils as the ink is frozen solid. This journal has been a constant companion throughout the last few years and I will continue adding to it, no matter what. Giving up my cabin, and *Terror* herself, is one thing but I am determined not to be thwarted from keeping this book of my recent past, present and future. I underline that word 'future'. I have a past and this is the present.

I hear a voice outside regaling his mates with a funny story about his children. To my left, Officers Fitzjames is fighting the same battle as me, equally determined to record this day in his notebook. Mr Goodsir is fighting an even tougher battle in his attempt to darn either a pair of socks or a pair of gloves. His head is bent solidly over his work as he draws the needle in and out of the material as carefully as he can. As I watch, his concentration is broken once more when the needle gets stuck in the finger of the glove he is wearing. I silently wish him the best of luck.

Wednesday, 26th April 1848

It has been a rotten day and I dare say that my writing is just as bad, if not worse. I am sitting in my tent, in a state of complete exhaustion. Thomas has just delivered my writing desk. It is after five o'clock and I can just about smell whatever is being served up as dinner this evening, the cooks having positioned their oven on the ground outside.

I had hoped to keep us all together for the long trek south but those hopes were dashed a few hours ago. Neptune and I were leading the way, over a hundred men behind us, working in shifts to help push and drag the sledges and lifeboat. It was my decision to take the longer but easier route since it would have been much too exhausting dragging the sledges, boat and ourselves up and down the jagged landscape with its snowy hills, deep and shallow crevices and ridges of varying lengths. The shorter route, across land, would involve spending most of our time and effort in just climbing. Therefore, it is far better to walk across the iced sea because it is relatively smooth.

As we trudged along, Officer Fitzjames caught up with me, calling out for my attention, 'Sir, we have a problem and a big one at that.'

I had not looked back in some time. As the commander, I need to set the example of only looking straight ahead as we march. It is of vital importance to keep up the pace and persist in heading south at all costs. Being forced·

to come to a halt did not sit well with me. Also, to stop moving is to be severely reprimanded by the temperature. To be sure, the walking works up a sweat in the sunshine but standing still allows the sweat to freeze. I tried to mask my irritation as I turned to face the officer, thus allowing me to realise that our crew was falling away into separate groups.

'What on earth?' I began.

I could hardly make out the stragglers they were so far back, and the glare of the white snow hurt my eyes even with my blue goggles. At this distance, I would have easily convinced myself that they were penguins, not men. This would not do at all. The crew may find fault with my stern and unyielding manner but to survive the coming months we needed discipline in the ranks, discipline first and discipline last. Even as I began to chastise the young man standing in front of me, I could not fail to notice how miserable he looked.

'Officer Fitzjames, I expect you and your fellow officers to understand the importance of maintaining ourselves as a tight group. Apart from anything else, it is the proper naval procedure.'

'Yes, sir,' he replied.

As he prepared to say more, I rudely interrupted him, 'Well, why the devil are they all the way back there? It just isn't good enough. They are too far away to count, never mind recognise as members of our crew. I cannot have a breakdown in communications. Might I also remind you of the ease in which such a slow-moving group can lose sight of the rest of us?'

Officer Fitzjames hung his head, obviously deciding that it was best to let me have my say before he spoke once more. I paused in my rant, thus allowing him the opportunity to explain himself. 'Sir,' he said, 'they are the sick, the invalids.'

I stared at the barely moving specks on the horizons and felt my stomach lurch. The officer continued, 'I have spent the last hour hounding them to stick closer to the rest of us. I threatened them with court martial and anything else I can think of. But ...'

'But?' I asked, guessing what he was about to say.

'They are just too weak.'

I briefly pressed my lips together. They felt like they were made of stone. 'Do they realise that we have no option but to keep moving?'

'Yes, sir. I told them that and they do not mean to disrespect your orders, but they would prefer to stop here and allow the rest of us to continue. More than a few of them are in pretty bad shape, sir. Mr Goodsir suggested I talk to you.'

'Talk to me about what?'

'Both he and Officer Peddie have offered to stay with them. He reckons they could build a shelter of some sort, like a sick bay, though I did hear some of them talking about returning to the ships. In any case, there is plenty of food to split between the two groups.'

I sighed deeply, unwilling to commit to this new situation.

'Sir, two men have just collapsed. Their flesh is black, just like we have seen with the others. Actually, sir, they look more dead than alive and that's the truth of it.'

Oh, God help us! As if I didn't have enough worries.

'How many men are there?'

Officer Fitzjames shrugged. 'Somewhere between twenty and thirty. Apologies, Commander. I should have counted them. I'll have a man do it now.'

He turned to summon one of the men forward, but I told him not to bother. 'It is alright, though I will need a list of their names. We must keep a record of what exactly is happening and to whom.'

He looked at me, waiting for me to decide what to do. I shook my head in annoyance. We had only left the ships four days ago. I felt that I was being tested for my leadership qualities and considered walking back to inspect the invalids for myself but there was no time to waste. A good leader must trust his officers. If Mr Goodsir and Peddie had already decided to stay behind then I had to accept that they felt it was absolutely necessary. Well, that was my first thought, but I just as swiftly contradicted it. Ordinarily, I believed in discipline and keeping a professional distance from the men. However, there was nothing ordinary about this situation. I needed to see the ill men up close before walking away and leaving them behind. It also occurred to me that maybe some of them would be inspired to keep going if I showed an interest in their plight.

Of course, I had known some of the men were ailing, but I convinced myself that they would somehow cope until we found help, that they would prefer to first get out of the Arctic before daring to allow themselves to succumb to their illness. How naïve I was.

'Sir?' said Captain Fitzjames, hinting at me to hurry up with my thoughts.

'Come with me, Captain, I want to inspect matters for my own sake.'

I wondered if he disagreed with me. Well, if he did, he did not betray any impatience in his manner.

'Yes, sir.'

'Have the rest of them march on, will you? We will only be a few minutes behind them.'

He passed on my orders to the men nearest us. 'You there! Take the lead and keep going. The commander and I are just inspecting the lines.'

As we walked back, I studied the men we passed. There was no denying it; we were already a raggedy-looking bunch. Most of their faces were covered by their scarves or whatever they could use to wrap around their heads, leaving only the eyes on show. And they could not hide the fact that they were freezing. They clapped their hands together, stamped their feet and pulled their hats down over their faces. Some of them were doubled over with dreadful fits of coughing. Those pulling the boats on the sledges hardly noticed me, so absorbed were they in their tasks. I could see they were putting their backs into it but, still, they were barely progressing. The dead weight of those necessary contraptions, all filled to the brim with our possessions and food, was fighting them, inch for inch. The biggest challenge I had was *not* to question if we could keep this up for the next two months. In any case, they were all healthy men compared to the miserable lot that were gathered around Goodsir and Peddie.

Now, they were a sorry sight to behold. Most of them were sitting on the ground, trying to shelter their bowed heads between their rounded shoulders. If they could, I am sure that they would have forced both shoulders to meet, like a sheet of paper folded in two.

'I'm too hot,' exclaimed one sailor. It was an incredible statement considering that his very breath was creating puffs of mist. As he started to unravel his scarf and drag his collars this way and that, his friend leapt towards him and a half-hearted tussle began, the sailor trying to shove the scarf off him while his friend tried to re-wrap it about his neck.

'But I'm burning up, I tell you. Leave me alone!'

'Hush, man. It's just your imagination. Why, it is freezing. Can't you see the ice in my beard?'

A third man whined, 'Oh, for God's sake, mind your own business and leave him alone. You're such a busybody!'

He might have continued except he was suddenly seized by a dreadful cough that only ended when he spat something into the snow. I did not look to see what it was.

The second man, who I did not recognise, decided that the cougher was ready to be challenged. 'You come over here and say that to my face. Nobody calls me names. Nobody!'

It was at this point that Captain Fitzjames decided to make my presence known by bellowing, 'Attention for Commander Crozier!'

I appreciated his efforts but most of the group did not

seem to care. Some staggered even as they turned to face
me. One fellow would have fallen only for his colleagues,
on either side of him, grabbing hold of his arms. At
least Doctor Goodsir looked up from his patient, who
was lying far too still. He patted the man on the arm
and stood up. Another fellow was lying on the ground
and I assumed the man bending over him was John
Peddie. I gestured to Mr Goodsir that he should follow me
and Captain Fitzjames as we took a few steps away from
the men.

'Well, Mr Goodsir?' I asked.

I could barely make out his features as his hat was
pulled down low while his scarf was wound tightly around
his nose and mouth. To oblige me, he plucked his scarf as
far as his chin and said, 'You see for yourself, sir.'

'If it were just one or two, we could put them into the
boat, or on a sledge,' I offered.

Neither the doctor nor Fitzjames answered me. We
were surrounded by almost a third of our total number.

As we stood there, I saw the doctor flinch and turned to
see what caused this reaction. A man was rolling about on
the ground, his feet pulled up into his chest, saying over
and over again, 'I'm so cold, so terribly cold. I'm so cold!'

It was a ghastly sign that some, if not all, of these
men were utterly unable for a two-month trek out of the

Arctic. And I was only a Royal Naval commander, not a magician.

Mr Goodsir spoke in a low voice. 'You have my word that I will do my best for them, of course, but ...'

There was that word again, *but*. Our entire situation was riddled with them.

I sighed and turned to ask my second-in-command his opinion of our dilemma. 'Well, Captain Fitzjames, what would you do if you were me?'

His reply was immediate. 'Let them go, sir. If we force them to keep moving, some of them, at least, will not survive. This way, staying behind, gives them a fighting chance. We can come back for them since we know where they are.'

My teeth chattered against the cold, biting air. 'Alright, Mr Goodsir, you have my blessing, but I want a list of your patients for my personal records. We will return for your party as soon as we are able. Although, remember, it is you who may rescue us if the summer temperatures release the ships.'

I did not bother to ask how many sailors were staying with the doctor or how far gone they were in their illness. For one thing, it was hard to identify who was who since everyone was wearing as much clothing as they could fit around themselves. And for another, it was more pleasant to believe in the possibility that those sick men might just manage to take either *Erebus* or *Terror* and come looking for us in the next month or so.

'You and Peddie are doing us a great service in looking after the sick. I wish you well.' I shook his hand. There was little else to say.

'Please, sir,' said Mr Goodsir as he ripped off a glove and reached into his coat pocket, 'might I trouble you to post a letter for me. It's for my family and, well, it is something in case ...'

I took the letter from him, saying, 'It would be my pleasure. Though, let us hope, for all our sakes, that in the months to come, we will remember this day from the safety of our drawing rooms and marvel at how we got through it.'

He smiled and shook hands with Captain Fitzjames. I felt that I should address the invalids; they were suffering so much after all we had been through and they had wanted to get home as much as we did. It would have been unfair not to include them in our goodbyes. As Captain Fitzjames jotted down their names, I took my position in front of them and began, 'Gentlemen, I want to wish you all the very best of luck.'

A chorus of coughing along with the rolling man who would not cease his cries of 'I'm so cold' forced me to talk louder. The cold air burnt the back of my throat and even my teeth hurt so I kept my speech short. I felt like I was also addressing miles upon miles of the landscape that surrounded us – the ice that refused to melt, the snow that refused to dwindle and whatever lay beneath it.

'You are in good hands, thanks to the doctors who have volunteered to stay behind and care for you. Food will be distributed and I hope you will continue to observe naval rules and regulations. They will keep you right.'

'Will you come back for us, sir?'

I could not see the speaker's face though his voice sounded young. I nodded and assured him, and his companions, 'Yes, of course. You have my word on that. It may take a couple of months but we will return. Eight or nine weeks at the most. In the meantime, you must ration your food and keep yourselves physically and mentally busy.'

As a few heads turned away from me, I thought I saw tears. My heart was heavy though I strove to impart some wisdom. 'As you well know, this is a harsh environment. Respect it. You will need to help one another and work together. This is the key to success, full co-operation. Look out for each other.'

Perhaps I was talking too much. Several exhausted looking men started to sit down. One spoke up, 'I propose we go back to the ships.'

Before I could respond to this, Mr Goodsir pointed to the man he had been tending, saying, 'No. This man is too weak to make that journey. We set up camp here.'

A row broke out and I saw, with rising horror, that my little speech about sticking together had not made a whit of difference. This splinter group of thirty or so was already divided in two, those who wished to return to the ships and the rest who would stay put. It was inevitable that the doctors looked to me for advice. 'Well, Captain Crozier, what do you suggest?'

I paused, suddenly flustered, because, in that moment, I felt keenly that they were all doomed no matter what they did. Each and every one of them. And I suspected that Mr Goodsir guessed as much too. He waited for my answer.

'Well, I ... I might suggest that you rest here until you are all fit enough to make the journey back to the ships, if that is what you are set on doing.'

'Thank you, sir.'

I wondered should I confess my misgivings and invite Mr Goodsir, even order him and John Peddie, to accompany us if he wanted to live. There was only one answer to that question: of course I should! I had no intention of spending the rest of my life wondering if I should have said anything. That sounds so selfish but it was what made me ask him for a final quiet word. I was relieved when Captain Fitzjames did not follow us. 'You are a good man,' I began, 'and I must tell you that I am rather torn about leaving you here with them. You are under no obligation to stay; I hope you know that.'

I was being discreet, trusting him to understand what I was saying, which was that I believed his charges had little chance of surviving whereas he was still healthy with everything to live for. He nodded in silence. We both stared off into the whiteness for a moment or two. Finally, Mr Goodsir said, 'I took an oath, sir, the Hippocratic oath. As a man of medicine, it is my duty to stay and care for the sick. And because it is my duty, I would forever hate myself if I chose otherwise.'

He put a hand on my arm. I could not feel the weight of it beneath my layers of garments, and added, 'So, Captain Crozier, if I left with you now, I would not survive intact anyway.'

I shrugged. 'I see. Well, we both have our duties to attend to. Yours is to tend the ill and mine is to lead the rest of the men on what may well prove to be a costly and tortuous march.'

In answer to the doctor's questioning look, I confessed, 'I could be making a huge mistake. It is impossible to know but, even so, it feels better than doing nothing at all.'

Mr Goodsir smiled. 'Yes, sir. Neither of us has a choice regarding our urge to fulfil our duties as well as we can.'

I managed a laugh when he added, 'And you never know, sir, we may survive this yet.'

'Very true,' I replied. 'At this point, anything is possible.'

We shook hands for the last time. Gripping my hand, he thanked me, saying, 'It was a pleasure to serve with you, Captain Crozier.'

His words were unexpected and moved me more than I cared to show.

Just then, I thought of something and called Captain Fitzjames. 'Make sure these men are given guns and ammunition so that they are able to hunt for fresh food. Just because we have seen little evidence of seals and bears and birds so far does not mean that they won't finally put in an appearance.'

'Aye, sir! I'll have them sent back this minute.'

I watched him leave. Then I faced the men and made my farewell. Standing as straight as I could, in my bulky clothes, I clipped my heels together and saluted them. Those who could not stand saluted me from where they sat. To my amazement, I watched Neptune run about them, making sure he nuzzled each man, with his cold nose, for a second or two. For this, he received plenty of rubs and tugs to his ears. When he was done, he strolled back to me. I turned and walked away.

As I headed after Fitzjames, I called out for Officer Irving. The thought of fresh meat was a tantalising one. It would lend a great boost to our spirits if we had a good meal to look forward to, one that did not involve the infernal tins of food. As desperate as our situation is, I have already promised myself, and Neptune, that once we reach home again, neither of us will ever eat food from a tin again, for as long as we both shall live.

Officer Irving sprang to my side. 'Yes, sir?'

'I want you to send out our best shooters ahead of us, to scour the area for fresh food. My God, but there has to be some sort of animals in residence. I refuse to believe that we are the only beings here.'

'Very good, sir.' He trotted back and started calling out names.

I was glad that I had thought of this. It helped to ease the guilt that I felt in leaving Goodsir, Peddie and their patients behind. It would not be so bad if we could provide them with fresh meat.

Four men skirted ahead of me, slowly fanning out to the left and right. I silently wished them God's speed. This march to freedom would benefit considerably if the hunters could provide even half our food intake.

The hunters have just returned, empty handed.

Friday, 28th April 1848

All day the only movement and sounds are of our own making. Since officers do not help with the pulling of the boats, it is just the grunts of the men that ring out, as they heave and tug.

Time and time again, I imagine that I could see something ahead, some dark form, but when I prop up the telescope to my eye, I only see more snow and more ice. Is it phantoms playing tricks on me?

Quite a few of the men are complaining of blindness due to the sun's glare being reflected everywhere we look, in the snow and ice. We may as well stare directly at the sun which no one can do for more than a moment or two. Only some of us have goggles. Well, what can I do? It is just another thing to worry about.

Thomas staggered in here with my writing desk, falling down in front of me. His breathing sounded forced as he gulped, 'Sorry, sir!'

'Are you alright, Thomas?'

'Thank you, sir. Just a bit dizzy, sir.'

I nodded. 'See if Doctor McDonald can give you something, maybe an extra shot of rum.'

'Very good, sir.' He staggered back outside again, leaving

me feeling that I should do something more. But, what?

Saturday, 29th April 1848

Doctor McDonald squeezed himself into the tent just now, to inform me that my steward is dead. I failed to show any sorrow, only asking that the body be buried as quickly as possible so that we could break up camp and move on.

'He was a good man,' said the doctor, watching me carefully.

I was both impatient for coffee and attempting to form my plans for today's march. All in all, I was in no mood for a talk such as this.

'Is there anything else, Doctor?'

'As a matter of fact, there is,' he said. 'I have remembered that the Inuit use wooden spectacles to protect their eyes from the sun. I suggest we have enough made for the men.'

Seeing my look of dismay, he hurried on. 'It should not take too long. What I am referring to is a mere slat of wood, the length of a man's forehead, in which two small holes have been punctured.'

In fact, I knew what he was talking about, having seen Inuit wearing them on other trips. I had pitied them for not having proper goggles, but now desperate times were upon us. I asked, 'Is there enough wood to go around?'

The doctor rewound his scarf around his neck. 'Yes, we think so. Well, perhaps a few of the larger books may need to be relieved of their outer covers while some minor slats can be removed from the lifeboats without causing too much fuss.'

I saw him glance at my little writing desk. Of course, Thomas had not returned for it and it had spent the night in here with me. I wondered if the doctor dared to ask for it. Well, he was not getting his hands on something so precious to me. I need to write every day. We are depositing notes as we walk, in the hope that someone will find one and then come find us. That little ornate desk could well be our only means for surviving this hell.

'Alright, sir,' he finally said. 'I will have those spectacles made as swiftly as possible.'

He turned to leave only to turn back again, saying, 'Oh, I almost forgot!'

Digging his hand into his coat pockets, he took out a pair of raggedy-looking gloves and handed them to me. I eyed them suspiciously. 'Yes,' he said. 'Thomas's last wish was that these be given to you … to make up for gloves he left behind at Beechey Island.'

Before I could say a word, he was gone and therefore missed my tears for the man who had cared for me every day, without fail, for the last three years.

18

Mama and Papa have
important news

L ast night, I dreamt it was snowing. I awoke to feeling my entire body freezing up, limb by limb: toes, ankles, fingers, elbows, shoulders, nose. The creeping chill was making its way for my heart and I could do nothing to stop it. I could not move. The bedcovers felt like sludgy water, sodden through. The cold air hurt my throat as I struggled to take deep breaths in an effort to calm the seismic beating of my heart. Was this what it was like to suffocate?

Just when it became unbearable, just when I decided to call for help, I recognised the tingling of my scalp and, instead of screaming, I gritted my teeth in annoyance and hissed, 'Go away, Weesy!'

It was just her. Oh, how I hope it was only her.

Within seconds, my body was returned to me. I flexed my toes and fingers before dragging my blankets as far as my nose. And then, as soon as I could, I cried.

Earlier that day, I had been standing in the parlour, trying to decide if I felt like walking in the garden. Papa was in his study and I heard him call me. I pushed the door open to find him at his desk with Mama standing beside him, a letter in her hand. Her cheeks were flushed as she glanced from the paper to me. She appeared quite bothered about whatever it was that she was reading.

Now, what had I done? Had some complaint been made about me? Why did Mama look so ill at ease? Had someone else died?

'What is wrong, Mama?' I felt a little afraid.

Meanwhile, Papa seemed his usual calm self. He was patently not looking at Mama, only concentrating on me as he said, 'Sit down, Ann. Your mother and I wish to discuss something with you.'

Hoping that he would prove to be my ally for whatever was going to happen, I asked him, 'Am I in trouble, Papa? Did I do something wrong?'

He shook his head. 'No, no, it is nothing like that.'

Mama continued to read, although I could see that the letter was not that long. She must have finished it by now.

I waited nervously, with no idea what was going on.

Finally, Mama sighed and let her arm drop to her side. Now they were both looking at me. I smiled, hoping that would help.

'So, Ann, my dear, it seems that we find ourselves involved in a rather extraordinary matter.'

'Yes, Papa?' I asked.

'Your map of the Arctic, the one you drew some time ago … do you remember?'

Well, of course I remembered. How on earth could I forget something like that? Naturally, I did not say any of this aloud but only nodded coyly.

Papa continued, 'I sent it off to Lady Jane Franklin, Sir John's wife.'

My eyes widened in surprise. I had been wondering what had happened to it. Papa had taken it to his study that day and it had never been mentioned again. He shrugged. 'It seemed the right thing to do. I had heard that she is beside herself, having no clue where her husband's ships are. Searches have been made of the area but, so far, nothing has been sighted of the men. No hints had been left as to where exactly they went, which of course creates great difficulty for those trying to find them.'

'And you think my map will help? You think I got it right?'

Mama began to fidget. 'No, that is not what Papa is saying.

Nobody is sure about that. Papa felt obliged to send it to Lady Franklin just in case it could help. It would have been remiss of us not to.'

'The thing is,' added Papa, 'I, that is, your mother and I could not ignore our obligations because of that word you heard, as you finished it.'

'You mean, "victory"?' I asked.

Thanks to Aunt Harriet pressing me as to whether I could add anything else to my map, I had remembered what I thought I had heard and had offered it shyly, in case it was merely the voice in my head congratulating myself on a job well done. Of course, this was before I had opened my eyes to see the squiggles I had produced.

'There is an area in the Arctic called Point Victory and the Victoria Channel and where you marked your map is within this area.'

'Oh, I see.'

Well, what else could I say?

I was terribly flattered but was doing my best to hide it. Mama would squash any hint of big-headedness and I felt her scrutinising my entire being for the tiniest sign that I was feeling full of myself. But, really, who could blame me? Lady Franklin had seen something I drew; she had actually held it in her hand.

'Did she like it?' I asked, careful not to sound the least bit excited. It was a reasonable question since any kind of an artist wants their work to be liked. I tried to visualise the map in my mind's eye; it has been a while since I have seen it. I wished I had had the opportunity to add some colour to it. If I had known it was to be posted off to London, I could have reworked and improved upon it. It was too bad that Papa did not let me know what he was planning to do with it.

Typically, Mama replied, 'Whether Lady Franklin likes it or not is hardly the point here, Ann. That is not why your father sent it to her. You should not be looking for compliments since there are most important things to consider, for example, that it might be of some help to her finding her husband.'

'Yes, Mama,' I replied meekly.

Papa winked at me. 'I can ask her if she liked it or not.'

I stared at him. Whatever did he mean? 'What, Papa … I mean … pardon? I don't understand.'

Before Papa could make a reply to me, Mama took over again. 'Her Ladyship has asked to meet Papa to talk about how you came to draw the map and what it might mean.'

Oh, my goodness!

I panicked. 'But, I don't know what it means. I drew it with my eyes closed!'

Surely such a boring explanation would fall rather short in Lady Franklin's eyes? My satisfaction over my artistic endeavour vanished and I was just me again, a young girl who knew very little about the world and needed to be rescued by her parents.

'Calm yourself, Ann.' Papa was laughing at my expression. 'There is no need to look so scared.'

'You see,' said Mama to him. 'I told you that she would not be able for this. It is too much.'

Wait a minute, I thought. *What was I missing? What was I not able for?* I did not like to hear such talk, that I might be unable for a situation. That was unfair. Should I not be given a chance to judge my ability for myself?

Somewhat huffily, I asked, 'What am I not able for, Mama?'

I assumed that this was the part that Mama was struggling with. She took a deep breath, flicked some dust off her skirt and spoke slowly. 'Lady Franklin has invited Papa to have tea in her house.'

'Her house, the one beside the Admiralty headquarters? Remember what Uncle Virgil told us, that she moved home to supervise the Admiralty.'

Mama tutted. 'That is not what your uncle meant. Anyway, as I was saying, your father is to visit Lady Franklin. Now, she did invite you along too but we do not think that is necessary.'

Was it just my imagination or did Papa look uncomfortable when Mama said 'we'?

'Lady Franklin invited me to her home? In London?'

Could it be true? I gazed at one parent and then the other.

'She actually wants me to come to London?'

'Well, yes, but only your father will go. You would need a female chaperone and neither your aunt nor myself are able to accompany you.'

My mind blazed as she spoke. I needed to find a solution and fast. 'But, what about Cousin Charlotte? She could come with me.'

In the few seconds I had, before Mama shook her head, I beheld the grandest vision of my dear cousin and myself, arm in arm, traipsing through London streets, on our way to see pictures at the National Gallery and spy on Her Majesty, Queen Victoria, through the windows of Buckingham Palace … and drink hot chocolates at a refined café … and … and … and. I had read so much about London that this vision would have continued on for some time had I not been interrupted by Mama. She may as well have picked up Papa's knife, the one he used to slice open his letters, and stabbed me in the heart. Of course, her attitude was entirely predictable. She did not want me to experience anything exciting, nor have Papa to myself for days on end.

'No, that would not do at all.'

I was shaking. 'But why not? I want to go. Please, Mama, I beg you!'

Tears stung my eyes and I was helpless to prevent them from gathering. My parents became nothing more than two shapeless blurs, which only added to my distress as I wanted to look like a responsible young lady instead of a little girl who weeps when she doesn't get her own way. In tears, I struggled for that perfect reason which would enable me to go. 'But Lady Franklin asked for me. How can I refuse her such a thing, with all she is going through?'

My mother actually had the temerity to smile sourly at me as if I had said something so ridiculous, it did not deserve a response.

'Please, Mama. Oh, please let me go!' I persisted.

She gave my father a look that stirred him from a stupor, forcing him to get involved once more with this horrid conversation. 'Lady Franklin will understand, Ann. It is just that your mother ...'

He faltered beneath my accusing look. Why wasn't he taking my side? Of all the people in this world, he knew my ambitions to travel. Spreading his hands before me, he continued, 'Well, it is just that we have one more piece of important news, you see, which explains why you cannot be spared.'

I pouted, pointedly refusing to show any interest in whatever he was taking about.

'You see, my dear, there is a baby on the way.'

Too frustrated to make sense of this, I stood in silence, still trying to concoct something that would allow me to go. To her credit, Mama recognised this and asked, 'Do you understand, Ann? Did you even hear what your father said?'

Lady Franklin would want me to go. She sounded like the sort of woman I hoped to be, independent and fearless. Perhaps I would write to her and ask her to petition Mama with a second invitation. After all, I was the one who had drawn the map. Of course, to write to her, I would need to get her address from Father without telling him why. That might be difficult but …

'ANN COPPIN, are you listening to me?'

I jumped in fright and shock that Papa – my own sweet father – had shouted at me. Mama looked on with a certain satisfaction as he addressed me. 'Young lady, I have had enough.'

The battle was lost. I would not be going anywhere.

Papa's anger had not yet abated as he peered at me, his voice sounding incredulous. 'Well, isn't there something you wish to say to your mother?'

I managed to gulp out what I supposed was expected of me. 'Congratulations, Mama.'

Laying her hand briefly across her stomach, she sighed, 'Do you understand why I need you here?'

'Yes, Mama.'

My tone was flat, all my excitement squashed. I needed to escape them and said, 'I have an essay to write. Thank you.'

I hardly knew what I was saying as I opened the door and

quickly closed it behind me. I galloped up the stairs two at a time in my desperation to reach the sanctity of my room so that I could give in to the sobs that were swelling up from my knees. Making sure not to display any temper in slamming my bedroom door, I eased it into place before flinging myself across my bed, almost swallowing the top cover as I strove to wail in secret.

I was crying because I wanted to go to London and meet Lady Franklin. After a few minutes, however, I felt something crumbling, as if I was sinking into a new level of grief. Now, I was crying for more than a lost trip abroad as I suddenly remembered my parents' news. A new baby. Poor Weesy.

19

April or May 1848

Captain Crozier's Journal

I cannot write much. I am tired and cold and am struggling to believe in myself. Or anything at all.

My rule that we stick together was dealt another blow today. Another thirty men gone. I tried reasoning with them and shouting at them too, but in the end my words sounded false even to my ears. I said, 'We must stay together. There is safety in numbers.'

'Begging your pardon, Captain Crozier, but safety from what, the ice?'

This was from Officer Irving. He held my gaze as if trying to see into my skull, as if I was hiding something from him. Then he shrugged and said, 'Look, sir, with all respect, we are too ill to keep walking like this. We all agree that we have a better chance if we return to the ships. At least they provide shelter from the cold. At least we will have hammocks to sleep in.'

Well, even my eyes watered at the thought of my bed on *Terror*. This was my difficulty, that the weakest part of me, which is to say the part that was cold and exhausted, which is to say most of me, wanted to be back on board my ship too.

Could it be that my thoughts were obvious? Officer Irving continued, possibly believing he was convincing me, 'Sir, maybe the ice is already melting. Maybe there are searches being made all around *Erebus* and *Terror* while we plough on to goodness knows where.'

My reply was unhelpful. 'That is a lot of maybes, Officer.'

Oh, but they were in a bad way. How can I force sick men to follow me across miles of ice and snow? Yet, I tried once more out of duty and, yes, desperation. My audience was not up to a long speech. One man kept trying to take control of our meeting. His friends hushed him but he became ever more vocal, calling out, 'I know where we are. I know exactly where we are.'

Doctor McDonald caught my eye and shrugged, possibly telling me to ignore him, but I had not the energy to talk over his ranting. Instead, I asked him, 'Pray tell. Where are we then?'

He threw back his head to laugh at me, at all of us. 'Don't you know? Oh, alright, let me tell you, my friends, that we are on the moon.'

Not surprisingly, his audience just stood and stared at him. 'Why, yes,' he cried, jabbing his hands at the air around him. 'Look, everything is white and shiny and quiet, just like the moon, see!'

In the very next second, his confidence evaporated. With sagging shoulders, he beseeched us, 'But don't you believe me? You must believe me!'

I could not think of a single thing to say other than, 'Yes, we believe you.'

My response was a flimsy kindness that was immediately taken up by the rest of the crew and officers. Our navigator, such as he was, flopped down on the ground, folding his gloved hands into the snow, and seemed almost happy that he had been able to put us right, in his own mind at least.

Few of us were in good shape. Some were doubled up in pain, wrapping their arms around their middles as if afraid of losing bits of themselves out here, in the middle of nowhere.

It felt like nowhere.

It feels like nowhere.

I told them, 'I know you are all tired but we must keep

going. We have a destination, a goal. This is not some pointless march, you know. We are making this journey to save ourselves.'

Thirty faces turned away from me. I realised that they meant to go this very second, actually turning and shuffling off. Comrades in arms, literally holding up the arms of those poor fellows who would never see *Erebus* and *Terror* again.

I flung an accusation at their retreating backs. 'Is this a mutiny?'

One of them, I don't know who, replied, 'There are no mutinies in Hell, sir.'

I pretended not to hear. But I had my responsibility to them. They were still my crew, whether they believed in me or not. I made sure they had plenty of food, to give them every chance of surviving their trek back to the ships. And I ordered them to take one of the lifeboats. I will pray for their success as I pray for ours, those who decided to stay with me.

I must say, though, I almost cracked wide open when I saw Neptune make his decision. That overgrown, shaggy mess of a dog looked left after those setting off to return to the ships, and then he glanced right, seeing me and the rest of my colleagues. How I would have preferred him to have looked confused about what was happening. As it was, he merely shucked his head before following the others.

I would not have thought it was possible that a mere dog could hurt my feelings so.

I was more shocked by this than by anything else that has happened since leaving the ships. How could he reject me? Was it because he felt the sick and broken needed him more? Or did he sense that the others offered him a better chance of survival?

There are forty of us now, who will make the walk to Great Fish River. If I can get forty men to safety then I will not have totally failed.

I will stop writing now.

So tired.

I wish ...

Well, what do I wish for? If I rubbed this bowl of mine and it turned out to be a magic lamp that could bring forth a genie who, in turn, granted me just one wish, what would that be? For running water? For Sophie's love? For Neptune's return.

No.

I wish for home.

20

Mama is finally convinced

Papa was back from London and not, I felt, telling me much about his visit to Lady Franklin. Apart from the usual, that she was polite and asked about all of us and was sorry about Weesy's untimely death. She was, he said, 'a lady of great intelligence'.

This was earlier at the dinner table.

'Did she like my map, Papa?'

Mama gave Papa a look that was loaded with meaning, making me suddenly suspicious. 'Why, yes, indeed, she did. Very much so.' He smiled at me, ignoring the fact that I was waiting to hear more. And I waited.

Aunt Harriet broke the silence. 'William, cut your potato into smaller pieces, or do you want me to do it for you?'

'Harriet, could you pass me the butter?' This was Mama.

There began a right chorus of clatter, clinking cutlery against the flowery-patterned plates. Mama poured tea into Papa's cup, the sound reminding me of rain being blown in torrents against my bedroom window. She filled her own cup halfway and waved the teapot in Aunt Harriet's direction. Next, she seized the big knife and energetically sawed her way through the loaf of white bread, showing off her skill at creating even thin slices. All in all, the only adult not acting awfully busy was Grandfather, who was feeling better now. All he did was chew his food, deep in thought or perhaps he was dreaming. I tried a different tack.

'But, what was she like, Papa? Was there any one thing that struck you about her person?'

Mama barely hid her impatience. 'What an odd question, Ann. I do wish you would eat your lunch before it grows cold.'

I smiled sweetly and obediently raised a forkful of carrots to my mouth.

'She has tremendous spirit,' said Papa, glancing at Mother to see he had not vexed her.

Aunt Harriet could not help herself and asked, 'What do you mean?'

Choosing his words with care, Papa replied, 'She is not prepared to believe her husband is dead until she hears otherwise. And this, she told me, is why she refuses to wear dark clothes. Because she is not in mourning.'

Aunt Harriet was intrigued. 'So, what colour was she wearing then?'

Papa laughed. 'Far be it for me to notice a woman's dress but it was colourful, blues and reds and pinks, I think. Yes, really quite colourful.'

After lunch, I pretended to believe what we were told. Papa said he would go to his office, while Mama and Aunt Harriet professed a need to sort out our winter clothes, but not one of them moved when William and I excused ourselves. I declared my intention to go to my room and read, whilst William, having extracted a promise from Papa to inspect his newest ship, took off to prepare for it. I followed my brother out of the dining room and halfway up the stairs before it properly occurred to me to hide here, in the alcove of the parlour, which is curtained off from the main room.

'Where are you going?'

William had thought I was right behind him until he caught me tiptoeing across the hall. Glaring at him, I put my finger to my lips. That was enough for him and he trotted down to join me uninvited but at least he did not bother to repeat his question. For once, the parlour door did not creak as I inched it open. We took up our positions and listened. It was quite a risk as I had to hope that they would not want to move from the table to the parlour, thereby pulling open the curtain to find my brother and me eavesdropping.

Papa sighed. 'She really was a character and her niece too, Sophie. I would not care to vex either of them. I mean, I would not be surprised if I heard that she was taking command of an office in the Admiralty's headquarters and issuing orders as if she were her own ship's captain.'

Aunt Harriet said, 'But she is a captain, in her own way. You said that she is funding her own ships to go in search of her husband's.'

'True,' agreed Papa. 'She told me that she is quite prepared to use up all her money to sponsor as many searches as she can afford. I hear the Franklins are not too happy with this, her besieging the family coffers as it were.'

To my surprise, Grandfather spoke up and asked about my map. 'Did she take Ann's map seriously?'

There was a pause before Papa answered in the most astounding way, 'Oh yes, she took it seriously alright. In fact, she was most interested in hearing all that has happened since Weesy's ... well, you know. She even asked if I thought my children were gifted.'

'Gifted?' Of course this was Mama who sounded so incredulous.

Papa smiled, or at least that is what it sounded like to me. 'I know this is going to sound fantastic but we can all imagine how desperate she is. Her husband and over a hundred men have vanished, with not a single word or sighting of them for over three years. Several searches have already taken place but, according to Lady Franklin, they have no proper idea where to look and she is desperate for any clue, any hint in which to steer new searches. And, as it turns out, Ann's map is not the first – let us call it – *supernatural* information that she has looked into.'

'Ooh,' said Aunt Harriet, 'pray tell us all!'

I heard more tea being poured as Papa said, 'I may not remember all that she mentioned but this is my favourite story, after's Ann's map of course.'

William tapped my arm, congratulating me.

'Alright,' said Papa. 'There is a man, a Mr Snow who, apparently, has psychic powers on account of splitting his head open when he was a boy. He and his powers are the subject of some magazine article. Anyway, he had a sad childhood, became a sailor but is now living in New York as a newspaperman. He wrote to Lady Franklin, describing how he awoke in the middle of the night to find himself standing at his bedroom window when ...'

'Wait,' said Mama. 'Is this going to frighten us? Are you sure you want to tell us?'

It was Aunt Harriet who answered, 'Oh, Dora, do let him continue. I want to hear it.'

I guessed that Papa checked with Mother before continuing. 'As I was saying. He is standing at his window and sees the curtains being parted and, instead of whatever is the usual scene, he finds himself gazing at what he believes is the Arctic. What he wrote was that he saw a flat, ice-covered triangle that he took to be King William Land, the very same land that Ann included in her map. And he saw bodies.'

I stifled a gasp and was not in the least surprised when William took my hand. I stared hard at the curtains, letting Papa's words paint a picture for me. *How funny*, I thought, *that the man's name was Snow.*

'He actually saw bodies?' Aunt Harriet sounded beside herself with excitement.

Mother tried to protest. 'Oh, now, this is too much!'

Either Papa did not hear her or he chose not to, so caught up was he in his storytelling.

'Yes, he claims to have seen it all, bodies of men lying in the snow and the two ships. Don't worry, not all the men were dead. He heard some calling out for help. They were in different groups, spread out over the area, but he pinpointed actual locations for Lady Franklin, urging her to have them searched. And, according to Lady Franklin, Ann's map matched up well enough with Mr Snow's vision.'

William squeezed my hand hard but I was too astonished to acknowledge him.

'It seems that Mrs Snow woke up to see her husband standing at the window but the curtains were closed. He was shivering with the cold and she said his skin felt like ice.'

'Honestly,' said Aunt Harriet. 'I think that is the most wonderful thing I have ever heard.'

Grandfather said, 'In other words, Ann was not making it up, not any of it, it would seem.'

I pictured Papa and Aunt Harriet nodding away.

At long last Mama spoke, saying quietly, 'Yes, I realise that. Now. And that Weesy has really been with us all along.'

There was a tremendous silence at this.

So, she had doubted me all along.

This was huge and I was meant to know nothing about it. In truth, I felt like jumping out at them in triumph, which would have been an error of the highest proportions. How grateful I was for William's hand in mine to remind me to keep still. I turned to him to, oh – I don't know – hug him or kiss his shiny forehead. I had to do something. Only he wasn't where I thought he was. Instead, he was standing behind me, both hands in the pockets of his knickerbockers.

'Were you holding my hand just now?' I whispered it, pressing my face close to his.

He shook his head in disgust, as if accused of a crime.

21

Arctic

My dear James,

I am writing this letter to you instead of making my usual journal entry. You see, for the first time in a long time, I know that I will see you again.

Let me explain.

It is some time since we last saw our companions. To be honest, I am confused as to how many days have passed since they left us because I have not been able to write or record anything until now.

However, this has been a better day. This is the new beginning that I have been praying for.

We began walking at first light and the going could have been a lot worse. There was no wind, just the freezing air biting at us, searching for any flesh not amply covered, blackening it. Frostbite. Yes, that's what it's called. Anyway, the sun came out, offering no comfort. This is the hollow, empty sun of the Arctic that merely dazzles us without providing any warmth. It reminds me of that saying, 'All that glisters is not gold.' Shakespeare, I think.

I was never one for poetry.

My mind is wandering across this page.

Anyway, with Neptune at my heel, I strode ahead, my back as straight as the wall of my father's house and I refused to look back, to check on the progress behind me. Of course, you know that I must be stern if we are to succeed. It is up to me to both lead my thirty-nine officers and crew and, as a role model, provide exemplary behaviour and confidence, showing that it can be done, that we can keep walking. We must keep walking.

You agree with me, don't you, James? How lonely it is to be a leader.

Although, of course, Neptune is not actually here. He left me, didn't he, to return with the others to the ships? But I am free to say he is here if that is what I wish and, therefore, I permit my imagination to keep him here with me. You would really like him, James. Anyway, I chatted to him because I needed to chat to someone.

'Well, my boy, are they keeping up with us?'

He could never resist looking back, such a curious dog.

He answered my question with a short bark and, I could swear, a look of reproach. 'Oh, no, you don't,' I told him. 'Don't you feel sorry for them! Pity is a luxury here.'

We had not been walking for too long before I thought I saw some movement in the distance. But was this another mirage of mine? For the last day or two, I could not shake the feeling that we were being watched.

'Neptune, can you see what I see? Am I mad or is that people up ahead? Actual people?'

I heard a bark which was good enough for me. Well, if we were on a floating ship, I could equate this marvellous scene with finding land. Remember, James, when we finally found the Australian coast. Wasn't that something? Wasn't it warm? So, it was that same feeling, of something miraculous happening even if land had been expected for quite some time. I had hoped and hoped that it was only a matter of time before we met with some form of life other than ourselves. I simply would not accept that we were the only ones here. I quickened my pace, although I did turn and use my arms to gesture to the others that wondrous sight.

Retrieving my telescope from my coat pocket, I put it to my eye. Oh, how it hurt, the steel being so cold to the touch that it scalded my skin. Do you remember our Antarctic expedition, James? Remember that we marvelled about never, ever feeling warm for months on end. We had to be careful with our instruments; they hurt us so.

I could have whooped in delight as I peered through the telescope. At first glance, I teased myself that I had discovered a new type of animal, one that was as tall as a man and walked about on two legs like a man. The glass circle of my telescope confirmed that I was looking at a group of Inuit covered in fur, from head to toe. Some of them carried spears, which delighted me further as this meant that they were hunting for food. They had their own dogs with them. And they saw us too. I watched them point in our direction. Two men, it seemed, were being sent to meet us. Since I had time to, I briefly inspected the rest of them. My heart thudded when I realised it was a family group. There were women and children. How long had it been since my men and I last saw a woman or a child? Oh, it gave me such a jolt.

Officer Fitzjames appeared at my side, out of breath, his panting causing pillow-sized mists that momentarily obscured his face, reminding me of bridal veils made from the finest Belfast linen. His breathing was laboured for a few minutes but when he could, he asked, 'What is it, sir?'

'Natives. A family, I would say. I should think they are

most surprised to see us here. Two are coming our way.'

'Do they look friendly? We should take the usual precautions, sir.'

I bridled at this. 'Why, yes, Fitzjames. Thank you for telling me what I already know. Have one of the marines load a rifle and follow me but tell him to hang back. You wait here with the others until I judge the lie of the land.'

'But should I not accompany you, sir?'

I was haughty because, as usual, I felt he was judging me and assuming he was superior to me in every way. I snapped, 'No, you should not!'

But then I sought to be understood. Willing myself to sound more patient than I felt, I added, 'I do not wish to frighten them away. We cannot afford to intimidate them or appear unwelcome.'

Looking unconvinced, Officer Fitzjames nevertheless replied, 'Very good, sir.'

I watched Fitzjames as he carried out my instructions. Our little procession came to a halt and, moments later, one of the taller men detached himself, rifle in hand, and made his way towards me. I raised my hand briefly, letting him know that he was to follow me, at a distance.

As I walked, a hundred thoughts slid around my mind. Surely this was the best piece of luck that we had had in years. God in His mercy had sent these natives to us in our hour of need. Possibly, young Fitzjames did not grasp the reality of our situation. We had guns and bullets aplenty which meant nothing out here. Over the last while, we had managed to shoot a couple of birds, but there were no oxen, no deer, no bears, not even a blasted squirrel. Only snow and ice. We were in a bad way. Most of our food was gone. I am not sure how this happened. Maybe we gave the others too much. Maybe we lost it. In other words, we were at the mercy of these strangers. If they turned away from us, I should not like to consider the consequences for our survival.

I gave them my best smile and dearly wished I could remember the Inuit word for friendship. There was a crack in the ice and the two fellows steered me there to meet, a river frozen beneath our feet. I know, James, I know. They were wary of us and wanted to keep us away from the rest of the family until they deemed me trustworthy. It was all down to me, to make them feel at ease and make them want to help us.

Could they see the hunger in my face?

They stared at my escort's rifle so I ordered him to lay it on the ground and look friendly. Once the gun was down, they focused on me, studying my clothes and my boots. I was charmed by the reverence they showed for the gold buttons of my coat. Perhaps this was their first

time to see buttons. Certainly, I could see no openings
in their attire. I wondered how many animals each was
wearing.

'Two ships,' I began, as I used my arms to draw *Erebus*
and *Terror* in the air.

Private Heather, my marine, muttered, 'Do they even
know what a ship is, sir?'

I ignored him. They watched me politely. I added
noises to my repertoire, the whirring of engines getting
slower and slower before dropping my head to my hands
to signify the ice moving in around us, getting tighter
and tighter until we were solidly trapped. It was a most
vibrant pantomime, I assure you, and they were an
attentive audience, graciously following my hands when I
pointed in the direction we had travelled from, where our
ships were held fast.

Hunger motivated the next act. I moved my hands
from my mouth down to my stomach several times and
told Private Heather to do the same. I mimicked putting
food into my mouth and then, rather cheekily, pointed to
the bags on their back. There had to be food in them.

You can imagine my delight when they gestured us to
follow them and turned to head back to the rest of their
group. I winked at Private Heather, delighted with my
success. Yes, James, you are right. This was quite out of

character for me to behave so with crew but you will have to admit that this was a special occasion.

Our two friends spoke to their family who each carried the same sort of shapeless, bulky bag made out of some furry animal. There was no need for small talk, no need for niceties because they knew no English and this is the Arctic, not a London residence. I pointed to their bags and prevailed upon them to open them, again pointing to my mouth and tapping my stomach to demonstrate it needed to be filled with whatever they could give me. Private Heather did not need to be urged a second time to copy me.

They did exactly what I asked and you can appreciate how my eyes watered at the sight of the meat in their bags. Thick chunks of seal meat. They had been far luckier than us since we had not seen a seal in months and months. I smiled and smiled to encourage them and, bless them, they all removed some of their meat and placed it in one pile for me. I was overjoyed. This was better than gold, to dine on fresh meat for the first time in years. The oldest man called one of his dogs, a big, shaggy thing that reminded me of Neptune. He carried his own bag which was tied to his broad back and which was now being filled with the meat. I shook hands all round, even with the women and the timid young boy who held back yet allowed me to take his hand. Or perhaps he was a young girl. Their exotic features make it difficult to tell the youngsters apart.

'Come,' I said, waving my arms once more. 'Come and meet the rest of us!'

Four of the men elected to go with me. I sent Private Heather on ahead to ensure that our men were busy setting up camp and that they should make our guests feel welcome. I started making plans there and then. We would befriend this family group and, with our weapons and their keen knowledge of the area, we would be able to provide fresh food for everyone. My heart sang as I thought about never having to open another tin again, not that we had any left.

Our four companions followed me back across the frozen river to where our chaps were erecting the tent. At our arrival, I am disappointed to say that my men stopped what they were doing to stare rudely at my companions. I was an anxious host and roared at them, 'Get back to work if you want to eat today!'

The natives looked startled at my tone. I smiled graciously and summoned Assistant Surgeon Alexander McDonald. He knew these people better than the rest of us as he used to hunt whales in Arctic waters and had spent some time with them, even learning their language.

He came forward and I wished he could have looked a bit less sorrowful. In any case, he translated for me, my name and rank, and how we came to be here. The four seemed rather surprised to hear familiar words spring forth from the surgeon's mouth. They glanced at another, raising their eyebrows in disbelief. As McDonald spoke, I beamed and nodded my head to compensate for my colleague's dour expression.

Once our tent was standing, the dog's saddlebag was emptied out onto the ice. My men beheld this fatty feast with a holy regard normally reserved for the inside of a church. I could not help myself and took a bite of the meat, uncooked, just enough to fill my mouth. I grinned at our guests, displaying my compliments for their food. Now, it was time for us to give them something. 'Open up our bags, open everything. We need to give these good people our thanks.'

My men were sluggish from lack of sustenance, which explains why I had to roar once more, 'I said, open up our bags. We owe these people our lives.'

Not one of them looked like they agreed with me. Dullards! How I wished that Thomas, my poor steward, would appear to carry out my wishes.

I suddenly fancied a break away from my men. Had I not been looking at their faces for days on end now? I had McDonald suggest to the natives that I accompany them back across the river, to where they were building their shelter for the night. How nice, I thought, to go and visit the neighbours. While McDonald translated, I rifled through our things, taking out a knife, large coloured beads and Sir John's medal that was jumbled up with everything else, more than enough to make them happy to help us.

My four new friends grinned like excited children as they led me back to their 'home'. We walked back in contented silence. McDonald had told me their names but I could not remember them. Never mind, I thought, there will be plenty of time for that later.

Their tents looked a far sight warmer than ours did, thanks to their outer layer of furs. I was invited to go into one of them, which I duly did, bending down almost double to step over the threshold. My height fascinated them. They stretched their arms to my shoulder and then compared it to the size of the tent's entrance. We all fitted in quite comfortably. A young girl was sitting there, gutting fish. I sat down near her and, on seeing a container of water, pointed to it. Guessing what I wanted, she poured me a cup. It made my teeth rattle with the cold. I knew she could not understand me but I told her anyway, 'I will have my men show you how to make tea

287

and coffee. I think we have a little left of each. Believe me, you are in for a treat.'

She smiled graciously and, just for that, I opened up my bag and gave her some of the bigger beads. She rolled them about in the palm of her grimy hand. 'See, you can make a necklace with them, if you like.'

I took out the small knife and handed it to the fellow that I took to be in charge. He was one the others seemed to check everything with. He held it in both hands and bowed his head. Maybe he was the girl's father. I passed out a few more beads, along with the medal which fascinated them. One of them, a younger man, rubbed it with his thumb, perhaps expecting to rub out the engraved head.

Just then, we heard shouting outside and filed out to investigate.

They brought us luck, these sturdy little people. Two of my men had followed the sound of running water and returned with a pink salmon, medium-sized. We cheered them, while I declared that fortune had finally swerved in our favour.

And here I sit, James, at this very minute, writing these very words to you. The young girl watches me write. I wonder has she ever seen someone write before. I draw some circles and triangles and hold them up to show her. She smiles nicely before returning to her work. Such an industrious creature.

I cannot describe to you the relief of sitting here and feeling that we have overcome the worst. The seal meat, the fish and the running water are just rewards indeed for what we have faced up to today. These simple folk will be our guides and protectors. It is madness to think that we could have done it by ourselves. We have maps but lack the native knowledge. They are the answers to our prayers. And we can teach them so much in return. We are going to make it home, James.

I find that I want to write that last line once more: we are going to make it *HOME*.

22

An Arctic farewell

I cannot write any more ...

I can only listen to the voice in my head as it composes letters and private monologues, which no one shall ever read or hear. My journal and notebooks are lost, with their pointless scribbles and scientific babble. All is lost.

Who am I?

I am Captain Francis Crozier of the British Navy, a native of Banbridge and proud resident of London. None of this is relevant any more. The snow wipes clean a man's history ... and future.

Do I blame the Inuit, for abandoning us after that first day? No, not now – now that I have realised that they had to in order to survive. Our extra bellies would have meant death for their children.

The Arctic is a callous murderer that has killed all my men and will kill me. Today, in fact.

I will let it kill me today.

Am I not grateful, now, that I leave no wife and children grieving forevermore? Sophie was right not to entangle herself with the likes of me. James was right to give up this life in exchange for a home that will never move.

My body is deteriorating fast. I can hardly see where I am going but that does not matter. I cannot feel my feet and have lost the courage to inspect them, to look at the blackened stumps instead of toes and ankles. Everything is black against the white of the Arctic. My fingers resemble dry twigs, ready to be snapped in two.

How can anyone survive here?

Just a few steps more.

I did my best.

Just a few steps more ...

23

Night-time visitors

They had me surrounded, confusing me with their cold smiles while moving in far too close. Tess, Katie and the others. 'Do you or do you not have a ghost in your house? You must tell us the truth!' Tess Bradley appeared to be in charge. We were in the yard, Mrs Lee having sent us out into the sunshine after it had rained for the previous ten days.

Feeling trapped, I glanced around, hoping for a friendly face. Tess shoved me in the shoulder. 'Ann Coppin, do you have a ghost? You do, don't you!'

I was not allowed to talk about Weesy outside our house. Nor could I tell anyone about Mrs Powell's visit or about the map or Lady Franklin or anything like that. Sticking her face into mine, Katie Bradley whined, 'Are you going to cry? Well, are you?'

'Do you want me to?' I asked, desperate to say something.

They sneered at me. 'If you do not tell us, we will send you to Coventry.'

I swallowed hard, admitting, 'I don't know where that is.'

'Oh, dear!' howled Tess. 'Fancy not knowing what Coventry is.'

She spoke to me as if I was a child. 'It means that we will not talk to you at all. You will be ostra ... ostrich ... ost ... well, none of us will talk to you ever again.'

'I never liked her anyway,' sighed Katie. The others considered this and then nodded their heads in agreement.

Someone behind me tugged my hair, just a short, sharp pull. I did not turn to see who the culprit was. They were all the culprit, making up one big awful culprit that would not let me be until I told them something, so I said, 'There might have been something months ago but it is gone now.'

To my mind, that was the safest answer I could give since I was not mentioning Weesy's name or anyone else's. If my parents were here, they would surely agree.

'Well, what?' asked Tess, sounding excited. 'What did you see? What did it look like?'

The earnestness of the question threw me, though I felt the change in the atmosphere as they awaited my story. Now, I was feeling a surge of pride in being the centre of attention and quickly leafed through the occurrences of the last few months for something interesting, and safe, to tell.

'What is going on here?' It was Mrs Lee. 'Ann, come inside and tidy the bookcase. The books are all muddled up. Girls, if you wish to take a book, you must put it back exactly where you found it. Do I make myself clear?'

'Yes, Mrs Lee,' responded the meek chorus.

They released me with reluctance and I followed my teacher indoors. The bookcase was beside her desk.

'Empty it and start again, putting the books in alphabetical order according to the writer's surname.'

I hunkered down and began pulling the books out, stacking them on the floor beside me. The room felt cool and calm after the blaze of sunshine and attention.

'Ann, what was going on out there?'

Not daring to look at her, I kept at my work, saying, 'Nothing, Mrs Lee.'

'It did not look like nothing to me. Tell me the truth, please.'

Everyone wanted me to tell the truth. I took up a book and wiped a smudge from its cover, *A Christmas Carol* by Mr Charles Dickens. 'D' for Dickens.

'Ann?'

I looked up, feeling exactly as I had done a few moments earlier outside. What could I say that would not get me into any more trouble? Mrs Lee was seated at her desk, her expression grave. But she was not alone. A girl by her side smiled at me and so I smiled too and she went back to what she had been doing, standing over Mrs Lee as if reading whatever she had written into her notebook. 'Were the girls picking on you, Ann? You can tell me if they were.'

I did not want to tell tales, but I could tell her something just as I had with them, enough to satisfy her. 'They might have been a while ago but then they stopped.'

Mrs Lee pursed her lips while her companion beamed at me in delight. How friendly she was. 'Are you a new girl?' I asked her. She laughed but made no sound. 'My name is Ann,' I said. She seemed much nicer than any of my old classmates so I was determined to secure her friendship before the others could turn her against me. The book in my hand slid to the floor and I made to grab it once more. 'Who are you talking to?' asked Mrs Lee, a peculiar expression on her face.

'Oh,' I said. 'She is gone. Is she coming back?'

Mrs Lee took up her pencil and readied to continue writing. 'Is who coming back?'

'Why, the girl who was just beside you. Did you not know she was there?'

'Describe her!'

Surprised at the urgency in Mrs Lee's tone, I replied, 'She had long, brown hair with a red bow ... navy dress with yellow trimmings and ... Mrs Lee?'

My teacher seemed to be near tears but she shook her head

to silence me, asking, 'Did she look alright? Happy? Sad? How did she look to you?'

'Well,' I gulped, feeling confused. 'She looked happy. She was smiling. I mean, really smiling.'

Gathering herself together, Mrs Lee nodded as if tremendously relieved. 'Good girl, Ann. Good girl.' Wiping her nose with her handkerchief, she said, 'When you are finished sorting out the books, you may go and tell the class to come back inside. We have a lot of work to do today.'

'Yes, Mrs Lee.'

* * *

'Ann, are you asleep?'

William was standing in my doorway and he had not exactly whispered. He had not woken me up, but I felt bound to protest all the same, whispering, 'I was fast asleep! And keep your voice down, for goodness sake. What do you want?'

'I don't know.'

I sat up and peered through the darkness, just about able to make him out as he hung back from me. Something was wrong. 'What is it? Did you have a bad dream?'

Again, he replied, 'I don't know.'

Sighing heavily, I reached out until I found my box of matches and struck one in order to locate my bedside lamp.

Lighting the tallow, I kept the flame low, and said, 'Come in and shut the door quietly. You can stay for a little while but then you are going back to your own room.'

'Thank you, Ann.'

Well, I could not fault his manners.

He shut the door very slowly but still managed to make more noise than he should have. It was a struggle but I managed not to complain.

'Where can I sit?'

I looked around my room but then accepted that there was only one place for this nocturnal visit. 'Here, just sit on the end of my bed.'

He trotted over and heaved himself up until he was sitting, his back to the end post, facing me while I moved my pillow so that it supported me better. It felt foolish, the two of us propped up, staring at one another. 'So,' I began, 'would you like me to read to you?'

'No, thank you.'

'Oh,' I said, surprised, as I had assumed that was how we would spend the time until I could get rid of him. Now what? 'So, was it a bad dream, is that why you are here?'

His eyes flickered as he considered his answer and he shivered, nicely distracting himself from having to answer me by asking me, in turn, 'Can I put my feet under your blankets?'

Stifling a grumble, I nodded. 'Just keep them away from

mine. Why are you not wearing your slippers?'

He gazed at me as if I was the strange one who had burst into his bedroom in the middle of the night. 'There was no time to put them on.'

'Whatever do you mean, there was no time?

He smiled shyly. I glanced at the door and, for some reason, leant over to turn up the flame in my lamp. We watched its flickering light spread itself out across the floor, stretching across the top of my desk. To my surprise, two of William's model ships were sitting there, atop my sketchbook which was open, providing a pristine white surface for the light to bounce off. William rushed to defend himself. 'I didn't leave them there. I know I am not allowed in your room.'

'I know, I know,' I said, before adding, 'and I didn't leave my sketchbook open either.'

We were quiet again, satisfied that the other was telling the truth. Just then, there was a sound, a gasp, a giggle, that barely registered but we both heard it and whispered together, 'Weesy!'

As if our saying her name aloud created a sudden gust of wind, the flame in my lamp went out.

'Ann!' cried William.

Trying to disguise my own fright, I whispered, 'It is alright, I am still here.'

I was about to tell him to come up beside me when he did

just that, his arms almost stopping my breath as he fastened them around my waist, plunging his legs beneath the blankets. 'What's that?' asked William, burying his head in my side. 'Is someone there?'

'Where?' I asked, swivelling my head from left to right, doing my utmost to penetrate the darkness. I thought I could see shadows but could not be sure. The dark can reveal what is concealed deep inside you: your fears, be they real or imagined.

'Look, William, it is just Weesy.' I persevered in trying to convince both him and myself. 'She is bored and is making mischief with us.'

'Call Papa!' My brother was pleading with me, but I could not bring myself to do it. Because it began to feel familiar. The temperature had dropped, my feet were numb and the sheets felt damp, even wet. Suddenly William exclaimed, 'It is the place from my dream.'

I saw 'the place' take shape around us as the darkness slowly receded, leaving behind a mist of silvery grey. Maybe William and I were having the same dream? Anything was possible now and I was so cold that it was hard to tell if I was awake or still sleeping. Thanks to the peculiar light, I could make out the pattern of the wallpaper on the wall opposite but I could swear to also seeing what looked like mountains, monstrous craggy peaks doused in bluey white.

'Can you see it too?' asked William.

'You dreamt about this place before?'

William nodded, his skull jutting into my side. We could see one another now which helped to keep him calm. Clouds of our own breath hung in the air. 'Look, William, your ships are standing up.'

And, indeed, they looked like proper ships, proud and purposeful, waiting to be released into the sea.

'The ice is melting,' said William.

Tiny fissures jutted their way through what I had assumed to be solid ground, fracturing it in half and then into more and more pieces that dislodged and broke away from one another. Meanwhile, something most precious was surging beneath, sparkling like Mama's jewellery when she was out in the sunshine, and reminding me how she used to laugh before we had any notion of death and white coffins. The palest blue water gurgled up between the cracks, full of promise, lapping over the ice, gently pushing it aside as if waving it on its way.

William and I looked at one another and grinned, glad we were in this together, whatever it was. Although, we were not alone. A blue oval shadow, far richer in shade than the water, hovered around my desk, the masts of William's ships appearing to support it.

'Weesy, we know you are here.' I also felt bound to add, 'Don't worry, I am not angry at you anymore.'

William was perplexed. 'Why are you angry at her?'

'I am not angry now,' I replied, somewhat huffily.

Much to my annoyance, he persisted, adopting a tone of arch accusation. 'But that is not fair. Why do you have to make her sad?'

I was suddenly reminded how irritating it can be to have a baby brother, and a baby sister, for that matter. 'For goodness sake, Will—'

A dog's bark silenced me, making us both jump. Relieved to change the subject, I asked, 'Is that Bobby? Mama will be cross. Why isn't he outside?'

But William only whispered, 'They are coming!'

The light in the room shimmered like ripples in the water that, by now, had seen off the jigsaw pieces of ice. It was a scene of tranquillity, a cloudless sky mirrored in a serene blue sea. Even the mountains shed their cragginess, their sharp edges and crevices now resembling the lightest strokes of grey charcoal made against the white page, easily rubbed out in order to begin again. Everything was changing.

I saw what William meant. As if bursting through a veil, a shroud of finest lace, a large group of men were walking towards us. There were maybe ten or twenty abreast.

We sat like two statues, watching their approach, which was framed by my bedroom door. As they crunched their way through the snow, it squeaked and groaned beneath their weight.

'Where are they going to?' asked William.

I shrugged for an answer.

Typically, he immediately asked another question, 'Can they see us?'

Before I could reply, he said, 'Look, there is the dog!'

The dog was huge, reminding me of a wolf, and appeared to be smiling broadly. His lower jaw hung open, with his tongue draped over the side. He sneezed once and twice in his excitement, earning himself a fierce rub on the head from the man beside him. This man stood out because he was the tallest man in his line. An older man, who beamed in delight, linked arms with the tall man. His smile was contagious and, whether they could see us or not, I smiled in dawning recognition. I had seen their pictures in Grandfather's newspaper.

All their faces were coming into focus now. They were handsome, in that their eyes and cheeks glowed with good health. I could find no traces of the tiredness or anxiety that I was used to seeing in the faces of my parents. They looked so happy to see us. In fact, their welcoming smiles reminded me of the girl that had stood behind Mrs Lee today. Awestruck, I quietly asked William, 'Do you know who they are?'

My little brother actually had the nerve to roll his eyes in front of all these gentlemen. 'Of course I do! It is Captain Franklin and his crew. See, they are wearing their navy uniforms and this ...' He flung out his arms as if to uphold all that he could see. '*This* is the Arctic.'

William was speaking quickly. 'This was my dream. They are lost and need our help.'

Weesy reminded us that she was near; the sails of William's model ships trembled as she flitted over them, her spirited performance bringing them to life. The air around us crackled with expectation on all sides. Suddenly, I found myself remembering a line from a book I had read. I no longer remembered its title or anything else beyond this one short sentence: 'Home. There is magic in that little word.'

'*HOME!*'

I blurted it out, causing my brother to put his finger to his lips, shocked at my loudness. I felt warm all over, and Weesy renewed her gleeful ballet above our heads. 'You are right, William. We have to help them. That is why Weesy is here; she is going to help us. They are stuck, like she is stuck here with us.'

To my immense joy, the tall one briefly lifted his hat from his head, saluting my efforts. I stared into his eyes and, in that instant, I knew exactly who he was. He held my gaze and I felt chilled and distraught by the loneliness that had consumed him during his final days.

Just then, I saw him as he was: Captain Crozier, a solitary figure, stumbling onwards, blinded by the glare of the snow. His tangled, wildly overgrown beard was a glistening mass of frozen teardrops. His cheeks, nose and lips were rubbed raw by the howling gales. His teeth were black and broken while his feet were swollen and bleeding, all his nails torn and gone. Hunger and thirst taunted him while his mouth was a mess of open sores. Yet, even though he was filled with remorse for his lost crew, he kept going, determined, even now, to master his fate. Eventually, however, he could walk no more. I felt his heart petering out and watched him fall to his knees, arms outstretched as the snow rushed to cover him, begging God above for help and, then, for His forgiveness. His last breath, a bitter testament to a life that he believed was only half lived.

'Look,' said William.

It was raining paper. Pages upon pages flitted about the men, like doves looking for a place to settle. Some were larger than others, the writing an assorted mix of loops and dotted 'i's, all in black ink that helped them stand out from the snow but not for long. Here and there were doodles, some more elaborate in detail, that captured life onboard the ships. I recognised a Christmas tree along with a cooked goose, sprawled across a massive plate, so good that I could almost taste it. I could not help smiling as another sheet displayed a shaky effort at reproducing, I think, two men playing chess.

Every single sheet, following its short flight in the sun, began to fall, the ink – that is, the words and the pictures – fading away, leaving the page clean before it dropped into the snow, no longer visible.

'What is happening?' asked William.

'I think it is their journals and, maybe, the letters that they never got to send.'

A bell rang out in the distance, reminding me how late it was. Assuming it belonged to St Columb's Cathedral, I counted off the chimes out of habit, not used to hearing more than nine or ten. By the looks of it, the men could hear the bell too.

'Is it the ship's bell?' asked William.

It was almost funny how we ignored Weesy, not on purpose, of course. Up to tonight, her presence had been the most important thing in our lives. She had always been the centre of attention. Her sickness had dominated our house when she was alive and her death left our parents adrift. I understood now that they would always miss her.

Thus inspired, I heard myself assure the men, 'I know you did not leave any words behind but you left people, your family and friends, who will always miss you. And, well, I think that is much more important.'

I was rewarded with the warmest smiles, including from my brother, who seemed to radiate pride in his sister.

I felt that time was speeding up now. Lights flashed around me like stars bursting across the night sky; years were racing by with lessons being learnt all over again. Everything was going around and around but always falling a little forward. It was something to rely on. Distance was forming between the men and us. They were growing hazy, as if I was seeing them through tears.

The light was ship-shaped. It appeared behind them and shone brighter than the ice and snow. Captain Crozier, Captain Franklin, their officers and their crew stared in fascination, uncertain about what to do next. Only Captain Crozier looked back to me. I nodded. 'Yes, it is for you, all of you. It is going to take you where you need to go.'

A line was formed and they were off, one following the other, disappearing from sight as they passed through the light. Captain Crozier and his dog were the last ones to leave. Just before he took that final step, he raised his arm in thanks and farewell. We raised ours in reply and, in an instant, they were gone. Snow began to fall once more, filling in their footsteps, wiping the surface clean just like the pages of their letters and journals.

I was exhausted and closed my eyes for just a moment, savouring those last seconds when I felt that I knew everything that was important.

'No, Weesy, not you!'

William's cry shattered my smugness.

My heart cracked when I saw the figure of my little sister edging towards that light. Why was it still there? It had what it came for.

She suddenly appeared to us as clearly as the men did. There she was with her brown hair in ringlets, her snub nose, her freckles, her crooked front tooth. After all these months of resenting her, I was suddenly terrified of losing her. Oh, it wasn't like the first time. Silly little coffin. Everyone dressed in black, young and old, grim and monotonous. Lengthy sermon in a draughty church. Vulgar wreaths that were too perfumed and heavy to lift. Candles in daylight, an empty comfort. No, that had never been real. Not like this.

'Weesy ... I ...' I could hardly speak. 'No, please don't leave us. Stay. Why can't you stay?'

But she looked so happy, her joy banishing the cold temperatures, allowing us to bask in what felt like the gold of the setting sun. William reached out for her, but she turned towards the light as if hearing someone calling her name and then she smiled at me and nodded, needing me to finally let her go.

New beginnings

We never told anyone what happened that night. William fretted that our parents should know, but I disagreed, telling him, 'There is no point upsetting them all over again.'

He harrumphed a little bit before promising to keep it a secret between us.

In any case, I had had an idea and was so pleased with myself that I boasted to my brother, 'I know what I am going to do. Actually, it is the most wonderful idea!'

William waited politely to hear it but failed to look much impressed when I declared, 'I am going to paint Weesy's portrait for Mama.'

Of course, he is far too young to understand.

Sitting myself down in front of a large blank sheet of paper,

I faltered immediately. The sheet was so empty and the picture that I wanted to paint, which was tucked away in the safety of my mind, was flawless.

I had realised that my mother's grief was made unbearable when she failed to see Weesy after she died. That was why Papa rejected his own sighting, that time he had returned from his trip. All Mama had was that moment of confusion and horror as Papa pulled down the lid of the coffin, shutting away Weesy's face forevermore.

Well, I would capture her for Mama. I would bring her back. There were no paintings of Weesy so it was up to me. Oh, if this painting was what I wanted it to be, Papa would have it framed and hang it in the front room, alongside our ancestors. 'There,' Mama would say, to her visitors, with pride and affection. 'There was my little daughter who died but is now here again thanks to her sister Ann.'

I picked up my paintbrush and readied myself, feeling awed by my own ambition. All I understood was that I would place Weesy in the garden to demonstrate that she could still be around but at a distance.

Moments passed and I was petrified, my hand holding the brush still hanging in mid-air as I struggled to even choose a colour. Should I start with the thick brown strands of her hair or smoky clouds lazing across a blue sky? What about the delicacy of blush on her cheeks and lips? Or the bold patterns of her dress that I liked? And, well, what colour exactly were her eyes again? And freckles, how many? Also, did her fingernails shine?

On I sat, searching for greatness in the white of my page.

Just then, the door was flung open. Sarah hiccupped loudly as she strode in, followed closely by William who was pretending to stop her. 'Oh, no, Sarah, we are not allowed in here. This is Ann's room!'

With that, he looked at me hopefully. Hiding my relief at this interruption, I pretended to sigh as I said, 'Oh, all right, then, you can stay but do not knock anything over.'

Sarah stumbled over to my desk. 'Me see, me see!'

'Well, I am only just starting. There is nothing to see yet.'

'Me paint!'

'I want to paint too,' said William.

'Really?' I tutted. 'Honestly, I can never get a moment's peace.'

Sarah giggled, knowing full well that I was going to give in to them. There was just about room for the three of us to work side by side.

'Now, you can each have a sheet of paper but promise not to get paint on your clothes or on the furniture. Do you hear me?'

As I spoke, I fetched a second chair and sat Sarah onto it. William was happy to stand. Sarah was too busy reaching for a brush to pay me any heed so I looked at William who shrugged, 'We know!'

And just like that they started painting. I moved the vase of water to the centre of the desk. 'Now, Sarah, you must wash your brush when you want to use a different colour.'

'Green!'

William explained, 'Today, her favourite colour is green.'

They did not worry about making the most perfect and meaningful mark on their sheets. Sarah began to hum to herself as she pressed her brush down, creating different-sized splodges that made her smile. Meanwhile, William ran his brush over the top of his page, watching it leave a trail of blue in its wake. So, after a moment, I took up my paintbrush, dabbed it in Sarah's favourite colour for today and began.

Notes from the Author

Captain Francis Leopold McClintock and the
Victory Point Note

Between 1847 and 1859, over thirty ships were sent out in search of Franklin's men. As the years passed, it was merely hoped to find a clue that would help to explain their disappearance. After the Navy lost interest, due in part to the outbreak of the Crimean War in 1853, Lady Franklin used family money to fund her own searches. In 1857, she bought the 177-ton, schooner-rigged steam yacht, the *Fox*, and chose Dundalk-man Francis Leopold McClintock to take command, instructing him to search for 'the unspeakably precious documents of the expedition'. She had chosen well.

According to Frank Nugent, author of *Seek the Frozen Land*, Captain McClintock was one of Ireland's greatest Arctic explorers. He developed the proper use of sledges to enable naval expeditions to travel further abroad from a ship beset in the ice, in order to survey and explore a larger amount of territory.

Captain McClintock was told to look for survivors which, of course, would have been a miracle by this stage. Unlike the Franklin crew, seventeen of his twenty-six crewmen were already experienced in searching the Arctic for *Erebus* and *Terror*.

An unfortunate start saw the *Fox* spending the winter of 1857 adrift in ice and making it necessary to return to Greenland for fresh supplies and dogs that would be used to pull their sledges. They reached Beechey Island early in 1858 and, from there, sailed to a point near Bellot Strait, from where they embarked upon a series of explorations using sledges. As well as searching for anything to do with Franklin's expedition, McClintock was also determined to chart the remaining gaps on his Arctic map.

On reaching King William's Island, McClintock dog-sledged the northern end of the island, whilst his second-in-command, Lieutenant William Hobson, investigated the south end. Captain McClintock had his first piece of good luck when he encountered an Inuit snow village hoarding real treasure. Using sewing needles for currency, McClintock 'bought' cutlery and delph belonging to John Franklin, Francis Crozier and Alexander McDonald. He also acquired uniforms and tunic buttons. Furthermore, an Inuit woman told him about seeing a large group of white men who fell down (died) as they walked, adding that some were buried and some were not.

A couple of days later, he found a skeleton, face down in the snow, wearing the tattered uniform of an officer's servant or steward.

On 29 May 1859, Captain McClintock reached the western

extreme of King William Island and named it Cape Crozier in honour of Banbridge man Captain Francis Crozier. One of the lifeboats had been discovered and McClintock marvelled at the enormity of the task for the Franklin crew to push and pull this boat over ice and snow. Two skeletons were found in the boat, but perhaps the most striking realisation was the amount and variety of unnecessary possessions that were carried in the boat: boots, clothes, towels, soap, toothbrush, combs, silk handkerchiefs, tobacco, twine, nails, a saw, ammunition, watches, novels, Bibles, lots of silverware and delph, including eight plates bearing John Franklin's family crest, along with forty pounds of chocolate. McClintock described this stuff as being nothing more than 'dead weight … and very likely to break down the strength of the sledge crews.'

Elsewhere, stoves were found along with a medicine cabinet and writing desk. It was as if the men had attempted to carry their very civilisation – their Bibles and plates and cutlery etc – in the face of the most uncivil environment and climate.

Meanwhile, his second-in-command, Lieutenant William Hobson, finally struck gold. From the cairn at Victory Point, he retrieved the only official document ever found from Franklin's expedition, an eleven-year-old piece of paper recording the commander's death, along with many others, and informing the reader that *Terror* and *Erebus* had been abandoned on 22 April 1848 – with Captain Crozier's final scribble about heading for the Great Fish River.

One can only imagine the feelings experienced by Lady Franklin on receiving McClintock's news. It was probably as much a relief as a dreadful shock finally to learn a little of what had happened to her husband and his men.

She and her niece Sophie never gave up searching for more information and were convinced that her husband's journals would be found at some stage. Sophie and her seventy-eight year-old aunt finally made a trip to the Arctic, reaching Alaska in 1870, where they bought some souvenirs. Four years later, Lady Jane Franklin was still offering a handsome reward to anyone who could find any letters, journals or notebooks from *Terror* and *Erebus*.

When she died in July 1875, Captain McClintock helped carry her coffin. Her last act for her husband finally bore fruit two weeks after her death when a bust of Sir John, which she had tirelessly campaigned for, was unveiled in Westminster Abbey.

She died, a celebrity in her own right, widely admired for her loyalty and fearlessness regarding her determination to know the true fate of her husband.

The Two Ships Found

HMS *Erebus* was finally found in September 2014, in the south of King William Island, eleven metres below water, sitting up straight on the seabed and covered in kelp seaweed. The cold

Arctic water had preserved the ship, although there were holes in the deck that allowed divers a peek inside. The leg of a table could be seen in Captain Franklin's cabin. Two brass six-pounder guns were also found along with the ship's bell, which was imprinted with the British government's broad-arrow mark and the year, 1845, when the two ships sailed from Greenhithe, England.

Two years later, in September 2016, HMS *Terror* was found further north in Terror Bay (so named in 1910 by the Geographical Names Board in Canada) in forty-eight metres of water and in even better shape than *Erebus*. Some of the glass panels in the windows of Captain Crozier's cabin were still perfectly intact.

Like Lady Jane Franklin, researchers and archaeologists hope to find written documents that might have been packed safely away into containers and, therefore, may still be legible.

The Coppin Family

There are quite a few supernatural stories regarding the search for the Franklin ships but my favourite is Weesy Coppin and her family. Her father William (1805–1895), originally from Kinsale, County Cork, was a well-known ship builder, engineer and inventor, having built his first ship, named the *City of Derry*, in 1839.

The family lived in a four-storey house, called Ivy House, at 34 Strand Road in Derry, which was sadly demolished in

1994 despite the efforts of the Foyle Civic Trust to save it. Four-year-old Weesy died there on 27 May 1849 from gastric fever and her spirit was seen by her sister Ann and brother William. At some point, the children's Aunt Harriet suggested that Ann ask Weesy for information on the missing ships in the Arctic – it was the hot topic of the day. As a result, Ann produced an Arctic map that included territory which had yet to be discovered.

We only know this thanks to a Liverpool vicar, Reverend J Henry Skewes, who published the story forty years later in 1889, in a book about the missing expedition. Of course, plenty of people did not believe a word of it, including Captain Francis McClintock. However, this spurred the reverend to publish his evidence, that is, letters between William Coppin, Lady Franklin and her niece, Sophie Cracroft. According to Reverend Skewes, William Coppin made approximately thirty visits to Lady Franklin to discuss Ann's map.

In 1850, Lady Franklin confided in the Admiralty's Second Secretary, Captain W.A.B. Hamilton, telling him that Mr Coppin had been in touch once more to say that the ship had been 'seen' in the same place, surrounded by ice. Only a couple of people knew the true origins of the map, but today, all things considered, the information provided by Weesy has proved to be the most accurate concerning the true locations of the ships.

Lady Franklin begged the Navy to send out a ship to search the area suggested by the map but they refused. She put together a search of her own, directing the crew of the *Prince Albert* to go south, on reaching the Arctic, but the ice proved impenetrable, forcing the ship to return home.

It is the assumption that after Lady Franklin died, Sophie, a devout Christian, destroyed any mention in her aunt's papers of contacts with the supernatural.

For my story, I made Ann slightly older. According to most books, she was nine years old at the time of the sightings. Also, I ignored the existence of an older brother, John, who was studying in Trinity College, in Dublin. Mrs Dora Coppin had another baby, after Weesy's death, a daughter called Harriet, but she died on 11 April 1859 at the age of eighteen months. Mrs Coppin died on 11 September 1866 and her husband William died on 17 April 1895. Both are buried with their family in St Augustine's graveyard. It does not appear that Ann ever married.

Beechey Island Bodies

In 1984, the bodies of John Torrington, John Hartnell and William Braine, buried on Beechey Island in 1846, were exhumed, or dug up, by a team of scientists and archaeologists, including writers John Geiger and Owen Beattie who recorded their experience in their book, *Frozen in Time*.

Things to Do

* Visit **Banbridge** to see the monument to Captain Francis Crozier and his house that sits across the road.

* Visit **Dundalk Museum** to see various items that belonged to Captain Francis McClintock.

* Visit **Westminster Abbey** to see the bust of John Franklin and the plaque to Captain McClintock.

* Visit **Dublin's Natural History Museum** to see the musk ox and polar bear that were shot and presented by Captain Francis McClintock.

* Visit **Derry** to see the Coppin family grave in St Augustine's Church.

* Think about what might have happened had Sir John and Captain Crozier decided, from the very beginning, that their best chance of success in the Arctic lay in learning more about how the **Inuit** lived and copying them.

Further Reading

Alexander, Alison, *The Ambitions of Jane Franklin: Victorian Lady Adventurer.* Allen & Unwin, 2013.

Beattie, Owen and Geiger, John, *Frozen in Time: The Fate of the Franklin Expedition.* Bloomsbury, 2004.

Fosset, Renée, *In Order to Live Untroubled: Inuit of the Central Arctic, 1550 to 1940.* Manitoba Press, 2001.

Hutchinson, Gillian, *Sir John Franklin's* Erebus *and* Terror *Expedition Lost and Found.* Adlard Coles, 2017.

Lambert, Andrew, *Franklin: Tragic Hero of Polar Navigation.* Faber and Faber, 2009.

Malley, Annesley and Mc Laughlin, Mary, *Captain William Coppin: Neptune's Brightest Star.* Foyle Civic Trust, 1992.

McCoogan, Ken, *Fatal Passage: The Story of John Rae, The Arctic Hero Time Forgot.* Basic Books, 2003.

Murphy, David, *The Arctic Fox: Francis Leopold-McClintock, Discoverer of the Fate of Franklin.* Dundurn, 2004.

Nugent, Frank, *Seek the Frozen Lands: Irish Polar Explorers 1740–1922.* Collins Press, 2003.

Palin, Michael, Erebus*, The Story of a Ship.* Arrow, 2019.

Watson, Paul, *Ice Ghosts: The Epic Hunt for the Lost Franklin Expedition.* WW Norton & Company, 2017.

Woodman, David C., *Unravelling the Franklin Mystery: Inuit Testimony.* McGill–Queen's University Press, 2015.

To follow the ongoing excavations of HMS *Erebus* and HMS *Terror*, check out the excellent blog: *www.visionsnorth.blogspot.com.*